The Pianoplayers

Manchester University Press

The Irwell Edition of the Works of Anthony Burgess

Series editors: Andrew Biswell and Paul Wake

Anthony Burgess (1917–93) was one of the most prominent
novelists and critics of the twentieth century. He wrote thirty-
three novels, twenty-five works of non-fiction and two volumes of
autobiography. Pursuing a parallel career as a classical composer, he
wrote a symphony, a piano concerto, a violin concerto for Yehudi
Menuhin, and more than 250 other musical works.

The Irwell Edition takes its title from a collected edition outlined
by Anthony Burgess himself in the 1980s but never achieved in
his lifetime. Each volume in the series presents an authoritative
annotated text alongside an introduction detailing the genesis and
composition of the work and the history of its reception.

The Irwell Edition of the Works of Anthony Burgess

The Pianoplayers

Edited with an introduction and notes by Will Carr

Manchester University Press

Published by Manchester University Press
Altrincham Street, Manchester M1 7JA

www.manchesteruniversitypress.co.uk

British Library Cataloguing-in-Publication Data
A catalogue record for this book is available from the British Library

ISBN 978 1 5261 2234 6 hardback

First published 2017

Typeset in 10/13.5 Stempel Garamond
by Servis Filmsetting Ltd, Stockport, Cheshire
Printed in Great Britain
by CPI Group (UK) Ltd, Croydon CR0 4YY

Contents

General Editors' foreword

John Anthony Burgess Wilson (1917–93) was one of the most prominent novelists and critics of the twentieth century, but for many years much of his work has been unavailable. A graduate of Manchester University, he wrote thirty-three novels, twenty-five works of non-fiction and two volumes of autobiography. Pursuing a parallel career as a classical composer, he wrote a symphony, a piano concerto, a violin concerto for Yehudi Menuhin and more than 250 other musical works. The Irwell Edition of the Works of Anthony Burgess is the first scholarly edition of Burgess's novels and non-fiction works. One of its purposes is to restore 'lost' novels to the canon of available work. The edition will include stage plays, musical libretti, letters and essays.

The Irwell Edition takes its title from a collected edition outlined by Anthony Burgess himself in the 1980s but never achieved during his lifetime. Each volume is edited by an expert scholar, presenting an authoritative annotated text alongside an introduction detailing the genesis and composition of the work, and the history of its reception. The appendices will make available previously unpublished documents from the Anthony Burgess archives held at institutional libraries in Europe and North America, in addition to rare and out-of-print materials relating to Burgess's writing.

The Irwell Edition is designed for students, teachers, scholars and general readers who are seeking accessible but rigorous critical editions of each book. The series as a whole will contribute to the ongoing task of encouraging renewed interest in all aspects of Anthony Burgess's creative work.

Andrew Biswell
Paul Wake
Manchester Metropolitan University

Acknowledgements

Many individuals and organisations have been generous towards this edition. I would especially like to thank the Harry Ransom Center at the University of Texas at Austin and the Trustees of the International Anthony Burgess Foundation, Manchester, for access to their collections; John Banville and Erica Jong for kindly allowing their work to be included; and Richard Cohen, Jonathon Green and Christopher W. Thurley for their assistance. In particular I would like to thank my colleagues Andrew Biswell, Anna Edwards and Graham Foster for generously sharing their knowledge and ideas, and for their tireless support and encouragement.

Will Carr

Introduction

Genesis and composition

Anthony Burgess believed he had a musical background. According to family legend, his mother, Elizabeth Burgess (1888–1918), was a singer and dancer on the music hall stage while his father, Joseph Wilson (1883–1938), had many jobs, including playing the piano in theatres, pubs and especially the cinemas in Manchester. Like other cities, Manchester in the early part of the twentieth century sustained a large number of small local cinemas, attracting customers from all over the region, and this part of the entertainment industry offered many opportunities for accompanists to the silent films of the era. Elizabeth died, along with Burgess's only sister Muriel (1910–18), in the influenza outbreak of 1918, and Joseph remarried a pub landlady called Margaret Dwyer (d. 1940). Joseph Wilson appears as a piano-player in Burgess's contribution to the collection of essays *Lives of the Piano* (1981), which details Burgess's love for the instrument. He writes:

> My mother was a soubrette and my father was a piano-player. He would not use the term *pianist* of himself, considering that it ought to be reserved to artists who performed on the concert platform, to which he was never good enough to be elevated. His place was the orchestra pit [...] He had, without being a virtuoso, as full a grasp of the capabilities of the piano as any professional performer I have ever known.

He could switch from ragtime to Chopin; he was a brilliant improviser.[1]

The piano was a fixture in the Burgess's homes in Miles Platting and later in Moss Side, Manchester, as it was in many English lower-middle-class households (as Burgess has it) in the early part of the twentieth century before the advent of affordable record players. Burgess described lying awake as a child in bed above the Golden Eagle pub in Miles Platting where the family lived in the early 1920s, listening to the combined noise of the three 'singing rooms', each of which contained a piano and each being played simultaneously.[2] Like his father, Burgess never became a concert pianist, but became confident in popular and jazz traditions and fairly effective in classical ones; he also wrote a great deal of music for the piano for many different ensembles and in very many styles.[3] None the less it is perhaps pride rather than regret that leads him to write in *The Lives of the Piano* that 'my father and I have been merely piano players' (p. 4), rather than pianists.

The Pianoplayers was published in 1986, but the first reference to a work called *The Pianoplayers* appears fully nine years earlier in correspondence between Liana Burgess, Burgess's second wife and literary agent, and Gladys J. Carr, senior editor at the McGraw-Hill Book Company in New York. On 29 March 1977 Gladys Carr writes that she is 'excited by word of Anthony's new work, THE PIANO PLAYER [sic], and, as requested, shall indeed not speak of it to anyone'; and by the early summer of that year it seems that a version of the novel is complete, as on 8 June 1977 Liana Burgess writes that 'THE PIANOPLAYER [sic] [...] has been sent to you

---

1 Anthony Burgess, 'The Well-Tempered Revolution: A Consideration of the Piano's Social and Intellectual History', in *The Lives Of The Piano*, ed. by James R. Gaines (New York: Holt, Rinehart & Winston, 1981), pp. 3–39 (p. 3).
2 Burgess relates this anecdote in the television film *Burgess at Seventy*, directed by Kevin Jackson and first broadcast in February 1987.
3 For a survey of Burgess's compositions for the piano see Paul Phillips, *A Clockwork Counterpoint: The Music and Literature of Anthony Burgess* (Manchester: Manchester University Press, 2012), pp. 198–213.

under separate cover'.[4] A possible composition date of between
March and June 1977 is supported by Anthony Burgess's review
at that time of Sidney Harrison's history of the instrument *Grand
Piano* for the *Spectator*. In that review Burgess describes 'the roman-
tic, indeed erotic, aspect of the walking or flying fingers conjuring
a complete edifice of sound [at the piano]', as well as writing of his
father and of himself as 'packhorses' of the musical world: 'I worked
in pubs, he in cinemas'.[5] Burgess also laments the way in which 'talking films wiped out a considerable body of musicians', counting his
father among them. All of these themes are explored in detail as *The
Pianoplayers* unfolds.

The first reference Anthony Burgess himself makes to *The
Pianoplayers* is in an interview with Samuel Coale that took place in
Monaco in July 1978:

> My father was a cinema pianist. I've written a little novel about
> him called *The Pianoplayers*, which I've not published yet. I
> think it's too short. It's a kind of structure which I'm surprised
> hasn't turned up more in fiction, the structure of a man who is
> thrown out of work by the advent of talking films.[6]

The 'little novel' survives in a complete typescript, undated and,
as is written on the front cover, purportedly by a writer called
'Josephine Kell'.[7] It is likely that this is the draft that was composed
in early 1977. Minor spelling and typographical errors are corrected
in Burgess's hand. Burgess wrote two early novels as Joseph Kell,

4 Letters between Liana Burgess and Gladys Carr (Anthony Burgess Papers at
  the Harry Ransom Center at the University of Texas at Austin (HRC), box
  84, folder 7).
5 Anthony Burgess, 'The Rules of the Game', *Spectator*, 5 March 1977, p. 23.
6 Samuel Coale, 'Guilt's a Good Thing', *Modern Fiction Studies*, 27.3 (1981),
  pp. 429–52. Reprinted in *Conversations with Anthony Burgess*, ed. by Earl
  G. and Mary C. Ingersoll (Jackson: University Press of Mississippi, 2008),
  pp. 115–34.
7 'Josephine Kell' [i.e. Anthony Burgess], *The Pianoplayers*, manuscript draft
  (International Anthony Burgess Foundation, Manchester (IABF), Manuscript
  box AAJ, folder 2).

Inside Mister Enderby and *One Hand Clapping*, on the advice of his publisher to prevent too many disparate novels by Anthony Burgess appearing in the market so close to each other.[8] This later third pseudonym of Josephine Kell did not survive into the novel as it was eventually published; however, there is a clear relationship between *The Pianoplayers* and *One Hand Clapping* in that these are the only two novels by Burgess that have female first-person narrators.

The first draft of 1977 is in most respects identical to the final published text, though there are some important differences. The first is in the opening section, which begins with a version of Chapter Two as it appears in the published text and omits Chapter One entirely: the action opens in the 1920s with memories of the narrator's father and his attempts to teach her to play the piano. The character of the narrator is outlined gradually with the business of the opening sequences being the business of pianoplaying. When the narrator is, almost grudgingly, introduced it is in details similar to those of Burgess's own biography: 'Who the hell's this "I"? Man or woman? Boy or girl? My name is Ellen Henshaw and I was born on February 25 1917 and I would now call myself a lady in retirement.'[9] Like Burgess, Ellen is born in Manchester on this date; and her mother and sister are killed, like his, in the flu epidemic of 1918. Chapter Two of the later drafts and the published novel omits the shared date of birth, and much of the detail of the house in 81 Bagshot Street, Harpurhey, though the fictional address is the same in both texts. Altogether, the quantity and specificity of the historical detail, and from this the identification between the author and narrator, is an important part of the autobiographical context of the novel. The changes between the first draft and the later versions show that Burgess diminished this to some extent.

A further major difference between the 1977 first draft and the final text is that Chapter Twelve and a Half in the published book – the final chapter, which is the story of Ellen's son Robert dealing with the dead body of his mother-in-law – appears as Chapter Nine

8 'Joseph Kell' [i.e. Anthony Burgess], *One Hand Clapping* (London: Peter Davies, 1961) and *Inside Mister Enderby* (London: William Heinemann, 1963).
9 'Josephine Kell', *The Pianoplayers*, p. 2.

in the first draft. This has the effect of pushing the ultimately fatal climactic piano marathon of Billy Henshaw to Chapter Ten of the draft text, followed by a Chapter Eleven dealing with Ellen's later career as the founder of a School of Love. As can be seen from Burgess's correspondence with his publishers, discussed below, his struggle with the structure of the novel in terms of how the various sequences were to be connected went on until the text was finally published.

A second draft, an undated complete manuscript stored in a folder marked '1982', is almost identical to the text as it finally appeared in 1986: again there are minor spelling corrections in Burgess's hand and a handful of changes in expression, but there are no substantial differences apart from an alteration to the conclusion.[10] The title page names the author as Anthony Burgess, and so by this point Josephine Kell has vanished. In this draft, and in the final published text, Chapter One begins with the narrator Ellen Henshaw sitting in a café in the South of France describing her surroundings. This provides a framing device for the novel to follow, whereby the narrator briskly dictates her story to a travelling writer called Rolf Marcus. This construction of the narrator also offers opportunities in the novel to compare the Manchester and Blackpool of the 1920s and 1930s with the France of the present day. The first draft does not develop this framing device as strongly, only later in the text referring to 'the young man who is helping me' and referring in passing to the use of a Dictaphone.[11]

In addition to the two drafts of the novel, there are ten surviving pages of manuscript fragments that relate to the final text, six of which constitute two different versions of the first few pages of the first chapter and which are abandoned abruptly. These false starts do not differ strongly from the published text though they spend less time on setting the scene in the French café where Ellen is sitting, and more time on establishing the character of the amanuensis Rolf Marcus. However, the remaining four surviving pages of manuscript fragments relate to the very end of the novel and are perhaps more

10 Anthony Burgess, *The Pianoplayers*, typescript draft (HRC, box 42 folder 5).
11 'Josephine Kell', *The Pianoplayers*, p. 40.

interesting in terms of the composition of the novel. They are identical to the final published version, and these pages are distinct from
the final pages in the 1982 and 1977 drafts. The latter drafts involve
an inconclusive visit to the British Consulate in Genoa, and then
the theft of the car containing Mrs Aldridge's body, before Robert
and Edna ultimately return to England alone. In these four pages of
fragments, however, a cartoonish encounter with the Italian police
is substituted and Mrs Aldridge is buried abroad. What is notable
about these fragments is that they are written on a word-processor
rather than on a typewriter. Burgess acquired his first computer, an
early Apple Macintosh, in May 1985, between the 1982 second draft
and the finalised text of 1986.[12] There is no evidence that a complete
third draft was completed on a word processor, but it may be that
these word-processed pages were used for final revisions to the text.
This is the only known example of Burgess using a word-processor
for anything other than letters and journalism, and the manuscripts
of his subsequent books are all composed on manual typewriters.

   In addition to these manuscript drafts and fragments, there are
two longer pieces of writing by Burgess that relate directly to *The
Pianoplayers*. The first of these is the short story 'An American
Organ', reprinted here in full as Appendix 1. This story was first
published in *Splinters* in 1968,[13] and is one of three vengeful stories
(the others being 'A Pair of Gloves' (1967) and 'I Wish My Wife Was
Dead' (1969)) from the same period, all on the theme of the murder
of an appalling wife by a down-trodden and resentful husband.[14]
Much of the material from this story appears as part of Chapter
Nine in the 1977 draft, as well as in the final chapter of the 1982
draft and published text. However, Burgess alters the ending of the
original 'An American Organ' radically to remove the murder itself.
Instead, Robert aborts his plan to kill his wife Edna in the bath

---

12 Anthony Burgess, 'Myself as a Chunk of Software', May 1985, typescript
   (IABF, Journalism box E, Articles 1982–1987).
13 Anthony Burgess, 'An American Organ', in *Splinters*, ed. by Alex Hamilton
   (London: Hutchinson, 1968), pp. 76–82.
14 For a detailed consideration of all of these stories see Andrew Biswell, *The
   Real Life of Anthony Burgess* (London: Picador, 2005), pp. 322–5.

as they grapple naked in the bathroom with them both becoming aroused by the encounter; and after this, 'the first time either of them had got anything out of Sex',[15] their previously unsatisfying marriage is saved. This cheerful conclusion fits far more neatly with the comedy of *The Pianoplayers* than does the somewhat gruesome original story, but the undertone of menace remains.

The second related work is called 'Trotsky's In New York!', an unpublished musical play dated 1979 that contains in much expanded and developed form the songs and plotline that Billy Henshaw composes during his ill-fated piano marathon.[16] The sequence is presented as farcical to an extent in *The Pianoplayers*, though the crowd is portrayed as being rapt with attention and Billy is described as having transcended piano-playing to become a 'Composer'.[17] The implications for labour relations of the changes in technology wrought by talking films appear in Burgess's claim in *Little Wilson and Big God* that viewing *The Singing Fool* (1926), an Al Jolson musical film that was one of the first to feature the innovation of recorded sound, 'was a great experience, but it had sinister aspects. The pit orchestra had disappeared: musicians were joining the industrial unemployed.'[18] 'Trotsky's In New York!' was never produced or staged, though large parts of it find their way into the 1982 novel *End of the World News*.[19]

Publication history

The attempt by Liana Burgess to interest Gladys J. Carr in *The Pianoplayers* in 1977 ultimately failed. This first version of *The Pianoplayers* was proposed by Liana Burgess for publication alongside two other possible works: *Jesus Christ and the Love Game* and

15 *The Pianoplayers*, p. 191. Page references to the published version of the novel are to the present edition.
16 Anthony Burgess, 'Trotsky's In New York!', 1979, typescript (IABF, Manuscript box AB/A/TRO).
17 *The Pianoplayers*, p. 138.
18 Anthony Burgess, *Little Wilson and Big God* (London: William Heinemann, 1987), p. 103.
19 Anthony Burgess, *The End of the World News* (London: Hutchinson, 1982).

Cat Day. Jesus Christ and the Love Game, a novel about the personal life of Jesus, eventually appeared as *Man of Nazareth* with McGraw-Hill in 1979; *Cat Day,* renamed *Puma* during this correspondence and an early version of a science fiction story about a meteor of that name approaching planet Earth, in the end formed one of the three narratives that intertwine in *The End of the World News.* The reasons why McGraw-Hill declined to publish *The Pianoplayers* are not recorded; although Burgess may have felt that the problem with his manuscript was its modest length, other short novel projects of this period such as *Beard's Roman Women*[20] and *ABBA ABBA*[21] did not find this a barrier.

Correspondence between Liana Burgess and Seymour M. Peyser, an attorney acting for the Burgesses in New York, shows that the Josephine Kell manuscript of *The Pianoplayers* was eventually returned to them by McGraw-Hill in April 1979. Burgess is described in a letter from his agent Gabriele Pantucci to Liana Burgess as 'still working on [*The Pianoplayers*]' in January 1981[22] and the novel does not appear again as a proposition until November 1985 in exchanges with Richard Cohen, editor at the publishers Hutchinson in London.[23] Hutchinson had begun to publish Burgess's novels in 1976 with *Beard's Roman Women,* and would continue to do so until the posthumous appearance of *Byrne.*[24]

Having received the draft manuscript via Burgess's agent in July 1985, Cohen contacted Burgess directly.[25] In his letter, Cohen laments that the scale of the project is not quite that of *Earthly Powers*[26] or *Kingdom of the Wicked,*[27] both successes for Hutchinson, and praises the humour of the book; but goes on to express serious reservations

20 Anthony Burgess, *Beard's Roman Women* (London: Hutchinson, 1976).
21 Anthony Burgess, *ABBA ABBA* (London: Faber, 1977).
22 Gabriele Pantucci, letter to Liana Burgess, 16 January 1981 (IABF).
23 Richard Cohen, letter to Anthony Burgess, 15 November 1985 (HRC, box 93, folder 2).
24 Anthony Burgess, *Byrne* (London: Hutchinson, 1995).
25 Richard Cohen, letter to Anthony Burgess, 16 November 1985 (HRC, box 93, folder 2).
26 Anthony Burgess, *Earthly Powers* (London: Hutchinson, 1980).
27 Anthony Burgess, *Kingdom of the Wicked* (London: Hutchinson, 1985).

about the final chapter dealing with the adventures of Robert and Edna in Italy and then in the bathroom. He writes:

> Particularly worrying was your bringing in of one of *the* old chestnuts, the story of the couple who go on holiday with the wife's mother, have her die on them, and then find that the body, and the car, are stolen. This is *such* a well-used story that even moulding it into the novel as you do cannot really make it more than it is. [...] I would ask you strongly for some kind of different killing off of the awful Mrs. Aldridge.

Burgess appears to have been rather stung by this, though his unusually long reply from Monaco the following week shows that it is this intervention by Cohen that leads him to change parts of the final section, using his word-processor as described above:

> The bits you find unacceptable I have rewritten. I agree about the old chestnut aspect of the original version, but ironically enough it seems to [have been] me who put the old chestnut about a good twenty years ago, when I recommended it to a creative writing class in the US (North Carolina). I had read it in a newspaper, then gave it to somebody who put it in a book about Urban Folk Myths and put it there as 'the disappearing mother-in-law'. It does not seem to be known outside Anglo-America, but you may be able to give it an earlier dating.[28]

The story of the theft of the inconvenient body of a despised mother-in-law or other relative appears many times and in many places and it has not been possible to locate the newspaper or book to which Burgess refers.[29] His claim of ownership over the popularity of the story does not seem credible as a result. Burgess goes on:

28 Anthony Burgess, letter to Richard Cohen, 25 November 1985 (HRC, box 93, folder 2).
29 See for example Jan Harold Brunvand, *The Vanishing Hitchhiker: American Urban Legends and Their Meanings* (New York: W.W. Norton, 1981), pp. 112–22. A variant of the story also appears in Katharine M. Briggs and Ruth L. Tongue, eds, *Folktales of England* (London: Routledge & Kegan

The substituted pages are as farcical, but this is right for a section that is intended to be farcical [...] I feel the theme and rhythm of the book require that descent into farce. I may be wrong, but I'd like to keep it as it is. Then I can leave it to reviewers to prove you right. Not that reviewers ever prove anything. A bad lot. Ever since the Americans carved off the final chapter of my A CLOCKWORK ORANGE and landed me into ghastly international difficulties chiefly to do with Kubrick's making a film out of a truncated version of a book which was known in its full version everywhere except in the US, I've been hypersensitive about cutting. I'd be happier if you left things as they are.[30]

The comparison with the revision of *A Clockwork Orange* for the US market is something of a red herring here as *The Pianoplayers* is still at this point in the pre-publication stage.[31] However, that Burgess should invoke probably the most dramatic example in his oeuvre of the effect editorial intervention has had on the reception of his work indicates the resistance he felt to the suggestions made, and the strength of his commitment to the Robert and Edna section of the narrative.

A contract for the UK and Commonwealth hardback publication rights in the novel between Burgess and Century Hutchinson was signed, dated 25 January 1986 and giving an eight-year licence with an advance of £25,000 against royalties.[32] Paperback rights were sublicensed to Arrow Publications for a further payment of £15,000. Richard Cohen wrote back to Burgess in February 1986, thanking him for the extra pages and confirming that 'everything on the script now seems fine', and scheduling the book for publication

Paul, 1965): it is described as 'an international migratory legend. [There are] various versions of the tale, some of them dating back twenty years' (p. 99).
30 Anthony Burgess, letter to Richard Cohen, 25 November 1985 (HRC, box 93, folder 2).
31 Anthony Burgess, *A Clockwork Orange* (London: Heinemann, 1962) and *A Clockwork Orange* (New York: Norton, 1963).
32 Memorandum of Agreement for 'The Piano Player' [*sic*], 29 January 1986 (HRC, box 93, folder 2).

in August of that year.[33] Burgess had no changes to make to the text after this point, and did not object to amendments made by the copy-editor in March 1986; however, on rereading the text he does write that:

> The impersonation of an illiterate woman is never easy, and I have failed in many respects to make my own convincing. I tried this before, in a novel called ONE HAND CLAPPING, where it seemed to come off, but something has gone wrong in this later effort. So into [the copy-editor's] hands I commend the body of the text, hoping that the intended spirit will come through and ignite.[34]

Ignited or otherwise, *The Pianoplayers* appeared in September 1986 in the UK, and simultaneously in the US with Arbor House. Arbor House had previously published US editions of Burgess's *Flame into Being: The Rage of D.H. Lawrence* (1985) and *The Kingdom of the Wicked* (1985). They had recently enjoyed particular success with *Mayflower Madam: The Secret Life of Sydney Biddle Barrows* (1986). Sydney Barrows was a businesswoman who ran an expensive escort agency in Manhattan that was shut down by the authorities in 1984, and her autobiography was a best-seller. Arbor House may have hoped to repeat the feat with Burgess's fictional version of a story with some similar themes.

The novel was translated into German, French, Spanish, Catalan and Portuguese.[35] After it fell out of print in the UK and US no further editions were made.

33 Richard Cohen, letter to Anthony Burgess, 7 February 1986 (HRC, box 93, folder 2).
34 Anthony Burgess, letter to Richard Cohen, 16 March 1986 (HRC, box 93, folder 2).
35 *Der Mann am Klavier*, trans. by Joachim Kalka (Stuttgart: Klett-Cotta, 1989); *Pianistes*, trans. by Jean-Pierre Carasso (Paris: Grasset, 1989); *El Hombre del Piano*, trans. by Jordi Gubern (Barcelona: Ediciones B, 1988), *Els que Toquen el Piano*, trans. by Elisabet Ràfols (Barcelona: Ediciones 62, 1991); *O Tocadordepiano*, trans. by Celso Noguiera (São Paulo: Editora Nova, 1990).

Background and contexts

There is music throughout *The Pianoplayers*. The travails of musicians provide most of the main action; music is the way in which characters are related to each other, as most clearly in Ellen's attempts to emulate her father through learning to play the piano and performing; music appears as a metaphor during its sexual interludes, and frequently elsewhere, such as on the occasion of Ellen's birth during the First World War 'banging and clattering away with the loud pedal down'; and music is used as a way of providing texture and invoking a particular time and place, as with the pages of lists of songs of the era. Beyond this, the novel itself is designed as a series of variations on a theme, with the different generations of the Henshaw family finding different outlets for self-expression through different applications of musical sensibility. The novel ends with a short piece of music, ostensibly taken from the Method of Billy Henshaw to teach 'any kid [to play] Mozart in a month' and evidently an exhortation to the reader to give music a try.[36] This treatment of music can be compared to that in Burgess's other novels where music provides an organising principle, such as in *Napoleon Symphony* which takes Beethoven's Symphony no. 3 (*Eroica*) as its framework, or is used to address questions of freedom and morality, such as *A Clockwork Orange*, where the work of Beethoven and other real and imagined classical composers is used to delineate the humanity of Alex.[37] However, the treatment of music in *The Pianoplayers* is possibly the most intimate and sustained, and relates directly to Burgess's own early musical experiences.

The opening sequences of the novel bear strong similarities to the account given by Burgess of his own life in the first volume of his autobiography, *Little Wilson and Big God*. The birth of Ellen, her father's wartime occupation in the Army Pay Corps, the death of her mother and brother in the 1918 influenza epidemic (Burgess here replacing his sister Muriel for a brother Dan): all of these events

36 *The Pianoplayers*, p. 195.
37 Anthony Burgess, *Napoleon Symphony* (London: Jonathan Cape, 1974).

exactly match the story told in *Little Wilson and Big God*, as does the short-term relocation of the decimated family to an aunt's house in Delaunays Road, Crumpsall, north Manchester, the terrifying picture of a gypsy woman on the bedroom wall and the remarriage of Ellen/Burgess's father to a pub landlady.[38] Just as Burgess's father was a 'cinema pianist', so is Billy Henshaw; and just as Ellen's Manchester is one of grime and squalor, 'not the best place in the world for a kid to be brought up',[39] Burgess's Manchester is 'an ugly world with ramshackle houses and foul back alleys'.[40] The narratives of *The Pianoplayers* and *Little Wilson and Big God* move apart after the marriage, as, while Billy Henshaw is evicted for an adulterous transgression, Joe Wilson remained with Burgess's hated stepmother. The early parts of *The Pianoplayers* are none the less shot through with the detail of Burgess's Manchester childhood, the same details appearing in substantially similar form in his recollections.

Much of the later action of *The Pianoplayers* takes place in Blackpool. Before he left home, Burgess visited a seaside resort with his family every year. As with the descriptions of Manchester, *Little Wilson and Big God* contains descriptions of Blackpool in the 1920s and 1930s that match much of the detail of *The Pianoplayers*: there are memories of drunken festivities, the famous attractions of the Blackpool Tower and the Big Dipper, the sea perennially full of jellyfish, the suspect sideshows of the impresarios and the song booths of the popular music composers and publishers of the day.[41] However, though many of the details are the same, the tone is noticeably warmer. Ellen's Manchester and Blackpool are more blighted by poverty than the Manchester and Blackpool of *Little Wilson and Big God*, but her resilience and good humour always triumph. Burgess's account of his early life is shadowed by loneliness and casual brutality, and the affectionately frustrated relationship between Ellen and her kind and generous, if weak and easily led, father is different from the rather more distant and

38 *Little Wilson and Big God*, pp. 18–22.
39 *The Pianoplayers*, p. 32.
40 *Little Wilson and Big God*, p. 23.
41 *Little Wilson and Big God*, pp. 126–34.

uncommunicative relationship that appears to have existed between Burgess and Joseph Wilson.

One of the main ways in which *The Pianoplayers* evokes a particular place and time is through its descriptions of food. Ellen remarks at the beginning of the sixth chapter that 'even though we were very poor it seems to me that the things we ate were tastier than what anybody eats these days' (p. 75), and embarks on sensual discussion of HP Sauce – described as 'the one thing in the world that has not changed' (p. 76) – fish and chips, tea and pork sausages. In a 1990 article Burgess expresses the same sentiment for himself: 'HP Sauce, from whose label I learned French when I was four, is rarely around. This, whose quality has not changed in all my seventy-odd years, recalls, when I sniff the bottle, the working-class kitchen of my Lancashire home. It is the lowly equivalent of Proust's madeleine.'[42] However, even as nostalgia proceeds through meals and foodstuffs in the same ways, the fiction of *The Pianoplayers* takes a more cheerful approach to the tastes and smells of the lost past than does Burgess's autobiographical writing, where somatic pleasures cannot fail to bring with them guilt and anxiety: 'Food tasted good, and that was in order, God's gift; flesh felt good, and that was wrong. But perhaps flesh was the devil's work, unless God stepped in and somewhat arbitrarily sanctified it in a wedding: after all, we were warned off the triad "the world, the flesh and the devil". There was, anyway, a contradiction hard to resolve. It is still there.'[43]

The treatment of religion in *The Pianoplayers* is striking when put alongside this, in that the Catholicism that Ellen affects to practise is a source of comedy rather than one of guilt. Ellen's confession to Father O'Casey after her encounter with the paedophile Fred, with the priest at first distracted by his reading of the newspaper and his sudden and prurient fury at learning of her sexual 'sins', is matched almost exactly by Burgess's account of his own confession in similar circumstances: however, in *Little Wilson and Big God* he is 'sick with fright' (p. 66) and describes a wrenching internal conflict between

---

42 Anthony Burgess, 'A Clockwork Forage', *Harper's and Queen*, May 1990, pp. 206–7, p. 206.
43 *Little Wilson and Big God*, p. 86.

the apparent heaven of sexual activity and the inevitable hell of dam-
nation for it. This is quite different from Ellen's response: '[Father
O'Casey] forgave me and gave me five Our Fathers and five Hail
Marys, which wasn't too bad all things considered, and off I went
to say them in front of the statue of Our Lady. And I stuck to that
way of doing things all the time, and no harm seemed to come to me'
(p. 72). And it is true that despite the grime and squalor and abuse
and misery in *The Pianoplayers*, no real harm does come to anyone,
apart from possibly Billy Henshaw, though his deliverance might
come from his sacrifice at the piano.

The treatment of sex is perhaps where the clearest distinction
appears between the novel and the memoir, and between this novel
and Burgess's other fiction. One of the main messages of *The
Pianoplayers* is that a cheerful and frank approach to sexual matters
is best for everyone in the end, and that repression and unhappiness
lead to conflict and – only narrowly averted many times, especially
so in the case of Robert and Edna – violence. Burgess's memories of
his early sexual life in *Little Wilson and Big God* are darker and more
complex. His accounts of being seduced, or rather abused, by the
maids hired by his stepmother at the age of nine, losing his virginity
at sixteen to 'a woman of about forty' whom he met in Manchester
Central Library, and later having furtive sex with another maid in
a hotel while on holiday in Cleveleys, a resort near Blackpool, are
presented as confusing and shameful, and Burgess is left accordingly
conflicted and guilty, castigated by priests in the confessional and
punished by his family.[44] These episodes are presented in altered,
ostensibly comic form in *The Pianoplayers*: Ellen is groomed by a
paedophile, pushed into sexual activity by a predatory older woman,
and assaulted by the man who owns the lodging-house where she
and her father are staying. All the sexual encounters in the main body
of *The Pianoplayers* are characterised by imbalances of power and
illegality due to Ellen's age and economic situation, but all of them
end in farce and are understood by her as positive experiences, ultimately turned to apparently good use in her later life as a successful

44 *Little Wilson and Big God*, pp. 66–8, 121–2, 131–2.

escort and then brothel keeper. Burgess's story of his own formative experiences contains no such redemption.

Critical reception

The Pianoplayers was Burgess's twenty-ninth novel, and his reputation as a prolific and successful writer in a variety of forms was well established by 1986. The novel was marketed as a comedy with a focus on the racy adventures of the protagonist. Burgess was complicit in this presentation to the extent that he saw and approved its UK cover design – showing a pair of female legs wearing tights emblazoned with a piano keyboard pattern, apparently being 'played' by a pair of male hands – prior to publication.[45] The US edition went further, and portrayed an entire female body in shadows that give the effect of piano keys, apparently reclining naked (no hands this time).

The book was reviewed in most of the major newspapers and journals on both sides of the Atlantic, and reached number three on the *Sunday Times* best-seller list, spending four weeks in the top ten in the month of publication, just behind *The Old Devils* by Kingsley Amis which had won the 1986 Booker Prize for Fiction. By November 1986 fifteen thousand copies had been sold in hardback in the US.

Enthusiasm from the critics for *The Pianoplayers* was general but not universal. Most positive reviewers compared *The Pianoplayers* favourably to the novel that immediately preceded it, *The Kingdom of the Wicked*, a fictional Biblical-era epic very different in style and content. There was much praise for its humour, inventiveness and frivolity: 'Nothing highbrow about this new novel. He has hit on a brilliant theme, low and heroic at the same time';[46] 'if some of Burgess's books seem as complex as symphonies, this one is noisy, good-natured ragtime'.[47] The most positive reviews tended to come from the US, where both national and regional newspapers responded

---

45 Anthony Burgess, letter to Richard Cohen, 18 February 1986 (HRC, box 93, folder 2).
46 Norman Shrapnel, 'Hero of the Joanna', *Guardian*, 29 August 1986, p. 15.
47 Susan Dooley, 'Ragtime Novel Spreads Burgess Cheer', *Plain Dealer*, 28 January 1987.

well to 'a delightfully bawdy jaunt',[48] 'a compelling entertainment
[...] Anthony Burgess's best novel in years'.[49] Many were charmed
by the detail of life in 1920s north-west England and the apparent
lightness of touch; an especially positive response that makes a virtue
of the apparent insubstantiality of the novel is 'Anthony Burgess and
the Music of Love' by Erica Jong, first published in the *Washington
Post* on 16 November 1986 and reprinted here in Appendix 2.

Some other reviewers, mainly those writing for UK publications,
were bemused or somewhat negative. *The Pianoplayers* was either
dismissed as 'a pleasant absurdity'[50] and an 'easy-flowing, easy-going
improvisation'[51] or compared unfavourably to Burgess's other work:
'How did the author of *Earthly Powers*, to name one among several
remarkable novels, move to the trivia of *The Pianoplayers* without any apparent transition? [...] He turned out the present novel
quickly to meet pressing monetary needs',[52] and 'A bit of a problem.
Compared with such vast and erudite productions as *Earthly Powers*
or *MF*, *The Pianoplayers* seems a relative trifle [...] Unconvincing
and faintly embarrassing.'[53] John Banville's piece 'Burgess and His
Mess of Pottage' sums up this kind of disappointed response and is
reprinted here in Appendix 2.

Biographies of Burgess have addressed the ways in which the
novel relates to Burgess's writing about his own life to some extent,[54]
but beyond this there has been limited critical engagement with

48 Lisa Hickman Bunn, 'Burgess' "Pianoplayers" a Delightfully Bawdy Jaunt',
   Commercial Appeal, 19 October 1986.
49 John Crowley, 'A Droll English Family from Anthony Burgess', *Newsday*,
   21 October 1986, p. 12.
50 D.A.N. Jones, 'Night-flights' *London Review of Books*, 18 September 1986,
   p. 40.
51 Victoria Glendinning, 'Vamps for the Memory', *The Times*, 28 August 1986,
   p. 28.
52 Francis Stuart, 'A Shadow of Burgess's Past Glory', *Evening Herald*, 19
   September 1986, p. 23.
53 Gene Lyons, 'She Was as Pure as Snow and She Drifted', *New York Times
   Book Review*, 2 November 1986, p. 7.
54 Andrew Biswell, *The Real Life of Anthony Burgess* (London: Picador, 2005),
   pp. 18–19, 322–4; Roger Lewis, *Anthony Burgess* (London: Faber, 2002),
   p. 57.

The Pianoplayers following the reviews on publication, mainly perhaps because new printings of the novel were not ordered and the
book became scarce. Burgess himself did not return to the work,
though he continued his writing about the piano in an introduction
to *Pianoforte: A Social History of the Piano* by Dieter Hildebrant in
1988.[55] Looking again at Burgess's contribution to *The Lives of the
Piano*, it is striking how extravagantly he describes the instrument:

> Ultimately the piano is a most ingenious structure in which,
> under the hands of Rubinstein, or the single hand of a
> Wittgenstein, opposites are reconciled and acts of magic per-
> formed. The note begins to decay at the very moment of strik-
> ing, but the illusion of durability holds. The instrument is
> a tuned drum, but it is also a human voice. Other stretched
> strings or vibrating air columns are competent to express a
> single aspect of the universe and the human life that tries to
> feel at home in it, but only the piano can attempt, in however
> miniaturised a form, the total picture. That is why it continues
> to deserve our homage and our wonder.[56]

Even if *The Pianoplayers* might be regarded as a work in a minia-
turised form, the novel still deserves some of our homage and our
wonder, not least for what it adds to our understanding of Burgess's
early life and work.

---

55 Dieter Hildebrant, *Pianoforte: A Social History of the Piano* (New York:
   George Braziller, 1988).
56 Burgess, 'The Well-Tempered Revolution', p. 39.

The Pianoplayers

*A Liana
che conosce tutta la scala
cromatica dell' amore*

One

You can see me any afternoon during the summer months, sitting at one of the tables in the square under the chestnut trees and taking a vanilla ice with a small whisky poured over it. The tables fill this square, which you could call like the social centre of the little town of Callian in the Var, which is in Provence, which is in the South of France. Half the tables belong to Les Marroniers and the other half to Le Petit Vatel, and if you're new to the place you can only get to know which tables belong to which café by sitting down and waiting. If it is fat little Philippe with the curly hair but going a bit bald who comes to ask you what you desire, then you are patronising Les Marroniers. This is a restaurant as well as a café, and some of their tables are set for meals during the summer months. There are three very pretty girls waiting on, and sometimes, it is force of habit, I look at them a bit commercially. There is Philippe's wife Jeanette, there is the German girl Trudi who is engaged to be married to the local butcher, and there is the jolie blonde French girl not yet married nor even engaged, but always kissing and cuddling the very dark boy that works in Bazin's garage, even when she should be waiting on. She is called Mirabelle and always looks half-naked, what with her shoulder-straps slipping down when she carries the dishes and her skirt slit almost up to her bottom. Ah well, she is as God made her.

The square is really a triangle, with the longest side by the main street which is the road to Grasse one way and to Draguignan the other but separated from it by shrubs in tubs and two big chestnut trees, the shortest side being the front of the church with a bench outside where Monsieur le Curé sits with his collar and tie on to show he is a priest. The other side is the Cascade, with water splashing down all the time through like tangled greenery into a big basin with candy and ice cream wrappers floating on it, then there is the house of Mme Guillemot, who mutters and comes down her front steps backwards, and then the shop which sells cigarettes and newspapers and stationery and sunbathing lotions and espadrilles. It has outside it a couple of revolving stands, one filled with newspapers and the other with magazines like *Paris-Match* and *L'Express* and some very dirty ones, all hot hairy hands and bosoms. A lot of us who sit here use both of these as public libraries, reading the reading matter but not buying it. Monsieur Rue, who runs the place, gets mad at this sometimes but he soon gets over it, human nature being what it is, especially here in the Var. It was while I was looking one day at a copy of a music magazine called *Gamme* that the idea of doing something for the memory of my poor father came into my head. For inside it there was an interview with my grandson the famous pianist and a photograph of him looking very handsome.

I might have let the idea pass, what with the heat and the laziness, if another thing hadn't happened and then another. The first of these was me lying awake in the middle of the night not able to sleep because of the heat and the mosquitoes and a bit of indigestion I'd got from a bottle of Côtes de Provence in Les Marroniers, French wine not being what it used to be. I was listening to the BBC Overseas Service on my little radio, and it was one of these request programmes, with Amazing Grace for Albert Nguzumu of Southern Nigeria, and Thus Spoke Zarathustra for Joseph Zarathustra, as it might be, of North-western Afghanistan. Miss Li Po Chang of Western Sumatra requested The One-armed Fiddler's Waltz, and here it is, Miss Li. This was a record very popular then and it still is, with ten thousand fiveyear-olds in South-Eastern Tokyo who had just started on the Sukiyaki Violin Method, which was really invented by my poor old dad. And it was my poor old dad who had written this thing, I'll give you a copy later, and he had not made one solitary penny, old or new, out of it. This put me into a sort of hopeless rage, as hearing it nearly always does, and I was just about

ready for the man who lives opposite, our windows all being open
because of the heat. This man is Italian I should think, with a name
something like Vermicelliano. He is a bricklayer with two cars and a
big family, you can see them sitting down at the table of an evening
for their dinner, the wife very gross and loud and him even grosser
and louder, stripped to the waist for his spaghetti and all boils and
hair. This man and his family can play their television screaming all
day, but let me put my little radio on in the middle of the night with
the insomnia and he wakes up and starts his abuse. I usually turn
the radio down, being desirous of being neighbourly so to speak,
but this time when he started I let him have it back. I gave him the
worst going over in really dirty French that he must ever have had
in his life. It shut him up all right, him just mumbling something
about denouncing me to the Maire, but then, with my desire of being
neighbourly, I turned off my radio and tried to read the latest John le
Carré which I'd bought from the Britannia Book Shop in Cannes, a
very dull writer who is good for sending you to sleep.

There is a big laugh, only it is a bit bitter, in the name of the street
in Callian where I have my little house for the summer. It is called
Rue des Muets, which means Street of the Dumb, but it is the noisiest
street imaginable, what with Vermicelliano and his wife and kids,
and the three homo Algerians always quarrelling, and dirty too what
with the big dogs leaving their *crottes* all over people's doorsteps.
Well, the dirty language I gave out with this night showed I was as
fit for the street as anybody there, including the filthy old widower
who lives next door to me with his filthy hairy great dog that shares a
bed with him and pees all over it, or so they say in the talk at Madame
Durand's the boulangère. Looking at me, though, you would never
think me capable of such a thing. I am a nice slim elderly lady, a bit
scrawny round the neck as is only natural, but with her white hair
nicely blued at the best hairdresser's in Cannes, which is where I
spend the winter, and nails nicely looked after and tinted cinnamon
and a little bit of lipstick and eyeshadow, and usually to be seen in
a nicely tailored blue or grey or off-white linen trouser suit. I pride
myself on being very English and even try to speak French with an
English accent, but old habits die hard as they say, and I find this

very hard to do. I have been called La Belle Hélène in my time, but I was born Ellen Henshaw and I stick to my maiden name.

You know, when you come to Callian as a stranger, when you're sitting in the part of the square that is looked after by Le Petit Vatel because it is a woman of about thirty-five called Claudine who crosses the road, sometimes having to wait till big refrigerated trucks pass, from where Le Petit Vatel is to ask you what it is you desire. She wears a dress with a bit of string round where her waist used to be and she looks like a picture by Picasso, one of those where there is a profile but you can see both the eyes. I knew Picasso for about half an hour because he came once in Paris for the use of my services but could not do anything, but that's part of another story. Le Petit Vatel used to be an auberge with a restaurant, but now all the rooms are shut up and it is only a café full of old men with caps on playing cards and dropping caporal ash over them. But some people think it is still a hotel and they go there looking for a room. This is what happened to the young man who is helping me with this story.

I felt really sorry for him when he trudged into the town from the Montauroux direction with his dirty shorts and his hairy legs all bitten by mosquitoes and his big pack on his back, and his face all streaming with sweat and his glasses all misted up. He asked Claudine in very bad French for a room for the night and perhaps longer, but all she did was shake her head at him very grim, so he sat down at the table next to mine in the shade of the biggest chestnut tree in the square and ordered a small bottle of Perrier. I know he doesn't mind me mentioning these things. After all, he's taking it all down off the cassette recorder. His name is Rolf Marcus and he says he comes from a place called Angostura or something in New Mexico.

'You looking for somewhere to stay, love?' I said, and he said:

'Thank Christ there's somebody here who speaks English. In that other place down the road, Monty Roo or whatever the shit they call it, they said they were all full up and I'd find a great big empty hotel here in this shit of a place.'

'I'll thank you,' I said, 'not to say shit to a lady of my age and appearance. And a great big empty hotel is just what you've come here and found. And they want it empty so it stays empty.' I couldn't help feeling a bit sorry for him, he had the look of my own son as he so often was, sort of frustrated. 'A lad of your age,' I said, 'should be sleeping under the stars. It's not even as if you shave.' Because he had this ginger beard. He looked in his late twenties but now I know he was thirty-one.

'I need a table and chair and a smidgen of tranquillity,' he said. 'In this pack on my back there's my typewriter, and I've come to France to break the block. You know what a block is?'

'A block is a word with several meanings,' I said, 'and one of them is a dirty meaning.'

'Would I be talking dirt to an old lady? I got this advance for a book and I can't write it, that's what block means. I want a nice cheap room so I can break the block. Where could I find such a place? What's the next town down the road?'

It was then that the idea started corning to me, him coming here being the third of the three things. 'What kind of a writer are you,' I said, 'besides being what is known as a book writer?'

'I did this thing on beachboy culture,' he said. 'Interviews all written up. Surf and Scurf it's called, they didn't take it in Europe. You French?' he then said.

'Why would I be French?' I said.

'You speak English with kind of a funny accent.'

'It is you that has the funny accent. My way of speaking is called a Lancashire accent,' I said. And then I said: 'In my little house there is what is known as a grenier. It is very long and has a very low ceiling, so you would have to watch your head.'

'Come again?' he said. 'You offering me a room? No kidding? How much?'

'Nothing,' I said. 'One condition is no use of the kitchen though you can use the bathroom and lavatory if you leave them tidy. The other condition is that you write down this book about my father.'

'But I don't know your father. Didn't know him is what I mean. You putting me on?'

'You will get all the facts from me,' I said. 'All you have to do is to write them down. I am not very good at writing, me having followed a different kind of trade.'

Now, at this moment a car pulled up across the road and a man and his family of wife and three kids got out, the kids clamouring for cokes and ice cream. He was a man of about fifty, bald and with a belly on him and a bit jowly, his wife a good deal younger, one of these washed out French blondes, and the kids young enough to show he'd left it a bit late getting married, or perhaps this was his second or third. The car was a big Mercedes, so you could see he was doing all right. Anyway, he suddenly caught sight of me, at first didn't believe it, then gulped, then his eyes popped, then he believed it, then started packing the kids back into the car, saying this place was too crowded and they'd go on to Montauroux. Oh, papa, non. Si, get on in. I didn't know him from Adam, but he knew me. A former client, many years back. It happens quite a lot, famous men too, ministers of education and economic planning, that sort of thing. I don't remember them, but they remember me.

My young man, Rolf Marcus, didn't catch on to what I might have meant by saying a different kind of trade. He knows better now, but he was innocent then and still part of a generation that thinks that older people not only do not have a sex life but have never had one. Each generation invents sex for the first time. He was thinking and drawing a little circle with his finger and some spilt Perrier on the Formica table top. Then he looked up and said: 'Okay, it might help break the block at that. Mornings only and afternoons I do my own thing.'

'Mornings,' I said, 'you do what you call your own thing. I consider myself to be what is called a lady of leisure, which is only right at my age, and I am not available until midday.'

So that was why, for one of the summer months that year, you could see me any afternoon at one of the tables, taking a vanilla ice cream with whisky poured on to it and talking to this young man's cassette recorder until two cassettes were full and he went back to the grenier to type it all out. It is his work, but the story is all mine. Meaning my father's story and mine.

Two

My dad always called himself not a pianist but a pianoplayer. Rolf Marcus says it ought to be piano player, with a hole between the two words, but I say that pianoplayer one word gives you a better idea of what he was. The piano. Pause. The player. There's the piano, waiting. Then the player comes on and you clap like mad. No, it wasn't like that for my poor father. Pianoplayer gives you the idea of him and the instrument being like all one thing, jammed together. In the pub, in the cinema, at the end of the pier in Blackpool he was always the pianoplayer. No applause for my dad. He was not Schnabel or Rubinstein or Horowitz or his own great grandson. He was the pianoplayer.

Pianist, he used to say, means somebody in white tic and tails who interprets Chopin beautifully and never, unless he's Schnabel, plays a wrong note. If he's Schnabel the wrong notes are expected and are part of his style. He used to say sometimes that Schnabel practised the wrong notes. My dad didn't have to practise them. They came natural, or sharp or flat as the case might be.

Perhaps I'm being a bit fanciful but pianoplayer somehow gives you the idea of somebody playing very fast with the loud pedal on all the time. My dad could play slow enough, and sometimes the piano he worked with had pedals that didn't work. But the kind of jobs he got usually called for hammering it out fast and loud over the other noise. I mean, no pianissimo for him. If he'd played pianissimo he'd not have been heard. They'd call out: 'Where's the bloody pianoplayer gone to?' When he wanted to play something nice and soft and they said they wanted a bit of noise he'd sometimes say:

'I'm playing p.' Then somebody very humorous would lift up his pint glass and say:

'And we're drinking it.'

'P. P. P. That means soft. It stands for piano, which is the Italian word for soft. Piano. Soft. This instrument's called a piano. Its real name is pianoforte, and forte means loud. If you want it loud all the time then what you want's an instrument called a forte. So bugger off and let me get on with the job. Such as it is.'

Such as it was. He was a professional pianoplayer. Professional. He wasn't too sure that he deserved that word. Professional meant white tie and tails and applause, it meant knowing it all and having a big repertoire. But, as I used to point out to him, professional also means earning your living by it. You can play like an amateur but still be a professional. He earned his living by it all right. If you could call it a living. My dad, the professional pianoplayer. I was a professional too, just like my dad, but I was more the piano than the player, and I was usually played on by players who could hardly manage chopsticks. Still, they paid for their bit of a tune. More of this later, if you can bear it.

I was born while the First World War was hammering and clattering away with the loud pedal down and my dad, even though he was officially a corporal in the Army Pay Corps, which they called the Apple Pie Core, was doing his bit to defeat the Hun by being a pianoplayer in khaki. He was C3 because of his chest and was with a lot of other seethree-ers in a Divisional Concert Party. He'd been in France, well behind the lines, ready to give a bit of diversion to the troops when they came back from the front. It was the usual kind of outfit that they had in those days and still have in Australia – I am thinking of Les Girls in Sydney, men in drag highkicking with fat hairy legs. They would have K-K-K-Katie glorious Katie, you're the only g-g-g-girl that I adore and hits from the Bing Boys and sketches with the sergeant-major bringing the troops tea in bed and so on. My dad had a pierrot costume over his khaki and would be on the stage knocking hell out of the old joanna. Doing his bit.

It was very nearly the end of the war that he had this dream in barracks that things weren't going too well at home, meaning the house we had in Manchester, No. 81 Bagshot Street, Harpurhey. He was in Preston, Lancs at the time, out of the concert party and doing imprest accounts, and he'd had this dream about seeing my mother with her nightdress all in flames and shrieking: 'Come home Billy and put the fire out.' He asked for a pass and they wouldn't give it him, so he just walked out of the barracks, caught the train and then the tram and put his key very shakily in the door. The house was very cold, dreams going by opposites, and there was not a sound except for me crying. He dashed upstairs and found my mother and my brother Dan who was four lying dead on one bed and me crying out alive in the other, a cot really. It was the flu. The flu, not the war, was the real killer, God's little joke or something. The woman next door, Mrs Rowbotham, was supposed to be looking after my brother and mother, who had just seemed to have had a bit of a cold when my mother last wrote, but she got struck down too and was lying dead at the same time, not getting into her husband's dreams out there in Flanders, because that poor bugger had just been seen off by a German bullet. What a bloody world. What a filthy stinking bloody mess of a world. And yet they say that life is good. The funny thing is that it is, God help us.

My father sent a telegram to the barracks saying what had happened, and they sent one back saying he had to come back right away and be put on a charge for being absent without leave. So he said bugger you, put that on the charge while you're at it (not in a telegram, just to himself), and saw about getting my mother and brother buried in Moston Cemetery. Then, or at the same time, or before, what does it matter, he took me to his sister-in-law's, my Aunt Bertha in Delauneys Road, Higher Crumpsall, and said: 'For God's sake don't you go down with the flu too.' She was a tough wiry old bird, some fifteen years older than my poor mother, and she would have sent the flu whimpering off with a couple of sharp backhanders if it had dared to come to her front door. So neither she nor I got the flu, nor did her two daughters that worked in the Ministry of Pensions and Slaughter, Slaughter and Sloane respectfully respectably and respectively, thank you Rolf, as shorthand typists. So my father went back to face the music in one sense and then in the other, because he'd done what had to be done and family came first and bugger the army and sod the war and the war came to an end then anyway, so that was all right. And he came out of the army and started looking for a pianoplaying job.

Most of the furniture we'd had in Bagshot Street was sold off, except of course for the piano, a French make, Garveau of Paris, *Médaille d'Or* 1878, and he had this shifted to the front room of my Aunt Bertha's house. My Aunt Bertha, by the way, had been widowed before the war, when my Uncle George, or Jud as he was called, who I never knew but still he was supposed to be my uncle in heaven, had been run over by a tram on Queen's Road, Miles Platting. The house was not all that big, but there was room enough for my father and me and my cot in the spare room, and there was certainly enough room for the piano in the front room. The idea was that my father should give lessons to whomsoever could afford to pay for them, a bob per lesson, and a card was put in the window saying PIANO LESSONS 1/- PER HR. The trouble was that people, when they wanted lessons at all, meaning usually for their kids, wanted them in the evenings, and in the evenings my father was pianoplaying at the Gem Cinema, on that same Queen's Road where my uncle in heaven Jud had been run over by a Manchester Corporation tram. And if they wanted lessons during the day, they could only have them on Sunday, which they didn't want, Sunday being a day of rest, or on Saturday mornings, Saturday afternoon being the kids' matinée, for which my dad of course played, not very well as a rule, as he'd usually had a liquid lunch in the Golden Eagle, Lodge Street, Miles Platting. Which meant that he didn't give many lessons on Saturday mornings.

Of course, none of what was going on in my father's life meant very much to me, seeing that I was a very young kid. I first came to life, so to speak, in 1921. I can remember a lot that happened then, Aunt Bertha cleaning the mats with tealeaves and a broom, feeding me too much bread and dripping and chip butties and fried fish and twopennorth of smalls, which is the name they gave to the bits of crisp batter which fell off the fish while it was frying, my dad sometimes waking me up with his heavy-footedness when he came home from playing for the second house pictures. Sometimes he and my Aunt Bertha would have a hell of a row about something and she'd yell 'Get out, I don't want you in the flaming house, get a proper job and get married again, go on, bugger off.' I often had nightmares. The biggest nightmare had to do with the big picture of a gypsy woman on the spare room wall, a big dark face with a lot of black hair and big black eyes staring out at you, and the name of the picture was, my dad said, BEWARE. The nightmare started off with this picture opening up like a door, and inside there were little men dancing about who I knew were made out of horse shit. There was plenty of horse shit on the roads in those days, and some quiet afternoons you could hear people shovelling it up for garden manure. The only way of following horses with success, it was called. When I saw these little men I would wake myself up with screaming, then everybody would be awake and into the room, and the light on and bare feet on the linoleum. They could have stopped that nightmare by getting rid of the picture, but they never did. People get very hidebound somehow.

My two cousins, the city typists, were named Freda and Ethel, and I always seem to remember them as one girl with two bodies, Frethel or Eda if you like. They were dark and dumpy and were not perhaps young enough any more to be called girls, and they had boyfriends who might have been the one boyfriend split into two for all I knew about it. Very dim people, like most people. My aunt was not dim, although she looked dingy, which was expected of a widow in those days, and she had a very loud voice. She would shout at me: 'Eat up your fish and chips, fish and chips costs money, you wasteful little bugger.' As for my dad he was about medium height and of medium intelligence, and he had a medium sized pot through the drinking of draught Bass. He also wore a pot, which is what they used to call a bowler hat. He had ginger hair growing thin, and he smoked Wild Woodbine cigarettes. I first learned to read from the empty packets. I also learned my first bit of French from the HP Sauce bottle: 'Setty sauce dee premier choiks,' so it began. In 1921 my father was courting hard somewhere, because it was in 1922 that he said I was to have a new mother and that we were going to live in a pub. By this time

I was calling my Aunt Bertha 'mother', and I screamed that I didn't want to have a new mother. But I had to have one just the same.

My father wasn't really getting married. What he was going to do was just live with a woman who kept a pub, a woman separated from her husband, her husband had gone off with a young girl, a barmaid I think it was. The woman had had the pub licence from the husband who had died previously, not the one who'd gone off. The pub was called The Grapes, though it sold no wine, except port and sherry, it was in a slummy district, it was big and full of brass rails, and it had two singing rooms, as they were called, as well as a lot of odd snugs and ladies' parlours and the like. I had a room to myself now, next to the one where my dad slept with the woman I had to call mother, whose name was Rosie O'Brien, Manchester Irish. My father served behind the bar and played the piano in the big singing room. He didn't have a wage, he told me later, only pocket money. I cried a lot, being lonely, and not liking the barefoot kids in the slummy street very much, nor the pub customers either, who smelled of beer and called me mardarse. There was a lot of noise and a fair amount of fighting near closing time. It was not the best place in the world for a kid to be brought up.

I was not brought up there for long. My dad had a hell of a row with Rosie O'Brien, who I was supposed to call mother. It was something to do with what her second husband had done, that is a bit of slap and tickle and then a bit more with one of the spare time barmaids. Before I knew what was properly going on, dad and I were in lodgings in Moss Side, a bedsitter it would be called now, dirty, dark and cheap I supposed, with a single bed for him and me sleeping on the ragged old couch, and a gasring, and a lavatory and bathroom for everybody on the same floor to use. It was in Lincroft Street off Moss Lane East, and my father was now working at the Royal Cinema, run by Jakie Innerfield. I remember him saying to me, while he opened up the *News of the World* wrapping of the fish and chips he'd just bought for our supper on Princess Road:

'Never again, girl. It's going to be just you and me from now on. There was no woman like your mother, and there never will be again.' He put the fish and chips on two old plates with the willow pattern on them, and he fetched the salt and vinegar out of the cupboard. 'Never again,' he said. 'Bugger the lot of them.' We had nothing of our own now, not even the French piano, but my father had this job, and he had hopes of getting a better job with the Piccadilly Cinema in Piccadilly, Manchester, people sometimes forgetting that London is not the only place with a Piccadilly, playing in the orchestra there.

I'd started going to school now, a Catholic one called the English Martyrs, run by nuns, and my father would take me there in the mornings, bring me back at dinnertime, take me back in the afternoon and be waiting for me at four o'clock unless it was a matinée day. Then he used to trust me to get back on my own. I could have got back on my own any time, but I think my dad wanted to feel less guilty about not being able to get a daytime job like everybody else in the world. The way he put it to himself was that he had no right to be working during the day, except for cinema matinées, when he had me to look after. In the evenings all he could do was to take me with him to the Royal Cinema, which was a real dirty old bughouse, and plant me there in the front row where he could keep an eye on me as well as the screen. This way I got to know films very well, though very big, with a fly on somebody's eyelid very clear to see, and a stiff neck which became almost a habit, though it was good as they said for my Deportment. I know the films from, say, 1924 to the time of *The Singing Fool* as well as anybody in the world, for I saw most of them at least three times. I did not always see them in the same cinema though, for my dad chopped and changed, was thrown out here, taken on there. He never got the big job in the Piccadilly Cinema. They said he was not good enough. In a way this was true.

This is the way in which it was true. My dad could not play with an orchestra. He didn't like having to bow and scrape to the leader or chief bow-scraper. The leader arranged the programme for the big picture, this starting with a march and going on with a waltz and then to a novelty intermezzo or something, and there would be whole chunks of the film which even to somebody who was tone deaf had music going on which had nothing to do with the action. The orchestra would still be playing Mendelssohn's Spring Song when the prairie was covered with snow. They would be playing the end of the Poet and Peasant Overture while the lovers were having their first kiss. My dad could not resist breaking away and playing what he thought was right – big loud chords for the fall of Jericho while the others were still on Rubinstein's Melody in F. This caused a lot of trouble. It happened not at the Piccadilly, which my father did not get within smelling distance of, nor at the Royal, which he left because he couldn't stand the bossiness of Innerfield's two daughters, but at the Star, where the manager brought in drums and fiddlers for Saturday nights, and my father would not tolerate it. What he said to the manager was this:

'Look, you're running a picture house so you ought to know something about pictures. Pictures are made with very short scenes. They cut, cut is the word they use, very quickly from one scene to something different. The music should do exactly the same thing, and that has to mean one man, meaning the pianoplayer. An orchestra is just a waste of the firm's money.'

'Who's running this place, Billy?' he said.

'Ah, don't talk bloody daft, you don't know the first thing about it. I was playing in picture houses before the war while you was trying to sell gentlemen's neckties.' Which was true because cinema managers were only silly little men who put on a dinner jacket at night to show they were running the shop, collected the money, paid the wages, and tried to get up the skirts of the girls who showed the customers their seats, usherettes they called them later. The manager, Fred Hawkes, knew my father was right. But he said one thing in 1925 that was like a prophecy:

'One of these days the music will come on like a big gramophone record along with the reels. All worked out beforehand and fitting exact. Then I won't have to have your lip or the lip of any tinpot pianoplayer who thinks he's Paderooski.' Of course his prophecy didn't go far enough. He was only a silly little man without much brains and smelling of beer and peppermint.

The piano that my father had to play on at the Star was a broken-down old thing that never got tuned, but my afternoon dad never complained. He showed me on Saturday once just before the matinée, with the kids screaming at the door wanting to be let in, just how a man of resource, as he called himself, could do big things even with a lousy piano.

'All those notes down there in the bass is just a lot of noise, but that's very useful for drums and thunder and so on. And that D there is gone, but it's fine for someone tapping at the window. And that E flat up there near the top has dropped down so it's the same as D flat, and that means I can do a trill on one note fast. Faster than what Paderooski could do on a proper piano.' My father had stripped all the wooden panels off the piano, so that he could bang the wires with a coalhammer that he'd pinched to make the effect of bells and zithers. As he said himself, he was more than a pianoplayer when it came to films, he was an effects man too. He took pride in having all sorts of little odds and ends he'd picked up or nicked to give what he called greater reality. He had a little clockwork bell for when somebody rang at the door on the screen. If a shepherd played a flute to his sheep in the meadows then he'd come in with a tin whistle. For rain he used to rattle dried peas in a biscuit tin. He once got himself a sheet of aluminium to shake for thunder, but he'd pinched it off a man who was trying to build his own racing car out in the street and there was a row about that. When there was a gramophone playing on the screen he had a real old portable with a record of Pretty Redwing. Somebody pinched this, though he'd pinched it himself. They were a pretty mean lot of customers at the Star, and they never appreciated what my poor dad did for their entertainment and enlightenment. Most of the music he played he made up as he went along. As he used to say, the buggers were getting Original Compositions for their lousy threepence.

The films he hated most were the comedy ones, Charlie Chaplin and Chester Conklin and so on because playing was really hard work then, very fast ragtime style, no real letting up at all, not even for the odd kiss and cuddle. He liked best a film with plenty of variety in it and the odd chance to slow down, playing a few chords with his left hand while he had a swig from a bottle of Bass's Pale Ale with his right. A fat woman next to me in the front row spotted him doing this one night and said it wasn't right him doing that, that was not what he was paid for, he was paid to play with both hands and at the same time too. So what he did then was to switch into the key of G flat or F sharp, the same thing of course, and play some nice little harp runs on the black keys with the base of the beer bottle. 'Is that allowed, missus?' he said, and she said, 'Cheek, that is.' One night he played a little tune in the middle of the piano with his nose, while his hands were busy at either end of the keyboard, but nobody appreciated it or even noticed it.

A film with plenty of variety was what he liked, as I just said, and this meant a railway train, a house on fire, a scene by the lake for lovers, galloping horses (a pair of wooden rickers in his right hand and quick chords with his left), a fist fight that did not go on too long, a ball scene with the Blue Danube waltz for preference, soldiers marching down the street coming home from the war, that sort of thing. Battle scenes were a big nuisance. He could get machine gun effects with the wooden rickers, but the big guns were not possible for him. He brought me into his special effects when I was nine. There was this Mary Pickford film in which she sings Home Sweet Home, with the words coming on the screen just to show what she was singing, and the second night of the showing of it he had me there next to him actually singing the song but not very well, and then of course he cut me off in the middle of a word or note while he went on to the next scene which was of two dogs doing a tug-of-war with an old pair of bloomers or something.

My poor dear, dead dad, how hard he worked and for so little money too. And all the time he worried about me, needing a mother and only having a father, but he was finished with women, so he said, and not eating the right kind of food, too much fish and chips, too many shop meat pies. When tomatoes or oranges or apples were cheap, he would stuff those into me for my Health's sake, as he said, but they only gave me diarrhoea. I drank plenty of milk off people's doorsteps as well as our own and didn't have many illnesses, only a lot of colds. He used to worry a lot about himself getting ill, because they'd get somebody else in at the Star and probably keep them too, there not being any trade union for pianoplayers to fight against the injustice of cinema managers, and he said to me, and me still not more than ten:

'Girl, you've got to learn, you've got to be able to take my place.'

'You mean I've got to take piano lessons, dad?'

'Not real piano lessons, no, like I had, scales and twiddly bits and such, not that. I've got to find a short cut for you, girl.'

One Sunday he brought in a long piece of like golden coloured wood that he'd pinched from a builder's yard when nobody was looking, and he got my school ruler and a thick black pencil, which he had to keep sharpening with a big German penknife he'd nicked off somebody in the war who'd nicked it off a dead German, and very neatly he drew part of a piano keyboard on this wood, two octaves and a bit to be exact. First of all he like ruled the white notes, then he said:

'One of the great things about having the black notes on a piano is that they show you just where you are with the white notes. See now, I'm going to draw the black notes.' And he started to draw them. 'Here you have two,' he said, 'and then you have a bit of a gap, and then you have three, and then a bit of a gap, and then two, gap, three, gap, and so all the way from arsehole to breakfast time, excuse my French. Now the white note just to the left of the two black ones is called C. It doesn't matter where it is on the piano, it's always C. C high up, C low down, C in the middle which is what we call middle C, but always C. Now you take that C and you go up, one at a time, till you've reached the next C. That's called the scale of C, see. It's C D E F G A B C. It's also *do ray me fa so lah ti do*. I want you to practise playing that now.'

'But that's daft, dad, there's no sound coming out.'

'Well, just you imagine we've both gone deaf, girl, and try to hear the sounds inside your head. Damn it all, Beethoven was as deaf as a bloody post, and he could hear it all going on.'

'Who's Beethoven, dad?'

'This German bugger who wrote the greatest music in the world when he was deaf. If you're a good girl I'll play some Beethoven tomorrow night when they do this film about the French Revolution.'

'What's the French Volution, dad?'

'It was when all these poor French buggers who were starved and treated like slaves rose up against their masters and sent them to the guillotine which was like a great big bloody razor blade hanging in the air that they let drop and sliced the bugger's head off, clean as a whistle. And don't ask any more questions, cause you're only trying to get out of your piano lesson. Go on, get your fingers on there and play the scale of C.'

So I did that, and he sang *do ray me fa so lah ti do*. Then we had some soup from a can, heated up on the gasring, and after that some cold beef from the cooked meat shop and some bread and butter and mixed pickles. And after that he made a good strong pot of tea. He was the best maker in the world of a good strong pot of tea. The French don't know the first thing about it, dipping their fiddling little bags in tepid water like Chinese dipping white mice into honey. There, that's surprised you, hasn't it? Stick around, kid, and you'll learn a lot.

Three

One thing you're going to learn now, and I don't just mean Rolf Marcus who's taking it down but anybody reading this, is how to play the piano. I had to learn it, so why not you? All right, for me it was an Urgency, a matter of being able to stand or sit in for my poor dad if he was ill, which he was later, as you'll see, and for you it's not worth your while, easier to turn the hi-fi on, and nobody's a pianoplayer any more, it's all nuclear guitars now. Still, you're going to learn the way I did.

The white note to the left of the first of the twin black notes, not the triplets, is always C. At the top or the bottom, it makes no difference, always C. The C in the middle of the joanna is middle C, which stands to reason. Then all the rest follow – D E F G A B, down as well as up: BAG FED. You can play the scale of C eight times over, very fast, from the bottom of the keyboard to the top, just by using your thumbnail. That was the first thing I learned when my dad had me there in the picture house half an hour before they started the advertisement slides on the screen. Then he got me on to chords. C E G. F A C. G B D. Those, he said, are the most important ones. Easy, really. Triads, he said, meaning chords made of three notes, tri meaning three like in a tricycle. If there are tricycles, I said, and bicycles, then there ought to be biads. All right, he said, there's C E and F A and G B, but you might as well have triads while you're at it, are you too bloody lazy to use three fingers? While you're at it, he said, you can use another finger or your thumb to turn those tricycles into fourwheelers. C E G B. Sounds a bit nasty, doesn't it? That is what

they call a discord. F A C E – see what that spells? – another discord,
the same sound as the C E G B one but four notes higher, a fourth
higher we say if we're proper pianoplayers. Try G B D F. That's not
so much of a discord, is it?

You can make triads, he said, and sevenths too for that matter, on
any note, black or white. What's sevenths, dad? Sevenths? Sevenths
are these fourwheelers, like C E G B and the others. They're called
sevenths because the distance from the bottom to the top is seven
notes. Count, you lazy thing. So then he had me playing chords on
all the white notes, and it didn't sound too bad, Then he had me
breaking the chords up – c e g c e g f a c f a c b d g b d g – one note
very fast after the other like the sound of water rippling or like a
harp. The Italians, he said, call a harp an arpa, as you might expect,
being too bloody lazy to sound the haitch, and anything like that is
called an arpeggio, meaning like a harp sound. Got that, girl? Now
let's fiddle about with the black notes.

The black note to the right of C is called C sharp. The black note
to the left of D is called D flat. But it's the same sound, dad. Ah my
girl, he said, there's a great mystery there, isn't there? You have a
choice between calling it C sharp and D flat, and let that be enough
for the time being. And so for the rest of these black buggers. Shove
F up half a tone, that means going to the nearest black note on the
right, and it's F sharp. It's also G flat. Try some chords, go on. I
liked the black chords, they were easier on the fingers than the white
ones. I played F sharp A sharp C sharp at the same time with three
fingers in my left hand, and with the fingernails of my right hand I
kept zooming up and down on the black notes. A nice watery sound,
dark water somehow though.

Here's a chord you can't do without, he said, if you're a picture
palace pianoplayer. You use it for fights, burst dams, thunderstorms,
the voice of the Lord God, a wife telling her old man to bugger off
out of the house and not come back never no more. And he showed
me. C E flat G flat A. Or F G sharp B D. Or E G B flat C sharp.
Always the same like dangerous sound, he said, as if something terrible's going to happen or is happening (soft for going to happen, loud
for happening), and you can play whole strings of these chords, each

one based on a different white or black note at the bottom. And you can arpeggio them to make them like very mysterious.

Here's just one more chord, he said, very very mysterious, I see the buggers are starting to come in so I'll have to show you quick, it's this one. C E G sharp. D F sharp A sharp. Make it on any note, good for ghost music, Frankenstein, that sort of thing.

And then he let me go and sit in the front row while he played music to go with the advertisement slides on the screen. Even this he did with the proper sounds for each thing advertised. If it was Stone's the Jewellers, he did wedding bells and Here Comes The Bride, very high up, all tinkly. For Harbottle's Garage he played Get Out And Get Under. For Ollerenshaw the Butcher he did The Roast Beef Of Old England, and once he did the Agnus Dei they sang at eleven o'clock mass at St Thomas's, this meaning Lamb of God, but nobody spotted his little religious joke. For Wilson's the Tobacconist he played what he told me was the Cigarette Girls' Chorus from the opera Carmen. He was never stuck. And after the advertisements the lights would go dark, and my dad would have to play by the light from the screen, not that light mattered to him, he could feel his way a treat in the dark, he said, and then there was the Pathé News. Usually he just played a march for this, Colonel Bogey or Blaze Away, but sometimes he would play the chord you can't do without, C E flat G flat A and its eleven brothers, for a building on fire, the diminished seventh's the name of it and I've never known why, and God Bless The Prince Of Wales if that Royal Personage (surprising you a bit, aren't I?) was shown smoking a cigarette and opening something by cutting a tape with scissors, and he would do Oh I Do Like To Be Beside The Seaside if they were showing Record Crowds at Margate for August Bank Holiday Monday. But the audience never properly appreciated all he did for them, nor did that great fool of a manager. And then we would have the comedy and then the big picture, and my poor dad would be at it all the time. And there were two houses, first and second, and matinées Wednesday and Saturday.

A funny life, when you come to think of it. A lot of cinema pianoplayers only did this job as an extra in the evenings and at Saturday matinées, doing another job, as it might be cutting hair or boiled

ham, during the day. But my dad said he was a musician, maybe a
bloody lousy one, but still a musician, that's what he was, and he'd
tried getting musician's jobs during the daytime but there didn't
seem to be any about. Besides, there was me to look after wasn't
there, me having no mother, and he had to give me dinner at half
past twelve (it was never much of a dinner though: fish and chips
or a meat pie with plenty of tepid gravy) and fetch me from school
at four. I do honestly believe there was a bit of laziness in him, not
really wanting another job, but there was nothing lazy about the way
he'd tackle the pianoplaying. He used to be quite done in when it was
all over. He always gave more than was needed.

Take this evening after he'd been giving me the lesson about the
chords and so on. The lesson must have been on his mind during the
comic picture, which featured Charlie Chase, I remember that very
clearly. While he was playing Ain't She Sweet he suddenly broke
off and vamped a long till-ready while he called me and cried out:
'Listen to this, girl.' And then he began to sing and play:

CABBAGE
FACE –
Cabbage face.
CABBAGE
FACE –
Cabbage face.
If we were in Paris you
Might be called mong petty chou
But you're in a different place
So I call you Cabbage face.

He was so pleased with this that he'd made up that he played the
tune over and over again, not only during the comic but during the
big picture which was Ben Hur. He kept using these notes C A B B
A G E F A C E in all sorts of ways, even during the chariot race, and
I heard one man in the fourth or fifth row say 'Oh for God's sake let
up on it.' He was trying to do two jobs at the same time, my poor
dad, teach me and accompany the picture, and it was typical of him.

My big chance came in 1928 it must have been, when I was eleven, and my dad went down with pains in the stomach, what he called colic which he put down to eating too many unripe bananas of which he'd nicked a bunch from a greengrocer's cart when nobody was looking. He had this habit of nicking things, nothing big, not money nor jewels, just the odd meat pie or a bar of chocolate or somebody's overcoat when he thought he could get away with it, which he usually did. He said he'd picked up the habit in the army, nicking things, you couldn't really call it stealing. Whatever you could call it, he had no real cause to complain if the dozen bananas he'd nicked were now getting back at him. Well, not the whole dozen. He'd only eaten seven of them. I'd refused even to think of eating them, seeing that they were green and hard and like raw. But he gobbled these seven, and now he was suffering, writhing in agony on the bed at six in the evening and saying he couldn't go, he couldn't make it, I'd have to go instead. I felt a horrible churning inside me when he said that.

'I can't, dad, you know I can't.'

'You've got to, girl, it's got to be you. It doesn't matter – ouch oh bugger it the pain – what or how you play so long as you're sitting there making some sort of a – ow the bloody agony – sort of a sod it noise. Those buggers are pig ignorant and don't know a semiquaver from a kick up the arse pardon my bugger it French.'

'What's the big picture, dad?' Because this was Monday.

'It's this big German effort about the City of the Future it's called Metro Polis – ouch damn and bugger the pain.'

'Metropole? That's the name of a big hotel, dad, that one in Blackpool where we had tea that time.'

'No, this is Metro Polis with robots and skyscrapers in it and the workers sod it living under the earth and the bosses supping champagne and that on top. Make us a good hot cup of tea, girl, that might help the agony, bugger it.'

'Seen it already have you, dad?'

'Seen the advertisements, that's all. Big effort it is, been coming shortly for the last six weeks, you must have noticed it and – oh God damn and blast those bloody bananas.'

'But there's the other things as well, the news and the comedy and the rest of it, what can I do about those, I mean, I can't do a march and Ain't She Sweet very fast. Oh dad, I can't, I can't.'

'For me, my dear girl. For your poor old dad do it. Do your best, girl, nobody can do more than his best, oh, ow, to hell with the pain in my bloody guts, bugger it.'

So trembling like a leaf and hardly able to do up the buttons, I put my Sunday frock on, which I never wore even on Sundays because I had to keep it for Special Occasions and this was a Special Occasion all right, and I brushed my hair and looked at myself all pale and haggard and shaky in the mirror, then I put my blue raincoat on and poured dad a third cup of tea and then was on my way, with dad sort of moaning 'Do your best, girl, oh the bloody pain' and I went out. I seemed hardly to have any legs when I walked into the Star. Hawkes opened his mouth very wide when he saw me on my own and he said:

'Where's your dad?'

'He's not coming. A pain in his stomach, real bad. So it's me who's playing instead.'

'You? But you can't. Oh Jesus, why didn't he let me know sooner I could have got Bert Cornthwaite that plays at the Crown Saturdays, oh God, this is a real mess. He's finished, you tell him that from me, pain in his belly indeed.'

'I can play, I tell you. My dad taught me to play.' And I marched down the aisle with my head up. The advertisement slides were just starting to come on. I took no notice of anybody, especially those in the front rows who said 'Where's your dad, love?' but I got under the dirty dusty black like surround of like curtaining that separated the bandpit as it was called from the audience, and I sat down and opened the piano lid and nearly was sick with fright on to the keyboard. Then I took a lot of deep breaths and looked up very cool at the advertisement slides with my hands on my lap, as if to say that that muck up there didn't deserve music. And then the lights went down and I began to feel a bit safer, since nobody could see me, and when the Pathé News started I plucked up my courage and banged out the chord C E G in one hand and the same in the other. The world didn't come to an end, so I did an F A C in both hands and then a G B D. And then I found that by mixing them up and keeping the time going with my left foot I was playing quite a nice little march tune, simple, yes, but nothing wrong with that.

One of the things that my father had told me was about what are called modes. Not moods, modes. He said: 'It's like this, girl. The ancient Greeks weren't satisfied with just C D E F G A B, what we call the scale of C major and all the tunes you can make out of it. They said you could make a scale on every single one of the white notes without bringing black notes into it at all, so to speak. Now try doing *do ray me fa so lah ti do* on the note D. Weird, isn't it, but it's nice. They called that the Dorian mode. The one on E they called the Phrygian mode perhaps because it sounds a bit frigid, you know cold, and the one on F they called the Lydian mode.'

'There's a girl in our class called Lydia Thompson.'

'Is there now, never mind about that. They had seven modes, one for each of the white notes of the piano, not that the poor primitive buggers had pianos of course, and each one was supposed to like have like a different sort of feeling and be used for one occasion and not another, if you see my meaning. Now we got rid of all the modes except two – the one you make on C and the one you make on A. The one on C is called the major mode, and the one that starts on A is called the minor mode. Sad, that is, useful for funeral marches.'

Now the first item of news was about a Boy Scout Rally, so my little march in C did all right there. But the next one was the funeral of some big bug or other in America, a gangster or somebody, so I started on the minor mode and did something solemn and sad. Then there was a big flood in New Zealand and I started on diminished sevenths and ended with quite a nice sad tune I made up in A minor, and I began to feel more confident. Nobody bawled out 'Get rid of her' and nobody seemed to notice it was not the regular pianoplayer, in fact nobody seemed to be listening, pig ignorant and ungrateful lot.

It was while the Pathé News was showing the Duke and Duchess of York in Tahiti or Swahili or somewhere, being treated to a big open air feast of roast pig and bananas, poor dad, that I discovered

a scale by accident that my poor dad hadn't shown me yet. A nice
foreign or tropical kind of scale, and I made it by playing C D E and
F sharp G sharp A sharp. In other words, three white followed by
three black. This made a kind of like native South Sea island tune,
and you could play any or all of the six notes at the same time and
make a nice weird chord of them. Later on, when I showed all this
to my dad, he said: 'Yes, Debussy, that is. He picked it up from the
Javanese or some such buggers. Very nice, but you can't do much
with it.' I did a lot with it that night.

The real trouble was the comedy that came before the big picture,
this calling for something fast and jazzy going on all the time, but I
remembered what my dad had told me – set yourself a nice easy pace
at the start and don't slacken off, and that will seem fast enough.
Play the chords on C, A, F and G over and over again in an oompah
rhythm, the oom being the note in the bass and the pah the chord
in the treble, you see that? So I oompahed along and they were all
guffawing away so much at the Keystone Cops that nobody really
heard me.

And so we came to this Metro Polis, as my dad had called it, but
I found out it was really all one word, with the accent on the Trop.
Of course, looking up at the picture, I got a very distorted view of
it, but I could see in a general sort of way what was going on. There
was a lot of the kind of variety that my dad liked, what with workers
trudging along to work in A minor, and machines in a factory and
skyscrapers, and a robot, and a big flood, and even a dance that the
robot does when it's made to look like a girl by the Mad Scientist,
and I found I had a lot of what was needed, what with diminished
sevenths and my new black-white scale and plenty of noise in that
part of the bass that didn't really play notes, only growled. It was a
long film and my hands were like bits of rag at the end of it, but it
came to an end with the Workers and the Big Boss shaking hands and
agreeing to be nicer and kinder to each other, and there was the big
chord on C major – C E G C E G – for THE END.

And then the lights went up, and there on the screen was the picture of King George V, and everybody stood up for God Save the
King, or at least the first half of it, and God Save Me, I couldn't play

it. There's only one way for a girl to get out of a sticky situation like that and that is to faint. I didn't really chuck a dummy of course, I just pretended. So there was a bit of sympathy in the audience, the first they'd ever shown to the pianoplayer, and people were bringing glasses of water from the lavatory and rubbing my fingers and putting hot hands on my head, and some on other parts too, dirty sods, and poor old King George V on the screen up there was forgotten and, seeing nobody was hearing his music, he just faded out. And then, thank God, my dad had arrived ready for the second house, which I honestly couldn't have tackled, my fingers all like having seized up on me.

He'd taken salt and hot water, he said, and got the lot up, it took a long time, and people kept banging on the lavatory door shouting 'How long are you going to be in there?' and 'Have you fell down the hole?' and so on. I told him it went not too bad, but never again, never, never again. 'No more of those green bananas,' said my dad.

But my dad could never leave well alone. He'd taught me the piano, in his queer daft way, and then one day he came home with a violin, complete with case, that he'd nicked from a furniture removers' van, shoved under his coat, and then run smartish round the corner with. He had some idea that anybody could learn anything, and quickly too, if that anything was not too much and if the teacher went the right way about it. 'Look at this fiddle,' he said, showing it to me. 'You see these four strings? Right, let me tune them,' and he tuned them by sort of listening to the proper notes in his head. 'Here you are,' he said then, 'that thick one's G, the next one D, the next one A, and this thin high one that looks very frayed and about ready to snap is E.' He didn't like the look of the bow, which he said needed resin or rosin on it, but he squeaked away on these four strings till somebody banged on the wall and yelled 'Shut it.' He said: 'Tomorrow night, before it starts, I'll show you what I mean along with the piano.'

The following night he showed me. He'd made up a little waltz tune, and the only notes were these four, E and A and D and G. You know the tune, everybody knows it, it's the tune I was listening to in rage and anger on the BBC Overseas Service, and if you don't know it you'll find it as a free gift at the end of this story. He showed me

how to bow along the open strings as they're called, and he made up
silly words to go with the rhythm –

GET yourcoatand HAT on
WHY didyouput THAT on

and he had me playing it during the comedy, me who'd never han-
dled a fiddle in my life, and it didn't sound too bad because of the
nice big fat chords in his accompaniment on the piano. Of course
nobody noticed and he said 'Ungrateful buggers' quite loud, then he
crashed into the music for what he still called Metro Polis.

Now I was getting on for twelve and well-developed for my age,
though I hadn't started the monthly blood bath yet, and my father
would sometimes look at me and say: 'The spitting image of your
mother, girl, that's what you are. What in God's name am I going to
do with you?'

'How do you mean, dad?'

'I mean, what sort of a future can I give you, me being what I am
and us living as we are. I mean, you're getting to an age now when
it's wrong for us to be sleeping in the same room, and I don't doubt
that that nosy bitch Mrs Etheridge downstairs will start talking soon
if she hasn't started already.'

'To be truthful, dad, I would like a bedroom of my own, some of
the girls at school have them, and I haven't even got a bed, have I, and
that old couch creaks too. Squeaks too.'

He sighed very deep. 'I must start looking round for a day job,'
he said, 'though they're hard to find. I've been a lazy old bugger. I'll
start looking tomorrow.'

'But what sort of a job could you do, dad? You're a pianoplayer
like you always say, and nobody wants pianoplaying during like
working hours.'

'If I could only sing,' he said, 'I might get a job in Lewis's Music
Department, selling the latest songs. I can play them all right, but the
customers want to hear them sung as well.'

'I've never heard you try to sing properly, dad. Try to sing something now.'

'The bloody ceiling will fall down, girl. Oh, all right, I'll try.' And he started on a silly waltz song that was popular that year.

It's a long long lane
That has no turning,
So follow the road to the end.
It's a long long time
That I've been yearning,
So follow the road round the bend.

Somebody started banging on the ceiling as though they were going to make it fall down, like dad had said, and dad said: 'I'm not much good, am I, girl? Of course, I was thinking, I could always try and write down my Violin Method, couldn't I, and get somebody to bring it out, Boosey and Hawkes, couple of disgusting names those are, somebody like that.'

'But you can't play the violin.'

'I know, that's how I know how to teach kids to play it. I must nick some music paper and some ordinary writing paper and a nice fountain pen and start writing it down. That could bring us in a fortune.'

'But what is this Method, dad? You mean just playing on the open strings like you made me do? I thought you had to put your fingers on the strings as well.'

'Right, girl. You start off with just the open strings, and then you add one note at a time to them. I've got some little tunes in my head that I could write down, with a piano part too. The easiest tune would be made out of open string plus semitone, do you see what I mean?'

'No.'

'Well, D and E flat, and A and B flat. Do you get the idea? You could make a nice little tune just out of those four notes. Listen.' And he started to lah a little tune, and the banging on the ceiling started again. 'You keep adding more notes all the time, and the tunes get harder but more interesting, do you see what I'm getting at?'

'No.'

'I'm a bloody fool, aren't I?' He sighed again, deeper. 'All right, I'll go out looking for a job tomorrow. I'm not cut out for bright ideas like a Violin Method.'

He was at the school gates at four o'clock the next day, although I told him as I'd told him before that I was big enough to find my own way home and the other kids laughed at me having my dad come to fetch me, but he said he'd got into the habit and it made his day and it was something to do in the afternoon and he loved his little girl so much he didn't like the idea of rough boys giving her the ki-yike on the way home through that slummy district. But the day after that he was not at the school at four o'clock, and it wasn't a matinée, so I supposed he must have got a job. I went home by myself, then, and dad wasn't there. He wasn't home till six-thirty, which hardly gave him time for some bread and a tin of Skippers sardines before going off to play. Yes, he'd got a job all right, and it was helping to sell pianos in Lodge's secondhand piano department, very small wage but you got commission, and he'd almost forgotten what it felt like to bang a decent piano, secondhand though these were.

With his first week's wages and his regular pianoplaying pay, less two bob for not playing at the Wednesday matinée, he was able to go down and see Mrs Etheridge, whose house this was, and find out that there was another room free on the same terms as the one we already had, but it was a bit smaller and it would not be available till the end of the month when the Indian gentleman, dirty people they are she said, went. And about time too, she said, your daughter's quite a young woman now, she said, leaving school she'll be soon and working. So there it was. A room of my own, with even a gasring for me to make my breakfast on, dad usually being so tired in the mornings. The first thing I did when I got into my own little bed for the first time was to start menstruating, so I knew I was a young woman now.

Four

The spitting image of my mother, my dad had said, and I believed him but I only had her photographs to go on, and these were mostly professional photographs, which are artful and lying and sell a product (thank you, Rolf) more than they show a woman. My mother, like my dad, was or had been a professional before getting married, being a singer and dancer and what was called a soubrette. Her name was Florence and on the stage Flossie, she used her maiden name Oldham, the name of a Lancashire town but not the town her people came from, Preston was their town, Priest Town, Proud Preston, and they were all as Old Catholic as my dad's family was. Flossie Oldham, Queen of the Soubrettes, as the song said.

> I say, Flossie,
> You're the Queen of all the Soubrettes.
> Let me be your beau
> For I love you so,
> Oh you sweet little pet.

I used to say that that wasn't a proper rhyme, but living in France showed me that it is and always was.

She'd been in the chorus of shows like the Lionel Monckton ones, never in London, only in Manchester and district, and she'd been in pantomime at the Ardwick Empire and on tour, and she was once Dick Whittington, and it was a joke I heard as a kid about a travelling pantomime company that put the idea in my head that that sort of life wasn't as Moral as they said it was and I shouldn't have been a bit surprised if my mother hadn't played around a bit in her time, but she was none the worse for that, who am I to talk? The story was about a parson of the C of E travelling in a railway compartment with some of the members of a panto troupe, and he had a big bag of peppermint humbugs that he kept handing round. Very interested he was in who did what, and he'd say: Who takes Dandini? I do, says a girl. Really, have a humbug. And who takes the Fairy Queen? I do. Really, have a humbug. And who takes Dick? We all do, they said, but not for humbugs.

She would do a Vesta Tilley routine while she was still slim, dressed as a soldier mostly, but then her liking for Guinness and pork pies with plenty of piccalilli and fried cod in batter and double chips started to show, and she'd do a saucy wink routine with saucy songs and a lift of the skirt to show the calf to loud whistles, less trouble than dancing about, all furs and paste jewels to catch the spotlights and God knows how many layers of frilly petticoat. One of her songs was this:

How'd you like to follow me?
How'd you like to learn what's what?
Let me take you home to tea
And give it you nice and hot
Straight from the pot.

I can't remember the rest, but it was all winks and what they call here *double entendres*, and her dances never overtaxed her, being mostly bottom wriggling and the like. My dad played in the pit band for a time before he had a hell of a row with the MD at the Ardwick Empire, and that's how they met and started courting.

My dad said to me that those were really the good old days, the music hall with beer and fights and rotten eggs thrown at rotten acts. You had to be good, or at least dominating, no mikes in those days for teeny weeny voices, and quick with back answers. My mother did an act in which she covered up her glamour and became a real vulgar fishwife type and she could outrazz and outshout any of the razzers and shouters in the audience. Once somebody threw a rotten cabbage at her and she caught it and threw it back. It hit the wrong target but it got a big hand. My father sometimes sang for me in his horrible cracked voice the song she used to sing:

A negg and some nam and a nonion,
A negg and some nam and a nonion.
Oh what a sight to see,
Spread on a plate with a nice cup of tea.
A negg and some nam and a nonion,
For a feed it sounds rather a funny un,
But all the world over its praise should be sung,
It's better than Kruschens for keeping you young,
Now what did Charles Peace eat the morn he was hung?
A negg and some nam and a nonion.

To my dad pianoplaying for the pictures was just a ghost, and I could see what he meant. He'd talk of the great days of Fred Karno and Casey's Court and the way he'd been in the pit to play for Stan Laurel and Charlie Chaplin before they went off to the States to be great names in the films. They became ghosts, my dad would say, and even the big money they earned was a kind of ghost money. I never properly understood what he meant by that. And yet if my dad regretted the old music hall days he had to admit that he was no good as a pit pianoplayer. He couldn't play with a band. So he was drawn to the cinema just as the others were. But they became big names. I see that I'm getting away from my mother.

The photos I had of her showed her in all her stage glamour, but there was no doubt she was a pretty woman, with a lot of blonde hair and these big saucy eyes, blue dad said they were, and the little upturned nose and the generous mouth and the firm little chin. And the bosom, of course, plenty of that, and I'd already got plenty of it, or them, by the time I was twelve, taking after her. I'd got the hair and the eyes but my dad's nose, a bit big, poking into things. She'd died at the age of thirty, fifteen years younger than my Aunt Bertha (there'd been a brother and sister in between that had died of typhoid and pneumonia respectfully respectedly respectively) and the same age as dad. Dad seemed old to me of course, but he was still really young, only a kid still, thirty in 1918 made him only forty in 1928, no age at all, but he didn't feed himself right, he liked his draught Bass and Wild Woodbines that gave him a nasty cough, he had this little pot belly and his eyes watered and his hair was going.

Anyway, I was now quite a young woman, spitting image of my poor dead mother, and I was beginning to know about Sex, going to the public library on the way home from school (when dad hadn't come to fetch me) with other girls and looking up OBSTETRICS in the encyclopedia, reading torn dirty books that the other girls had and the boys too even more so, about priests having it off with nuns and 'his handsome moustached face grew stormy with passion' and 'as he took me in his strong arms I seemed to melt like a snowflake in the heat of his desire'. The boys in school tried to get a feel in the cloakroom and one girl, Brenda Barrington, used to sell feels for a halfpenny. One or two boys would show their ugly red things for nothing. Dirty and all that, but it was only Nature coming out. There was one shy very dark and handsome boy called Terence McDonagh that I kissed once in the geography lesson when Sister Anastasia was drawing the Amazon River on the blackboard. It's very hard to get away from Sex, and I've never really tried.

But my dad knew the dangers and watched me like a cat watching a mousehole. He still insisted on me going with him in the evenings, but one night I sort of rebelled.

'I'm not coming with you tonight, dad.' And like a fool I said 'I'm going to the pictures instead.' He didn't see the daft humour of that and said:

'A lad, is it? You're going with some lad, that's what it is.'

'No, it's just my friends Brenda and Annie, it's Annie's birthday and she's like invited us to tea and the pictures after.' It was in the morning I was telling my dad this, no last-minute lie, but it was a lie of course. Dicky Duckworth had asked me to go to the Gem Cinema with him, and his dad was a bookie and gave him plenty to spend, a fattish boy but sort of clean and with a very sweet breath.

'Heard that sort of tale I have before, girl. You're going out with some lad, so you think, but I say you're not going, your poor dead mother wouldn't allow it, and it's up to me to stand sort of in her place. There's time enough for that, listen to your old dad, he knows all about it, about how some lads get carried away and do things they oughtn't to do, there's plenty of time for that. I don't want to be harsh, love, but I've got my duty.' So that was that. I was blazing but I got round it in a way he didn't expect. I asked Dicky Duckworth to meet me in the front of the Star, a thing he didn't want to do, being a bookmaker's son, he was used to the back row or the balcony front row, and he was bound to complain about getting a crick in his neck. But there we were, sitting together just near my dad, and we were as good as whatsit. Dicky had a big box of King George V chocolates which he kept feeding me, and my dad spent as much time looking at us, blazing, as he did at the screen. He couldn't say that I'd done anything wrong, but he saw that I was in a way having my own way, and he didn't like it.

He was worried about me, which was only natural in a father, and he worried about my future. I'd sat the exams for scholarships for three secondary schools but my heart wasn't in it, I was no scholar as they said, and I'd failed, so I'd be staying on at the English Martyrs till I was fourteen and then have to get a job. I didn't mind, I've never been much of a believer in book learning. I couldn't see myself in black stockings and a gym slip at the age of eighteen knowing Trig, whatever that was or is, and Latin. The trouble was I had no Talent, as my dad said, very worried, my mother had had Talent and my dad had it, but I had no Talent. Oh, I was nosy and liked poking into things, sex, and who the black man was that visited Miss Tarrant on the ground floor, and what they did together but you could guess, and Siamese Twins, and abortions, and what nancyboys did or had done to them, and how you could tell when Sister Agatha was menstruating and so on, but I see now that my only real interest was really sex. I didn't want to play the piano for a living or go on the stage. No Talent. Somehow I'd let dad down, and my dead mother in Purgatory too.

To add to my dad's worries, he lost his job in the secondhand piano department in Lodge's. He'd done his best, demonstrating Beautiful

Tone and Fast Action and so on, but he'd not sold a piano in five weeks. The floor manager said that they didn't keep him on there as a Resident Paderooski but to sell pianos, and my dad said how the hell could he sell pianos if the buggers didn't want to buy, so he was given a warning to get on with it and also to keep a civil tongue in his head. Then he wandered into the department where other instruments were for sale, and he demonstrated his Violin Method for too long, and there was somebody who was interested in buying a secondhand piano for his little girl, and there was nobody there to demonstrate, and there was a hell of a row which ended up with my poor dad's being given the push. So he only had his job at the Star and, God help him, he didn't keep that job much longer either. What happened was that they put on this religious film about which there'd been so much trouble in the States where it was made, the life of Our Lord, everybody saying it was too Reverent a Subject to be made into a movie for people to watch chewing chocolates and puffing fags and having a feel in the back row. You didn't actually see Our Lord in the film, that not being allowed, but you saw his hands being held out and people looking with their mouths open and very reverent to a great white shining light, which was supposed to be Him. It was mostly the camera that acted Our Lord. Anyway, this film came to the Star, and my dad was given strict instructions not by the manager but by the Rector of the Holy Cross Church, which was Church of England, about Due Reverence being needed in the music he played. It seemed that some big Religious Council or other was sticking its snout into the distribution of the film and insisting that a clergyman should say a few words about it, giving a sort of sermon really, before the film came on. No advertisements, no news, no comedy. Just a few holy words and then this film, which was called *The Light Of The World*. Anyway, this Rector was with the manager and my dad in the manager's office, telling him all about Due Reverence.

'The thing for you to do,' said this Rector, 'is to play Hymns Ancient and Modern all the way through. That would be Reverent and Altogether Appropriate.'

'But I don't know this Ancient and Modern thing,' said my dad, 'me being brought up a Catholic.'

'Oh really? A Roman Catholic, are you? A pity, but never mind. I will lend you a copy of the hymnal and I think you'll find them easy enough to play.'

'So,' said my dad, 'Our Lord has become the private property of the C of E, is that it?'

'Well,' said the Rector, 'the Church of England is the Established Church of the United Kingdom. It is logical, is it not, to consult the traditions of the Established Church in a matter of General Public Enlightenment.'

My dad showed him the poster that was hanging on the wall. 'There,' he said, 'look at the names of those who have made this film. Sid Schwarz. Emmanuel Rubinstein. Real C of E, aren't they? I reckon it's an imposition what you're asking.'

'Watch it, Billy,' said the manager, very quiet and like menacing.

'Oh, all right,' said my dad. 'I've no alternative, have I? Just the same as it always was, the Catholics getting the shitten end.'

'Watch it, Billy,' the manager said.

'All right,' my dad said. 'I'll need a light over the piano if I'm going to have to play from music. First time I've ever had to do that.'

'Most members of the Church of England,' the Rector said, very haughty, 'know these by heart,' and he gave dad a list with numbers on it – 64, 26, 77 and so on.

'Like Housey Housey,' my dad said. 'All right, God help me, I'll do it.' And he did it, and it was just like being in church. My dad gave out a great big sarky yawn when he had to play Abide With Me during the Crucifixion, which really called for diminished sevenths and the like. They showed the picture all the week, except for the Saturday matinée, knowing that the kids wanted their usual Our Gang and cowboys and Indians. And now my father did something terrible which he shouldn't have done. He'd put money on the horses, which he did sometimes, a bob each way according to a system he'd got, and he usually just about broke even. But this Saturday he put a bob to win on a horse called Salted Almond, running in the two o'clock at Ripon, Joe Muggeridge up, and he'd been told it was a dead cert. Well, it couldn't have been, not at 100 to 1, but it came in all right at that price, so there must have been some fiddling. Dad hadn't collected yet, of course, but he went into the Coach and Horses at five-thirty opening time, after the kids' matinée, and drank fast and solid, pints of draught Bass with double scotches, all on an empty stomach. I wasn't there, of course, not being allowed in pubs at my age, but I heard all about it. As a matter of fact I was just getting ready to go over the street to see Polly Logan, my dad having become a bit more reasonable these days and admitting that having to go and see *The Light Of The World* six nights running was a bit of an Imposition and not objecting too much to me going over to hear the Logans' new HMV portable with its six new records so long as I didn't bugger off after with Polly looking for lads, the other way round of course really. It was Mr Bamber who worked on the Telephones who knocked on the door to say he'd seen my dad weaving his way to the Star and shouting the odds and he'd heard about his win and him getting kalied in the Coach, so I'd better get over there and see that everything was all right.

Everything was *not* all right, I can tell you. I got in to the Star just in time to see dad throwing on the floor the electric light that had been put there for the Ancient and Modern, that was while the Rector himself on the stage was saying a few Holy Words. When the Rector had done, my dad said 'Three jeers for the Rectum,' but not too loud, and then when the picture started he seemed to me to be playing not too bad, though not Ancient and Modern, more something in the Dorian mode or the Hyperfrigidaire mode or something, very solemn and like more ancient than anything in that hymnbook. Then we had the birth of Our Lord and dad played Adeste Fideles and he sang and tried to get everybody to join in:

Venite adoremus
Venite adoremus
Venite adoremus
Dominum.

I got over to him and he hardly knew who I was at first, but then he knew and sobered up a bit and listened to me when I said cut it out do you want to be sacked.

So when camels came on he contented himself with playing In A Persian Market but in a kind of hymnlike way. When it was Mary Magdalene he did a kind of holy arrangement of I'm a Girl What Works Hard For Her Living, so that I don't think anybody noticed anything wrong. The manager Hawkes was not around, so I suppose he'd been sort of lulled by my dad playing what he was told to the last five nights and he thought everything would be all right and he was most likely round the corner not at the Coach and Horses, where he'd hear about dad getting kalied, but at the Queen Alexandra where dad didn't go. But soon what got into dad was terrible, but it was sort of fascinating as well, because he started to make a kind of grand opera out of it, singing in a high voice I'd never known he had, and making a kind of very solemn like waltz out of the Eight Beatitudes:

Blessy
Dartha
Peacemay Curs,
For theyshallbe Caaaaalled
The Chill drenov
Gawwwwd.

The Rector had gone off, most likely to get himself in fettle for Sunday morning, and there was nobody in like Religious Authority around, but I could hear one or two murmurs, and then more, but some of the younger ones seemed to be enjoying it.

But the draught Bass and whisky in my dad was having a new effect now, and he began to doze off with his fingers just trailing along the keys.

'Dad, dad, wake up. Come on, let me get you home.' Oh God, it was a proper bloody mess. I couldn't help looking to see how much of this the audience was taking in, and what I saw was the manager Hawkes coming down the aisle very heavy footed. 'Dad, dad, for God's sake,' He came to then, smacking his lips, which must have been very dry, squinted up at the screen and said:

'Who's that bugger there then?'

I squinted up too and could make out this bearded man leering and counting money he was pouring from a bag in to his hand.

'Judas, dad.'

'Judas, right.' And he began to play very severe solemn chords, and I thought thank God and went to sit down again. Hawkes was there now, leaning over me and his breath very sour with beer and saying:

'What's going on here? What the hell's bloody well up?'

'Don't you use words like that to me,' I said. 'Especially with this film on about Our Lord,' I said then. Then my father began to sing a new waltz song he was making up as he went along, doing big runs up and down the keyboard:

Thiiiiiiirty pieces of silver,
That's what I sold him for.
Thiiiiiiirty pieces of silver,
I am the son of a whore.

His runs weren't all that like accurate, but his voice was very loud and clear, and it seemed to me that he could do that singing job with all the latest songs in the Music Department of Lewis's so long as he stayed drunk all the time. Of course Hawkes was furious but didn't know what to do, especially as we were on the Crucifixion now, with just Our Lord's hands and feet with nails in them showing and all the women round the cross weeping like mad, and my dad had gone back to these very severe loud sad chords in the Laestrygonian mode or whatever it was. And he stayed on like that till the scene changed. He couldn't see what was happening up there so he kept squinting and his fingers were very like uncertain on the keys and then he called:

'What's happening up there, girl?'

'He's rose again from the dead, dad. Do something like cheerful.'

And by God he did, Oh Christ Jesus Our Lord help us. He started playing For He's A Jolly Good Fellow with like descending octaves in the bass, then he put the tune in the bass and did like all tinkling bells up there in the treble, oh Jesus help us all. And then the film

ended and he was still at it, Symphonic Variations on For He's A
Jolly Good Fellow, even when the lights went half up and King
George V came on to the screen. And then he didn't play God Save
The King but that old Catholic hymn Faith Of Our Fathers, singing
it too, very loud and hearty:

Faith of our fathers, living still
In spite of judgment fire and sword.
Oh how our hearts beat high with jo-oy
Whene'er we hear that glorious wo-ord
Faith of our fathers, holy faith,
We will be true to thee till death.

Then he banged out a big like triumphant Amen which shook the
piano and then he rolled off his seat on to the floor, flat out, and his
head appeared from under the black curtaining so that it looked like
it was St John the Baptist's head lying there under the feet of the
front row of the audience.

That was the end of the first house, and the second house was
ready to come in, and I could see the Rector ready to do his second
lot of Holy Words of the evening.

'It's the end,' cried Hawkes, 'he's bloody finished. He's not sitting
at that bloody piano again, not here he's not. I'll have him blacklisted
all over the town, he won't get another job in a flaming picture palace
as long as he bloody lives.' So then I began to beat at Hawkes with
my little teeny fists as they were then, shouting:

'You don't talk like that about my father, you bastard as you are.'
And my father's head from the floor said like the voice of doom:

'Language, girl, language.' Then he was snoring.

With the help of one or two people who'd been very drunk themselves in their time or truly liked what dad had been playing, I
managed to get him out by the side exit, and he sat in the alleyway
near the dustbins in all the cold and dirt and the cats yowling and
the cold air began to wake him up, as well as me banging him on
the face, calling him a bloody fool. He still sat there, his legs having
no strength in them, while the second house was on, you could tell

when it started because the audience went quiet, but there wasn't any music. In about ten minutes though we heard a hymn from Ancient and Modern played not very well, so Hawkes must have got somebody out of the audience who played for Sunday School or something. The Rector would be pleased about that.

When dad was able to totter a bit I managed to get him home, stumbling and falling and saying 'Let me sleep it off, girl' just near the 44 tram terminus with the punch clock for the drivers, but I got him home and up the stairs and on to his bed. I made up my own bed on the old couch, just like before. I'd better get used to it again, we not being able to afford the other room any more, and perhaps we wouldn't be able to afford this one either. Dad had really done for himself this time, he had that.

Five

I didn't sleep much that night, wondering whether dad would wake up in the small hours shouting the odds or looking for the lavatory in the wardrobe which we used as a food cupboard, or even whether he'd be sick and drown in it. However, he slept very solid, now and then choking on his snores and once or twice laughing at something. At eight-thirty, it was Sunday remember, he was still sound at it, so I got up though feeling tired, got dressed and then got out and went to St Edward's for mass. It had been cold the night before but this morning held what they call the promise of spring, and somebody let off a stockingfeeter during the Elevation. When I got back dad was up, bright as a lark, drinking a mug of tea and reading the *News of the World*, which we had delivered. He liked the Newserthe with its abortions and scandals with scoutmasters and in those days they used to print a popular song, words and music, in the middle pages, also photos of girls showing their legs right up their bottoms, what is called provocative. Dad looked up at me very cheerful and said:

'Sorry I couldn't manage it, girl, mass I mean, I had a bit of a head. The tea's still hot, I'll pour you a cup,' and he did. I sat on the couch looking at him. I said:

'You mean you can't remember?'

'Remember what, girl?'

'Last night. Oh my God, you can't remember?'

'Won a bit on the nags so I had a couple, that I do know, but did the job all right, didn't I? Ancient and Modern and a nice smile for his arseholiness the Rectum, pardon my French?'

He went a bit white when I told him the gory details, but he said:
'Nowt to worry about, just a lapse, only human, soon forgotten.
You'll see, lass.' I couldn't knock it into his loaf that he was out of
a job. He said: 'Read about this murder, have you?' knowing that
I'd not yet had a chance to. 'He pulled out his wife's intestines and
glued them on the window spelling her name, Lily.' He loved a good
murder, one of his few diversifications. He had a book he'd pinched
from the Public Library called *The Killer's Craft*, all about Charlie
Peace and Dr Crippen and Smith, the Brides in the Bath murderer.
It sort of fascinated him, the idea of these girls drowning in the bath
while Smith played Nearer My God To Thee on the organ in the
parlour. Well, it was harmless I suppose, reading about these things,
a very mild man, my dad, who'd not harm a fly. But it's funny how
ideas get passed on from one generation to another and become not
quite so harmless, as you'll see later.

Sunday dinner was always a bit of a problem, we not having cook-
ing facilities except for the gasring here and the one in the room I'd
have to give up, but what I used to do was buy some cold beef at the
Swiss Delicatessen on Princess Road on Saturday afternoon and heat
up some baked beans in a saucepan, not much of a Family Repast,
but it had to do. Dad had a good appetite today, he ate a hearty
dinner, if you could call shives of meat you could see the willow
pattern design on your plate through and one of Heinz's 57 varieties
hearty. Things had better change, and of course they were going to
change but not for the better.

Dad went round Monday morning to the Star. That was when
they had the new films in, delivered by the milk train or somehow,
and they would run them through and dad would have a look at
them and work out what music he'd play. Well, Hawkes was there,
and Hawkes was blazing still, and there was a hell of a barney which
dad told me of, which ended up with dad saying well stick the job
up your jaxy anyhow. I've not had one word of appreciation for
what I've done for you, being real artistic in my Approach and not
just hammering out a load of old tripe like the rest of the buggers,
and you've never had that bloody thing tuned no matter how often
I've asked you, so bugger you and yours mate. Hawkes said it was

a week's notice and he hadn't got a replacement yet and dad would have to work out the week, but dad said up your arse and put the money there too, you bloody ungrateful skinflint and so on.

It was a miserable week, as you can guess dad wandering round the proper smelly bughouses, not the refined bughouses like the Star but the real ones where, as they used to say, you could go in with a blouse and come out with a jumper. For the posh places had no vacancies, and there was already what they called a whiff of Coming Depression in the music business nobody taking lessons any more, people preferring the wireless to the joanna in the front room, and there was even talk of the Talkies coming, they were already on their way in the States, but a lot wanted to shut their eyes to that and you can see why, what with cinema musicians out of jobs and the cost of wiring cinemas up for the New Phenomenon as it was called. Anyway dad got a job at the New Electric, in the heart of the slums of Chorlton on Medlock, at the wage of twenty-five bob a week, and we were back to sharing the one room again, me on the couch as before.

This New Electric was near empty every night and there were no matinées, not even for the kids on Saturday, and the pictures were old and rainy and cut to ribbons and nobody seemed to care. My dad soon saw what the place really was, a cover for something else, and it took him no time to find out it was a place where men picked up prostitutes in the dark and where stolen goods were received and paid for, and my dad like a mug playing for pictures that nobody was looking at unless the police walked in, and then everybody was as good as gold and nice as pie. There seemed to be three brothers running the place, Italians from their name, which was Tagliaferro, more Sicilian, Rolf says, and it must have been pretty bad because dad not only didn't mind me not being there with him to have an eye kept on me but he actually said, 'Stay away girl, I don't like it, you're getting to be a big girl now and there's funny business going on and I don't like it but beggars can't be choosers.'

The piano he had to play, so he told me, only worked from middle C down. Everything above that note was all like jangling wires, useful enough for ghost scenes and thunder and lightning over the sinister forest, but you couldn't do Mendelssohn's Spring Song or the Maiden's Prayer. It was no good complaining, though, you might get a knife in your guts if you did, so life was pretty miserable in the thirteenth year of my Precious Girlhood.

It's here now that l have to speak of something very shameful, but what I did or had done to me was all in a good cause. My dad no longer called for me at the school at four o'clock, even he saw it was a bit ridiculous at my age, I felt quite a fool, is your daddy coming for you then babbywabby, but in a way he had the right sort of idea, girls always need care and protection. Anyway, when I used to come out of school in the afternoon there was often a man standing at the gate watching us girls come out, not anybody's father and he had a kind of hungry look as if he was lonely or perhaps he'd had a daughter that had died young and he was Rubbing Salt in the Wound as some people do by sort of seeing this daughter of his turned into one of these Winsome and Laughing Schoolgirls and then going home to have a lovely good cry about it. We girls used to laugh at him among ourselves, saying here he is again, there's your boyfriend Elsie, isn't he handsome, eh, and all the rest of it. He was a man about my dad's age, thin, with a moustache that could have done with the nail scissors being introduced to it, and like very pale mournful eyes. There didn't seem to be much harm in him, he used to just stand there watching and looking hungry and sad. Now whether it was by chance or intention when I was coming out late on my own, having had to Stay In for being a Bad Girl and scrawling a balloon with I LUV YEW in it on one of the illustrations to the tattered old reading book we had called The Adventures of Ulysses, who we used to call Useless, he was still standing there though just about ready to go off when I dropped my battered old satchel that had had my lunch sandwich in it, bread and marge and a scrape of Bovril, washed down with water from the tap in the girls' cloakroom, and he picked it up and said 'You've dropped this, miss.' It wasn't a Manchester voice he spoke with, more of a poshish London one, but all London ones used to sound posh to us, what with saying Barth and Parth and Clahss. Then before I knew what was properly happening I found he was walking my way down Princess Road.

Anyway, this man said his name was Frederick Gosport, very eager to talk he was, Fred they call me, and he was a widower, his wife having died of what he called Mortification of the Womb, if you'll forgive the expression he said, and he'd not been as sad as he should have, because she was a Domineering Woman who'd liked to have all her own way, if I saw what he meant. I thought I saw what he meant, but I soon found out that I didn't really. There was more to it than just her taking all his wage packet and saying we're going to Margate this year not St Leonards for our holidays, although that came into it too. His wife, he said, had been a Manchester woman who he'd met on holiday in Scarborough, they'd married in Ealing or somewhere, and then she'd insisted on going back to Manchester because she couldn't really stand Southerners, a cold hearted lot with no life in them she said, and so they'd come up and got this house on Claremont Road, not far from where my dad and I were lodging, and he worked nights at the Electricity Works, going on duty at midnight and coming off at eight in the morning. He'd got into the way of liking to do nights, he said, because of his wife wanting so much of her own way, and I still didn't see what he meant. He'd got into the habit of doing nights and he couldn't get out of it, he said. He said:

'It's not too far from here if you'd like to see it. The house, I mean, where I live. It's gone a bit to rack and ruin, me having nobody to look after me, but I do my best. If you'd like a cup of tea you can have one, I always make myself one about this time, with some Cadbury's Milk Chocolate Fingers, which I like.'

'I've got to get home,' I said. 'My dad expects me.'

And then he got on to what does your dad do, and I told him, and he was very interested. 'Works evenings, does he? Well, if you'd like to come round some evening to my place I could let you listen to my wireless, I made it, a sort of hobby of mine, me being in the electrical trade, not crystal sets, dear me no, but ones with valves and loudspeakers.'

Then I thought I'd show him what I suspected he had in mind, so I sort of pulled myself up straight and said: 'Do you know how old I am?'

'What's that to do with anything?' he said. 'I'd say you look about sixteen, but you can't be, still going to elementary school, but why do you ask that question?'

'It's just as well for you to know, isn't it?' I said. 'There's no harm in me saying how old I am, which is getting on for fourteen.'

'Will you come round?' he said, sort of low and panting, 'and listen to my wireless?' He made it sound as though he could pick up foreign stations which were like dirty and suggestive.

'Well,' I said, inventing it on the purse or fur of the moment, 'I'm supposed to be starting this job in the evening, as from next Monday.' It was Friday now. And I racked my brains to think of some sort of job a girl my age might do in the evenings, and of course there it was readymade and on a plate. 'I'm to go round at the Star Picture House in the evenings during the intervals, selling chocolates.'

He said, very careful: 'If you want a sort of job I can give it you. A bit of tidying up, washing the dishes, that sort of thing. Making the bed,' he said, and he swallowed hard on that one. 'How much do they pay you for selling chocolates? About five bob a week and a free chew of something?'

'Oh, more,' I said, having no idea how much.

'How about coming round tomorrow evening?' he said. 'Then, er, we could have a talk about it.'

'I don't mind,' I said, and my ticker was going like mad. And it was as if he could see it bumping away through my blouse, anyway that was where he was looking.

Well, to cut a long story short, when dad had gone off to do his job at the Eyetie fleapit, as he called it, the following evening, I put a bit of lipstick on and a couple of dabs of Juillet, which in those days I called Juliet. I'd bought both a bit ago, out of some money dad had given me when a horse had come in and he was sort of jubilant, and I'd kept them hidden away in my vanity box which was an old chocolate box with kittens and flowers on the outside. Dad never looked into it, respecting as he said a Lady's Privacy. And then I went out in the spring evening, wishing it was a bit darker, for there were some of the lads of Moss Lane East circling round on their bikes shouting 'Do you like bananas and cream?' the dirty young buggers. The house I was going to was No. 88 Claremont Road and when I banged the knocker it wasn't the only thing that went bang bang.

Well, there he was, and there was the house, pretty bare and dusty but it wasn't the cleaning up he was interested in, as you can guess. And there were his three wireless sets, home made, and he put them all on at once, some daft Lancashire comedians on 2ZY, one of them saying 'I've got blue blood in mah veins,' and the other saying 'What yer think ah got in mahn, dandelion and burdock?' And then Fred, as he asked me to call him, got down to it, not wasting any time. He said:

'I'm not after much, I'll be straight with you, but she was a Very Domineering woman.'

'How much?' I said.

'Half a dollar every time you come,' he said. 'I know this is going to be Against the Law, you being under the Age of Consent, but I reckon you don't want to be put away as a Young Person in Need of Care and Protection any more than I want to be put away for having Seduced a Minor. Not that there's going to be any seduction. I've nothing more to say than that if you've come here a virgin, then you'll go out one too, that I promise.' I knew what a virgin was, having been brought up a Catholic, but I was a bit vague about what was meant by staying one. 'So no nattering about this,' he said, 'to your schoolfriends, or you'll be for the high jump as much as me.'

Then he had me on his lap in a big creaky armchair by the fire, it being spring but still cool enough for a fire, and he was kissing me and putting his hand up and all the rest of it. Then he said he was Going Down, and I like a daft fool I said where to, and he soon showed me. This was when I first realised what it was all about, and for some reason I saw my poor dad playing away at the piano. I didn't know what to call what happened to me then, but he gave me the word. 'You've come,' he said, then he jabbed his hot thing against my bare leg, near the top, and then he said he'd come too. So that was it. 'Enough for one evening,' he said, and while he was wiping himself with a dirty handkerchief he said, 'Very nice it was too. Tomorrow being Sunday I'll like stay with my dreams, and I'll see you Monday same time. Very nice,' he said, as though I'd cooked him sausage and chips, then he pulled his trousers up, all the money in his pockets jangling along with his keys, then he fished a handful out and gave me a half dollar. 'As we agreed,' he said, 'and don't spend it all at once.' Then he gave me a smacker and sort of shoved me to the front door.

I went off at once and bought things – a tin of pink salmon, some ham and beef from the delicatessen and some Russian salad as well, and two jam puffs from Shaw's the confectioners. All this was for dad's supper, but how was I going to explain about the money? Say I found it? Say a kind lady gave it to me? Because, and I worked it out, I'd be bringing in fifteen bob a week, as much as dad made, if this Fred stuck to the arrangement. If the Law had me leave school now instead of at fourteen I could always have pretended I had a shop assistant's job during the day, but that idea was out, so what could I do? Of course, perhaps dad wouldn't notice at first, just thinking that the money he gave me to buy things was stretching further than he thought it would, and that was possible, because things were getting very cheap, especially what they called Dumped Japanese goods, and this had something to do with the Depression that was going on, though I've never understood how or why. I ended up by deciding to pretend I was earning a bit by helping Miss Hampton clean up her flat, as she called it, very posh, Miss Hampton being the teacher who taught Singing and the only teacher at the school that wasn't a nun. I'd keep some of the money I earned tucked away in my Vanity Box, and that would come in for an emergency, though there again the explanation would be difficult. Still, don't cross your bridges till you come to them is my motto, though how you can cross a bridge before coming to it I've never properly understood, like the Depression.

Then it dawned on me that what I had done this evening and intended to do other evenings was a Mortal Sin, and I felt my stomach sink to the floor of our little room as I put the food I'd bought into the wardrobe. I normally went to confession at St Edward's on Friday morning, along with the rest of the senior girls, the idea being to make bloody sure we went to confession, we being a Wild Lot. It was not the Sin of Adultery but it was the Sin of Impurity, and I'd have to confess it and promise not to do it again. Well, I could always do that and then break my promise like everybody else. I mean, if everybody kept their promises there'd be no more confession and the priests would be out of a job except for saying mass. Another thing was that I didn't do anything, what happened was done to me, not the same thing at all. Right, but you go to his house knowing what will happen, and that's doing something, isn't it? But going to a house isn't a sin, for God's sake, and it isn't certain that he'll do this time what he did last, he might say I'm a bit jiggered up, let's just listen to the wireless. I made up my mind that it was really a Venial Sin, because what happened helped my dad and I didn't start it. They wouldn't put me in Hell for helping my poor old pianoplaying dad, would they?

It didn't work out at every night, anyway, because in the next week Fred said, 'Don't come tomorrow night or the night after,' and I wondered, a bit jealous, funny really, if he was seeing somebody else those two nights. The two nights I wasn't to come were the Friday and the Saturday, which made it easier when I went to confession on the Friday.

There was Father O'Casey behind the like wirework, and he was reading the *Daily Mail*, which seemed to me to be cheek, not paying attention sufficiently to what we were confessing to him, but we were only kids and our sins would not be of great importance compared to the Adult Sinners he got on Saturdays. I said:

'Bless me father, for I have sinned exceedingly in thought word and deed through my fault through my fault through my most grievous –'

'All right, my child,' he said rudely interrupting, 'what have you done?'

'I was inattentive at Holy Mass and I missed my night prayers twice and I lost my temper with my father and I joked and laughed during Religious Knowledge.'

'Anything else, my child?' And he turned the *Daily Mail* over to the racing.

'Sins of impurity, father.'

'By yourself, my child, or with somebody else?' You could see he was getting interested now, he was not looking at the racing page.

'With somebody else, father. Somebody of the Male Sex.'

'What did you do?'

'I didn't do anything, father. He did it all.'

I listened very carefully to what he said then, ranting and raving about purity and shocking Our Lady and not being pleasing to God, and then he said: 'Do you promise not to commit that terrible sin any more?' So I said.

'I promise not to do anything ever again that is a Sin of Impurity.' And that was true too, I wasn't lying, I didn't do a thing. So he forgave me and gave me five Our Fathers and five Hail Marys, which wasn't too bad all things considered, and off I went to say them in front of the statue of Our Lady. And I stuck to that way of doing things all the time, and no harm seemed to come to me.

But now the bad times were really coming not only for my dad but for all people who played music in cinemas, I mean the Talking Pictures. One day there was a holy day of obligation, which meant a day off from school after going to mass, and so I treated dad and me to the afternoon matinée at the Deansgate Cinema in town, and the place was crammed because of the Novelty. The picture was *The Jazz Singer* with Al Jolson, and it wasn't a talking picture at all, it was singing, with Kol Nidrei and I'd walk a million miles for one of your smiles my mammeeeeee, and the talking was ordinary titles, nothing new at all. But the thing that my dad and I both noticed was that the musicians' pit was empty. There was not even a piano there any more and you could see that the place would get dusty and dirty and perhaps in time they would fill it in with concrete or something. It seemed strange at first, Just the feeling of something not being there that should be, with music coming from loudspeakers during the advertisements, very tinny and harsh and like threatening (like Hitler I suppose, although Hitler was not just yet) and then the same kind of harsh tinny music playing all through the film, but fitting the scenes just like my dad's pianoplaying, very professional, the Vitaphone system it was known as, sound on disc. Hawkes's prophesying had come true, I said to myself. My dad kept shaking his head.

'It's what they'll want, God help them, the stupid bastards. It won't be long now for any of us, poor bastards that we are.'

It was going to take time, we all saw that, before all the cinemas got themselves fitted up with sound machinery, but on the other hand not many of them were going to survive unless they did. Dad's horrible fleapit place was in no hurry, of course, and it wasn't worried about surviving as a place where you went first and foremost to see films. But as the only silent place around in the whole of Manchester it would sooner or later get itself talked of and the police would get very interested indeed, so dad said.

I remember most of the early Talkies, those that were on Vitaphone and those that had sound on film or a sound track, those being the two systems in use, and we know which of the two won. There was *The Singing Fool*, with Al Jolson again, and this time there was talking as well as singing, but there were whole long patches when the dialogue was in the old style, written down or up, very weird, as if the actors weren't allowed by some deep and secret law to talk all the time. The first picture I saw which was all talking from start to finish was called *The Doctor's Secret*, a very short one, with Ruth Chatterton in it. But then we started to get them all in this way, nearly all of them with a Theme Song as it was called, even *The Doctor's Secret* having a theme song called Half an Hour. There was *Weary River*, with Richard Barthelmess, and *Broadway*, with Regis Toomey, and the others called backstage musicals, such as *The Fox Movietone Follies of 1929*. And there was *Broadway Melody*, which I saw six times at the Tower Cinema in Blackpool, but I'll come to that later. There was *Innocents of Paris*, with Maurice Chevalier and the song Louise in it, also Claudette Colbert. The cinemas had to give in, because all the films they were making now were Talkies. I remember one cinema, the Princess, which pretended one week it had talking pictures, but all it had was *The Jazz Singer* without sound, and it played Al Jolson's gramophone records through the loudspeaker. What they call nowadays the lipsink was very bad. And the Royal, Jake Innerfield's place on Princess Road, was bold as brass with its poster saying NEVER MIND THE TALKIES WE WILL MAKE YOU TALK, and old German silent films with titles like *The Secrets of the Soul* until they too had to give in like every-body else.

But the New Electric got a supply of Italian silent films with the titles in Italian, and the audiences were just the same as before. The police were getting very suspicious, and they started questioning my dad, picking him up a few streets away where he was waiting for the tram to come home to me, poor old devil, plainclothes men of course, and offering him a couple of pints and a quiet chat in the snug of a pub called The Earl of Stanley. They were quite nice about it, only asking questions like 'What's going on there then?'

'They show pictures,' my dad said, 'and I play this lousy piano, and that's all I know.'

'You don't know anything, for instance, about men picking up girls under age in the dark?' said one of these CID men or Coppers In Disguise as they were called.

'I just get on with my job,' said dad. 'If you can call it a job.'

'You seen things changing hands?' said the other one.

'What sort of things?'

'Like this,' he said, and he pulled a lot of like jewellery out of his raincoat pocket, dad said. 'Picked these up off a man called Norbert the Snark coming out of the first house last Thursday. He said they'd been planted on him.'

'I can't tell you more than I've told you already,' said my dad. 'Honest.'

'Right,' they said, 'Thanks,' not really meaning it.

There came the day when dad reported for work, they were doing some picture about Dante in the Inferno or something, and he found the place locked up. There was nobody around. The Tagliaferro brothers had skipped, and that was the end of my dad's job. He was the last of the picture palace pianoplayers.

Six

I've said nothing in that last bit about how my Contribution to the Finances was getting on, the story of my father and the end of pianoplaying in cinemas being more important and being really part of History, while me collecting a few bob from this man for playing about and later putting it in, which had to happen sooner or later and it hurt like hell the first time and there were these sticky french letters, is sort of not historical but goes on all the time. Anyway, he moved his place of work, to Doncaster I think it was, and a good thing too because a policeman asked me one night why I kept going to this house and what went on there. I said it was my uncle Fred and I cleaned up for him, and he made a note of that, which I didn't like. But he'd gone now and it meant there was hardly anything coming in at all for a bit, except what dad earned in the Wheatsheaf, a very rough pub, playing at nights. But in the summer of 1930 I think it must have been things seemed to be looking up.

Rolf is still taking all this down and then writing it up but now he says I ought to tell my Younger Readers, which includes him, a bit more about life in the days of my youth. Well, first of all there's the things we used to eat, and even though we were very poor it seems to me now that the things we ate were tastier than what anybody eats these days. It was not what is called a Balanced Diet that we used to have, but it was a Tasty Diet. We used to have HP Sauce a lot to add taste to things, and sometimes Daddies and A1 and OK and Yorkshire Relish, but HP was best and still is. Take the top off an HP Sauce bottle and have a good sniff, and you'll be sniffing what

I sniffed as a kid, no change at all. It is the one thing in the whole world that has not changed. A nice sharp sort of fruity smell, vinegary and yet sort of full-bodied, that's what it is. We used to have it on everything, fish and chips, corned beef, tinned salmon, but my dad used to prefer just malt vinegar on his chips and his tinned salmon. Here in France we have wine vinegar, but it can't hold a candle to what they made out of good British brewer's malt, alegar as it was sometimes called. The chips we got in those days were gold and fat and crisp, I remember, and I liked nothing better when I was clemmed coming home from school on a winter day for my dinner than a chip butty which was hot chips with salt and pepper and HP Sauce laid between two slices of bread and butter or marge. When we were really hard up I would eat sugar butties, which were just bread and marge covered with white sugar, very unhealthy they say, but they filled you up. There was a time when if we had some fruit cake we had it between slices of bread to make it go further.

A threepenny fried fish we used to help out not only with chips but with a pennyworth of smalls, the crisp fish batter that I've already mentioned. A pennyworth of peas, grocer's peas they were, with salt and pepper and vinegar, they were good too. I sometimes used to cook a lobscouse on the gasring, a Liverpool thing that is, though they have it in Hamburg and also in Stockholm, and it consists of cubed potatoes and onions boiled together, then get rid of most of the water and add a tin of corned beef, fork it in, cook a bit, serve with plenty of HP, delicious. We used to like a tin of salmon just with boiled potatoes mashed. For sweet things there were Eccles cakes and jam puffs. A hot barmcake toasted at the fire with plenty of marge was all right too. We used to drink only tea, never coffee or cocoa, and it was always my dad who brewed it.

We had a brown teapot with the spout cracked and it held about a quart. He used to make sure it was warm not by swilling hot water in it, which is what most do, but by putting it by the gasfire to get really nice and warm. Then he would put four good heaped spoons of Liptons or Seymour Meads in the pot and pour the water on while it was still boiling. Then he'd let it stand to draw for about three minutes. We always had Nestle's condensed milk in it, which we preferred to cows' milk. I miss all those things now, I can tell you, and there's no real way of calling them back. I mean, what's to stop me making tea that way here in the South of France. I have all the things, but somehow it's not the same. The atmosphere isn't the same, the little smelly room with the fire on and the window closed, my dad's bed not yet made and so on.

I nearly forgot to mention pork sausages, which had plenty of meat in them. We used to fry these over the gasring and eat them with bread and HP. You don't get sausages like those now, all fat and crisp and bursting out of their skins with the goodness in them. And then there were the threepenny meat pies from Shaw's the confectioners, they used to pour hot gravy into a hole in them from a jug. Cabbage? That smells the place out and it's nearly all water anyway. Lettuce is rabbit food, no nourishment at all. Cucumbers and radishes make you repeat. Tomatoes were all right when they were mushy and you could fry them with a bit of bacon.

It's easy enough to see the other differences between now and then, because they're in books and in films, old newsreels and the like. I suppose the time I remember best is the summer of 1927, when we had the Total Eclipse of the Sun, and everybody trooped up Princess Road in the early morning to the hill by Southern Cemetery with bits of smoked glass so as not to get blinded. There was a lot of talk in the newspapers that summer about the End of the World coming and this eclipse being the sign of it, but it didn't make much difference to the way people behaved. Skirts were very short and girls wore fancy garters that you could see quite clearly and were meant to. Funny, girls' legs seemed shorter then than they are now, something to do with the wrong diet, though mine were long enough and still are. The big dance that year I remember was the Black Bottom, Woolworth's was really a place where nothing was over sixpence. You could see old people buying themselves a pair of spectacles for sixpence, take your pick from the tray, no nonsense about having an eye test. You could buy a motor bike in sixpenny parts. Money was a very solid thing then, and a tanner was worth having. Those days will never come again.

Still, it was a bad time just after, but my dad had a really big stroke of luck and he deserved it. He was playing one night in the Wheatsheaf, and a man there asked him if he knew the old music hall song He's Got 'Em On. My dad said yes and played it and this man sang it:

> He's got 'em on
> He's got 'em on
> He's got 'em on agyne.
> Just been to the boozer
> At the bottom of the lyne.
> Oh now he's here
> With his belly full of beer
> And he's larfin like a dryne.
> He's got 'em on
> He's got 'em on
> He's got 'em on agyne.

You can see from the way that's written down that it was sung in Cockney. Now this man who sang it and my dad kept looking at one another, even while the song was going on, and they could hardly wait for the last note to start banging at each other as men do to show they're pleased to see each other again after a long time, and it turned out that this man was Robbie Partridge, the comedian from my dad's concert party during the war. He'd been doing his turn at what was left of the variety theatres of England, and now he'd got a concert party together, or most of it anyway, and had a booking for the Central Pier, Blackpool, for the summer season starting Whitsun. What they hadn't got yet was a reliable pianoplayer experienced in concert party work, which surprised me a bit, knowing how many pianoplayers there were out of work, but this Robbie Partridge was very choosy. But he knew how good my dad was, and so he got the job.

I was going on fourteen, and I should have to leave the English Martyrs before the end of the school year, as dad and I had to set ourselves up in Blackpool. Really he should have got me put into one of the Blackpool schools, a lot posher than ours, even the free ones, but education wasn't much use to me, I was going to leave anyway at fourteen, and I looked about seventeen now. So we decided to risk it with the authorities, who wouldn't be likely to find out so we thought, so now I was a school leaver at Whitsun and in Blackpool with my dad.

Now in all towns they have boarding houses that cater for the theatrical profession, which includes concert parties, but the two rooms dad and I got were in a boarding house which had had no experience of such people, but it seemed a nice little place and clean, not far from Yates's Wine Lodge. He had his rehearsals, for he was expected to do more than just play the piano, there were little parts in sketches and so on, and I was able to set out looking for a job for myself, temporary of course like all jobs in the summer season. The job I managed to get after three days of my dad's start of rehearsals was not much, it was waiting on in a caffy off the Prom, lunches and high teas. I know perfectly well that I have not spelt café correctly, but it seems to me to be wrong to use the same word for two very different things, a French café bearing no likeness at all to the British variety, especially in Blackpool, which is where you get meals but nothing alcoholic – a nice plaice and chips or a nice chop and chips and a nice portion of spotted dick, a very rude name that, I wonder why it's allowed, with custard. For that matter, I wonder why everything always has to be nice, a nice cup of tea, a nice plate of bread and butter, but it always has to be. Sometimes the Father of a Family would plonk his wife and the kids down and say: Well, miss, we'll all have a nice helping of The Roast Beef of Old England and two veg, though he must have known it was frozen beef from the Argentine. People could never be straight about food in England, they always had to prettify everything up with nice or a little song about

Roast beef and Yorkshire pud
By God it does you good

or

When there's a snice smince pie
I ask for a helping twice

Cause I do like a snice smince pie
Cause it's snice snice snice.

The job was all right, with the odd copper and sometimes sixpence
left for me under the plate, and Mr and Mrs Hargreaves, who ran the
caffy, were all right really though very stingy, I never saw anybody
in my life carve the meat as fine as Mrs Hargreaves, razor thin, you
could see right through it. Of course, there were one or two lads who
tried to get off with me over their spotted dick and custard and even
the odd lonely old man having a bit of a holiday on his own, his wife
having just died or something.

Blackpool was all right in those days, very bracing and plenty to
do. There was the Blackpool Tower and still is, a copy of the Eiffel
Tower in Paris that most of us kids knew from the drawing on the
Eiffel Tower Lemonade Crystals, and there was the Tower Zoo
and Cinema and Ballroom, lots of other cinemas besides, lots of
sideshows, like the Fat Lady and the Man with Two Heads, and of
course the Amusement Park with the Noah's Ark and the Big Dipper.
There were the three piers also, all with slot machines and concerts
at the end, and the place was crammed with caffies and boozers. It
was a great resort for people coming from Bradford and Chorley and
Bury on the Wakes week, when the whole town would close down
and everybody go on their holidays together, not much of a change
I'd say. The beach was a good one, with the sea not too far out as it
is at Southport, but it was full of kids screaming because they'd got
stung by jellyfish, the sea being full of jellyfish.

Now I have to say something about the concert party my dad was
in, and I have to say a lot for the benefit of the Younger Generation
who don't know about such things any more. My dad was in the
Cockadoodle Doos, a silly name, and to give you an idea of what
they did I'd better try and remember the whole programme, which
began with everybody on stage in pierrot and pierrette costume singing the opening chorus to say who they were:

Cockadoodle doo
Cockadoodle doo

We're here we're here we're here we're here
To do our best for you.
When the cock crows in the morning
You know the thing it crows
Cockadoodle oodle
Just to get you on your toes.
So Cockadoodle doo
Cockadoodle doo
There's Jimmy and Maggie and Robbie and Jack
And lots of others too.
With a bit of a joke
And a bit of a laugh
And a bit of the old soft shoe,
We'll crow away
And make your day
With a cockadoodle doo.

That's awful, written down, but it didn't sound too bad sung, because you couldn't hear all the words. After the first chorus of it Robbie Partridge, who was what was called the Low Comedian, would do a bit of a quip with Rutland Wiltshire, whose real name was Ron Butcher, the baritone who was also the Straight Man. Robbie's what he called his speciality for this spot in the programme was just some gag about something that had been in the newspapers that morning if it was an afternoon show, papers that evening if it was an evening show, very topical, as he was always saying. One afternoon he went too far, so they all said, but none of the audience reported him to the authorities or anything, after all they were on holiday. It was this time of the scandal of the vicar in the village near Reading who was carrying on with what he called his housekeeper, a little whore really and only sixteen. Her name, I remember, was Doris Semple, everybody knew it then. Well, Robbie brought two coins out of his pocket, a penny and a half-crown and asked Rutland Wiltshire which one he'd like to have.

'The half-dollar, no two ways about it.'
'Ah, but this penny here is Doris Semple.'
'That penny? How do you know it is?'
'Well, what's the half-dollar got that the penny hasn't got?'
'Nicks on it.'
'That's right, I told you it was Doris Semple.'
After this bit of a gag they'd all dance the first half of the chorus in slow time and then finish it by singing it quick again and dancing off, all except my dad of course. My dad didn't play by himself in these chorus numbers nor in the jazzy ones, because there was Styx Davies who played the drums and later on a xylophone solo. But now there was Rutland Wiltshire coming on to give a ballad. One of his ballads went:

Sun, I don't want your sunlight
Moon, I don't want your moonlight
The one light I desire
Is the lovelight
Flashing like fire
From my loved one's eyes –

Nobody really wanted to listen to the ballad as the first item after the opening chorus, but they had to have it whether they liked it or not. It was like Duty, or the Holy Mass in a way. There was my poor dad in his pierrot costume crashing away at his piano, stage right, and Rutland Wiltshire like glued to the boards as though they'd nailed his feet to them, making with the big gestures at the moon and sun and then at his loved one who was supposed to be like in the audience. He got a lot of applause because everybody was glad it was over, and then there was the first sketch, to everybody's relief.

This had Jack Rowbotham, who was like the Light Comedian, and he was with Maggie Paramour the soubrette, just like my mother had been, and they were embracing and kissing standing up there in the middle of the stage. Then there's a knock offstage and Maggie runs off to hide, and who comes in but Robbie Partridge with a postman's hat and a parcel, and he says 'Mr Throstlewhistle?' and then it's 'Sign please'. This routine goes on for three parcels, but the last time he comes in without knocking and catches Maggie and Jack Rowbotham hard at it. He says 'That's my wife' and the other two go into the guff about we love one another and we can't live without each other. So then Robbie brings out his book and his pencil and says 'Sign please'. Blackout. Then Maggie herself came on to do her number, dressed as she was in the sketch but this time with no skirt on.

This Maggie had a snub nose and a bit of a double chin coming on, but she had these very lovely legs, I'll say that for the little bitch. They were very long and you could see them right up to her bottom, and they were in sheer black silk stockings with the seam absolutely straight up the back. They were very beautiful legs, and she didn't really deserve to have them. They were like the legs you see much more of post-war, legs having got longer due to better nutriment or Marshall Aid or something. My dad played her song for her, but while she did her bit of a monologue I couldn't help notice that he kept looking at these legs with a kind of longing, he could hardly keep his eyes off them, and I should have smelled trouble early on but didn't. There weren't a single man's eyes, married too, that weren't on those legs in the whole place, but my dad was fairly prominent up there at the piano, and a lot who were looking could see him looking too, sort of hypnotised. Maggie was married to Ray Morgan, a sort of dirty looking man with a lot of black hair who played the violin, but not with the opening chorus along with the piano and drums, too big a man for that, and called himself The Great Romano.

Anyway, Maggie Paramour, who was really née Maggie Bamber, had this saucy soubrette number, with a bit of a dance and showing off the legs, and it went something like

Oo la la oo la la
I'm a leetle meedeenette
Everyone near and far
Wants me for their leetle pet.
You should see

In gay Paree
How all ze monsewers stare at me
When I walk my merree way
Down ze Roo de la Pay.

And so on, all done in this like phony French accent. Then she told
a story about how a man took her for a drink and she asked for a
port and brandee, and she had five of these, and the man said do
you always drink port and brandee, and she said, oh no, it is only
when I am catching the train to see my mothair, I ave to dreenk zees
queeck because ze train he go in five minutes. Then she did her song
again, half a chorus, and ended up by saying oo I ave a laddair in my
stockeeng, and my poor dad had to run after her with a bucket and
a washleather saying Let me get up that ladder, missis, I'll clean your
windows for you. Poor dad. But this staring at these legs wasn't just
part of the act, I could see that and I knew it later on.

After this there was Robbie Partridge and Rutland Wiltshire in
their crosstalk act. Do you tennis, Dennis? Do you hockey, cocky?
You don't rugger, do you? Do you put manure on your rhubarb?
Yes. Funny, we put custard on ours. And at the end they walked up
and down the stage singing a song I thought wasn't as stupid as most
of them:

We're brand new friends
And if you should want to know why
The answer is simply because he's he
And I chance to be I.

He lends. He spends.
But it isn't really a loan
Because it already belongs to me
And what's his is his own.

When we first met
Each saw in the mind of the other
The thing that you'd find in a brother

Or, better, in
A Siamese twin.

If friendship ends
It won't be through him or through me.
If fate contrives
To take one of our lives
We'll throw in the other one free
And that's what brand new friendship ought to be.

I never did find out who wrote that song, because all my dad was given was a tattered bit of old manuscript to play from, but Robbie said he'd bought a whole bundle of original songs from some poor broken down drunken old bugger in a pub who'd been very good in his day but had never made the name that he should have done, got the lot for five bob and a double whisky. Anyway, the first half of the programme was well away now, and what followed was bloody Romano, Ray Morgan really, with his fiddle. He didn't wear pierrot costume for this number, what he had on was like loose blue trousers and a kind of silk blouse and a red neckerchief and cummerbund to match, like a gypsy, and what he played was Monti's Czardas, very slow at first, then speeding up, then prestissimo, with him shouting at my dad, Faster! Faster! One day my dad took him at his word and went so fast that he finished long before bloody Romano did, and that helped the trouble that was brewing as you'll see later.

Then there was a sketch in which Robbie and Jack Rowbotham and Jimmy Latham, who was called an Eccentric Dancer, sat down squatting near the footlights, and my dad played like Chinese music and the drummer Styx clacked away on the Chinese blocks, and these three were supposed to be in the Tasting Department of a Tea Blending Establishment, and they went on clowning about, gargling and spitting until Rutland Wiltshire came in and said:

'Okay, boys, break for coffee.'

Then it was time for the soprano solo, which was done by Robbie's fifteen-stone missis, whose real name was Margery but who called herself professionally Madame Estrella de la Roche. She did a number

I always liked when it was done properly, meaning sort of relaxed, and it was Dancing On The Ceiling, by Rodgers and Hart, but she did it a bit too solemn like a sort of classical piece of grand opera. But the song was built up into what they call a production number, with Jimmy Latham doing his eccentric dance, drums and piano and even fiddle, with the Great Romano very disdainful, and the company doing a kind of harmony thing my dad had arranged for them, humming. Then the idea of dancing led to Dancing With Tears In My Eyes from Jack Rowbotham, then a number from Jimmy Latham about dance rhyming with France, which gave Maggie Paramour a chance to show off the legs in a can can, and then all the company did Dance Dance Dance Little Lady with Rutland Wiltshire in the lead, and that brought the curtain down and there was the interval.

That like summary ought to give the Younger Generation an idea of what the old concert parties used to be like. For the second half the company was all in evening dress, some tails and some dinner jackets, my dad in the darkest ordinary trousers he had and a loose sort of black jacket that Robbie lent him, and the two ladies in frilly organdie stuff, with Maggie's skirt split up to the bottom so that the legs could get plenty of play. The first item was a very posh kind of ballroom display with Jimmy Latham in tails, very tall and smart with it, and Maggie Paramour all frills and gunmetal silk stockings and a flash of camiknickers. First of all they sang this duet that went like this:

> With you
> I can do
> Anything at all
> I can build the Eiffel Tower
> Or the Chinese Wall
> I can drive an express
> At a thousand miles an hour
> More or less
> If you'd only say Yes.

Then they did the dance, and when Jimmy Latham steered Maggie to the wings she seemed to disappear and then come back again, but she'd changed to Robbie wearing the same kind of dress as her and with makeup and a wig on like hers. So then it was funny, with Jimmy putting his hand on her titty and having it knocked away, and then Robbie's knickers coming down and finally his brassiere came off and you could see his hairy chest. Then there was a sketch with Maggie and Margery or Estrella de la Roche in which Margery said 'What do you think of Jack Rowbotham?' Maggie said, 'Oh he's terrible, he undresses you with his eyes.' Then Jack came on with his hands over his eyes crying 'I daren't look, I daren't', and when he tripped over something he dropped his hands to see where he was, then he looked at Maggie and her dress dropped off, she standing there in her underwear with the legs in all their glory, and then a blackout.

After that Rutland Wiltshire sang Up In The Garret Away From The Din Someone Is Playing An Old Violin, and of course there was Romano as a battered old fiddler doing Beethoven's Minuet in G, and then Jimmy Latham had his big solo, very hard work for my dad on the piano, shifting from one tempo to another. It was all made out of a song about dancing the world over:

Everybody's got two tootsies,
The French and the Swiss and the Dutch
And the Lithuanians
And the Scandinavians
And such like
Much like we folks.
But see folks what I do
With my two
Tootsies.

So he danced in different ways, Russian frogdancing and all, and he even did a bit as a man with a wooden leg. After that it was Robbie and Jack Rowbotham got up as tramps looking for fag-ends and pretending to start songs with titles like I Don't Like Fat Girls Cause They Roll Off My Lap or You've Worked All Your Life For Me Mother Now Go Out And Work For Yourself or else She Was As

Pure As Snow And She Drifted. Then they did a duet about being Kings Of The Road.

The next sketch was the old one, done by Jimmy Latham and Maggie Paramour, about the married couple at the breakfast table, the husband saying where's the marmalade and she saying I forgot to get it dear and he saying where's the *Daily Mail* and she saying I forgot to pay the newsagent dear, and he saying I never forget anything, and right at the end he gets up from the table he's sitting behind to say I'm off to work now and let me leave you with this thought: be very thankful you're married to a man who never forgets anything. And then you see him going off and of course he's forgotten to put his trousers on. Blackout. Now what looked like a breakfast table in this sketch was really Styx's xylophone with a bit of board and a cloth on the top. These were whisked off by Styx himself as the lights came up again, and there was the instrument in all its glory and he played two pieces – Sparks and then On The Track, using four hammers in this second one – with my dad oompahing away on the piano.

After this it was Maggie again, and she had a song that was one of the five-bob lot written by this poor old devil Robbie had met in the pub. She was dressed very demurely with her hair in a bun and glasses on and a long skirt, like a schoolteacher, and she sang this verse:

Scientists maintain
That they can explain
Everything on earth or in the skies above.
Why, if they're so wise,
Can't they analyse
This common phenomenon called Love?

She made a bit of a mess of that phenomenon, but never mind. Then the time changed, my dad played eight jazzy bars while she took off her glasses, shook her hair down, and yanked off her skirt as you might have expected. And so she did a song and dance to these words:

There's a reason for spring
There's a reason for the fall
But why did we get together?
For no good reason at all.

Have you heard a bird sing?
There's a reason for its call
But we are birds of a feather
For no good reason at all.

Reason revolted and cried
Better beat it and hide
But my heart was too quick
For that vanishing trick
Something went click inside.

There's no unknowable thing
Be it great or be it small
But I'm at the end of my tether
Why did I, why did I fall?
For no good reason at all.

Now during her dance part her husband came in with his old fiddle
and did a bit of Hot Club de France stuff, double stopping and all,
while Styx came in with the drums. After that there was a very long
sketch for all the company, it was supposed to be a theatrical agency,
and everybody did something that was supposed to be no good,
Margery singing Pale Hands I Loved and Romano being Paganini,
and at the end everybody got shot by this agent, played by Robbie,
with a toy machine-gun he took from under the xylophone, while
Styx did a rat-tat-a-tat on the drums. Then Robbie tried to sing and
didn't like it so he shot himself, and everybody lay dead on the stage
except Styx and my dad. So Styx and my dad shot each other with
kids' water pistols and that was that. Then everybody came back to
life again, just like in the old mummers' play I'd seen as a kid, and
they sang the closing chorus:

We've had our joke
And we've had our song
And a bit of the old soft shoe
Now we'll go to roost just like a rooster
With the words that you are used ter
Cockadoodle
Cockadoodle
Cockadoodle
Doodle
Dooooooooooooooooooo.

It wasn't such a bad show really. It was supposed to go on all through the summer, afternoons and evenings, except Sundays, but my dad was out of it long before August Bank Holiday.

When I saw Maggie Paramour for the first time, complete with the legs, I went straight back to our digs, shut myself up in my little room, and had a good look at myself in the old cracked mirror, having to stand a good way back from it to see all of myself. Without clothes on that is. It wasn't too bad a body, nice firm titties with the points sticking up in the air, good smooth skin without a pimple or a boil or a birthmark on it, and then my own legs, which were as good as hers and not all that much shorter either. Still are as good, I'd say, old as I am.

Seven

The caffy where I worked opened at ten in the morning for Morning Coffee, which was not what the French would want to call coffee, as it was made with Camp Coffee Essence and very weak, but that's how they used to like their coffee in Blackpool, the idea being that if you wanted strength you got it in a Nice Cup of Tea. Lunch started to be served at twelve-thirty, and I used to write out the menus for the ten tables we had. There wasn't a lot of choice, this one was typical:

Soup
Cod and Chips
Roast Beef Cabbage Boiled Potatoes
Steamed Raisin Pudding and Custard
Tea or Coffee
Minerals

There was only me and Mr Hargreaves to do the waiting on, but it didn't take the customers long to make up their minds what to have, and Mrs Hargreaves had all the stuff ready cooked to be warmed over, not very healthy, but that's the way it was. We'd be finished serving lunch just after two, then we had our own lunch, and then tea would be served from four till six-thirty, this of course being High Tea – a Nice Plate of Bread and Butter, fish and chips, cold beef or ham and salad, fruit salad or rhubarb with custard, and of course a Nice Pot of Tea. Only the posh people went in for dinner

at the Grand or the Imperial, but I used to think that was a waste of
time, dinner taking up too much of the evening and all the delights
of Blackpool going on outside. I forgot to mention that the Soup up
there on the menu was just soup, bits of left over meat and veg sort of
boiled up together, but Soup in the posh hotels was a different matter
being clear and thick and Julienne and Mulligatawny.

Anyway, when I'd finished my own high tea at the caffy I had all
the evening to myself, and a fair bit of spending money too, what
with the tips. But of course there were plenty to take me out, serious lads I mean, not the guffawing lot in the caffy who showed off
their Manhood by trying to get off with me. There was one lad, Jim
Birkenshaw, who used to come for lunch (it was dinner really, if by
dinner you mean the main meal of the day) and actually worked in
Blackpool at a printer's called Grigson's who had a lot of work as
you might expect in a place like Blackpool, full of posters and leaflets
and things. Jim was a nice serious lad and not bad looking either and
he knew how to dress. His spelling was very good, as it had to be in
a printer's, and he first got talking to me when he pointed out, nice
and quiet and apologetic, that I'd spelt Cabbage with one *b* on the
menu, a funny thing for me to do when you consider that little song
that dad made up for me, of which I remembered the tune all right.

I'd better say now before going further that I didn't see all that
much of my dad these days, except from a distance when I went on
the pier and he was playing or rehearsing. Back stage he'd usually be
arguing with somebody, usually the Great Romano, about him being
too fast or too slow or too loud, and he had his lunch in a pub, a sausage roll and a pint, and he had his high tea usually with members of
the company in the caffy on Central Pier, special cut rate for resident
concert party. We had breakfast together at first in the digs, in with
the monthly rate, and the others were mostly commercial travellers,
and dad got fed up with talk about new lines in corsets over the
bacon and egg, so he gave up having breakfast and just had a couple
of bottles of Bass up in his room. He looked awful in the mornings,
very gloomy and unshaven with it.

Anyway, Jim took me out and gave me some nice evenings. We
went to the Tower Cinema and saw *The Broadway Melody*, with

Anita Page and Bessie Love, more times than I can count. It was a
bang up to date thing then, of course, but now it seems very old-
fashioned and the girls in it very dumpy. In the middle of it there
was *The Wedding Of The Painted Doll* in colour, terrible colour I
suppose it was, but it didn't matter because it was all supposed to
be dolls with very unnatural colour. We were all singing You Were
Meant For Me in those days, and

Don't bring a frown
To Old Broadway
You gotta clown
On Broadway
Your troubles there are outa style
For Broadway always wears a smile.

He also took me dancing in the Tower Ballroom. He didn't dance
well being a lad, but I could dance anything though I'd had no lessons, like most girls. Some of us girls at school used to try out things
during playtime and that's how I learned I suppose. We went to the
Zoo and on the Big Dipper, and it was in the Tunnel of Love that he
first put his arm round me, not having done that even in the Tower
Cinema back row. Then of course he had to follow it up by kissing
me, and his breath was nice and sweet really, even though he'd had
sausages for his tea with Lea and Perrin's (he had his tea with his
mother, and we usually compared what we'd each had for tea, that
sort of being the beginning of the evening's conversation). But, I
suppose women are funny and I was a woman though only thirteen
and a half, I liked him less like that than when he was just a friend.
I didn't want his hot breath on me, I wanted us just to be pals. So
that night when he took me back to the front door of my digs, after
a supper of fish and chips just round the corner, and he tried to give
me a good night kiss for the first time, I had to turn my face away, I
couldn't help it. He said:
    'Did I do something wrong in the Tunnel then?'
    'Oh, I don't blame you for trying. I mean, everybody has to try.'
    'But you didn't like me doing it?'

'Well, it's like our, well, you know –' I meant relationship, but not many knew the word in those days. 'I mean, well, like you're a nice boy, and I'm very fond of you, but not in that way.'

'Not in what way?'

'Kissing and cuddling and what not.'

'I see.' He looked very downcast then, as lads will when they've heard that sort of thing from a girl. Then he said: 'You mean never? Not ever, is that what you mean?'

'It takes time, that sort of thing.'

'Not too much time, I hope,' he said, and I didn't like that sort of cheeky tone, lads always getting that way sooner or later in any relationship. 'Same time same place tomorrow?'

'No,' I said, 'sorry. I've got to wash my hair.'

'It's not Amami night,' he said without any humour. That was true. The next day was Thursday, and all the adverts for Amami said that Friday night was Amami night. And I hadn't even thought of washing my hair till that minute when I said I was going to. 'You're going out with somebody else, is that it?'

'No,' I said truthfully. I was going out with another lad on Saturday, I forget his name, and there was another one, Irish called Dempsey like the boxer, that I met after mass on Sundays (my dad had stopped going to mass, by the way, a very bad sign) and sometimes we had a walk and sometimes he said how about a walk tonight, and I wouldn't have minded a bit of a cuddle with him, but he went on a lot about his dad and his dad hating the English, I don't know why looking back I put up with it, but I was really not booked up for either Thursday or Friday. Feeling a bit sorry for Jim, I said: 'How about Friday?'

'No,' he said. 'I've got to go with my mother to Cleveleys to see my uncle and auntie. How about Saturday?'

'I can't manage Saturday,' I said, and I thought I'd leave it at that. I knew he'd be in for his lunch every day, so he wasn't just going to walk out of my life. He could if he wanted to, in a way, I didn't care one way or the other, but no girl likes to see anybody just go like that, it's a sign of your lack of power so to speak. It will seem silly to many that a girl of thirteen, although she looked seventeen, should think that way, but there's no flying against nature, and it's only the fact that the Old rule the world that makes them want to make the Young believe they know nothing about life. 'How about Monday?' I said. And I thought, well, if he did want a kiss and even a bit of a feel, no harm done. And I thought, yes, a lot of harm done, because the relationship would not be the same. The Difficulties of the Relationships Between the Two Sexes.

'All right,' he said, 'Monday.' And then he leaned forward and gave me this little peck on the forehead and it nearly made me cry, Life being so awful and at the same time Beautiful. And then he went off home to his mother, who would be waiting up for him, poor lad.

Well, I did wash my hair the next night, and not with Amami but with Solar Satin, which was supposed to bring out the High Lights, and I had trouble. The man who ran the boarding house was a bit of a lazy kind of lout whose wife really owned the place, she'd been left it in her father's will, and all he had to do was just stand around and pretend to be in charge. He was dark and looked a bit dago, about thirty-eight I'd say, and his name was Mr Flushing. He must have had a lot of jokes played on his name in his time, like you're flushing, Flushing, and you want flushing down the lav, you do, Flushing. On the other hand, I never heard anybody try that sort of joke on him, not even his battleaxe of a missis, as though they knew it must have been worn out long ago, and perhaps for that reason nobody had ever tried the joke, except perhaps when he was at school. But there was a girl at the English Martyrs called Nora Dare, and I never once heard one of the teachers say How dare you, Nora. It's an important thing, your name, and there's perhaps an instinct in people that tells them to leave your name alone. Anyway, Flushing was a man with a Roving Eye, but I never thought he'd rove it at me. He knew my age, dad had told him right at the start, perhaps he was quick to spot the roving eye and wanted to put him off. But there's no putting some men off, and to tell some men that a girl who looks seventeen is really only thirteen is like, as Mme Perpignan used to say, putting Spanish Fly in their Pernod. While I'm on the subject, there's a lot of foolishness talked by Headmistresses of Secondary Schools, trying to make growing girls look unattractive to men by making them

wear gym slips and black stockings, when most of the strip joints in
Soho and such-like places have their strippers start off with just that
sort of schoolgirl outfit.

Anyway, this is what happened. The bathroom was just opposite
my bedroom, and I washed my hair in the washbowl with just my
slip on. I came out of the bathroom near blind, what with water in
my eyes and my hair in them too and towelling away, and there was
Mr Flushing waiting for me, the sly and dirty devil. He said:

'Haha. I thought it was Friday that was Amami night.' And then
he grabbed me or tried to. I got into my room and tried to shut the
door on him but he was too quick. Then he was in the room with
me grabbing me and saying 'Hm, such a lovely smell of lovely clean
hair,' and started sniffing all over it like a dog and then kissing me on
the nape of the neck and then by God he had my slip down over my
shoulders and was kissing me on the back. 'I've wanted to do this,' he
sort of panted, 'ever since I –' And then by God he had me down on
the bed and was kissing me very hot and hard on the mouth, and his
right hand was on my Left Breast and was sort of circling with the
palm of it all over the Nipple. I yelled when I could:

'Stop it you dirty bastard. I'll scream, you filthy pig,' and I tried to
but then he had his big hot mouth on mine again and all I could get
out was Ilffy Hig Hop If.

'No good yelling,' he said panting. 'The missis is away at Bispham
seeing her sister. And everybody else is out on one job or another.
It's just you and me, love, so lie back and try to enjoy it.' But I
banged away at him with my fists and then when he took no notice
I started to scratch. He was very strong though this Flushing and
he just sort of bundled my little hands into his big left paw and held
them while he got his right hand under my slip and his mouth glued
on my mouth, and I crossed my legs very fiercely and he couldn't get
anywhere there. So he said very coarsely I thought, 'I don't want to
put it in, love, I just want the heaven of your lips and the loveliness of
your titties, I love you, I love you,' I Love You being what that class
of man always says when he's after nothing more than what they call
a quick bash, that being dirty soldiers' language. The trouble is that
sometimes it's not worth fighting, you might as well give in, espe-

cially when what's being done to you isn't all that unpleasant. This Flushing had a nice sweet breath on him, very surprising that was, but he'd probably been sucking things to give it him, planning this like Assault, and his kissing was a bit fierce but exciting in a way, so I just lay back and let him get on with it. Before I knew where I was he had his mouth down there, slopping and slurping away and going yum yum and then plk plk which was his spitting out the odd hair, and then I started to Come, which I didn't want to really but I had to.

Now the funny thing was that while I was Coming my brain was very clear and sharp and like far above all this hanky panky down there. And what my brain was saying was something like: no, never be like the thing that a man just uses for his pleasure and then when it's over he just says thanks love be seeing you around and buggers off whistling. If they want it make them pay big for it. At the same time make the bastards learn what it's all about. A Female Body is not just a piece of liver from the butcher. It is not just a pleasing shape with a hole in it. It is more like a musical instrument made of flesh and blood that has music waiting inside it but only for properly trained hands to coax out. Make the bastards learn.

Well, what this bastard Flushing was doing while he was slurping away down there was Coming himself into his trousers, I could tell by the way he was moving himself up and down in like rhythm getting faster and faster, making the bed creak, while he had a hand on each of my Breasts. Then he came I could tell by his going aaaah and like dithering, then it was all over as if it had been no more than a sneeze and he took his hands away as though he'd only put them where he'd put them in like a Fit of Absent-Mindedness, and there he was looking at me in like smirking embarrassment and yet like triumph and I was looking at him quietly blazing. I could see the wet seeping through his trousers at the crutch, the trousers being light grey flannel, and I was properly disgusted. I said:

'I'm not going to tell my dad, it's not worth it, you'll only say that I led you on or some such filthy lie.'

'No,' he said, 'to be fair, I wouldn't say that unless I had to. Fair's fair, love, all said and done. It was nice, that, by the way, it was nice, you have to admit.'

'It was like animals,' I said. And then, not really understanding why I said it or what it meant, 'There ought to be a key. Only proper players should know where it is.'

'Eh?'

'You're a bit stupid,' I said, 'I can see that. No use talking to you, is it? But I'll say one thing, next time you try anything like that I'll use violence.'

'Oh, come off it love. And I don't like what you said about me being stupid. You're only a bit of a kid, all said and done. Who are you to talk about me who's old enough to be your father being stupid?' And then he said, 'What do you mean, Violence?'

'A knife,' I said, 'or something. I haven't thought about it yet. I'm not having people grabbing me like that and just using me.'

'You're like all of them,' he said. 'Love it while it's going on and then get all full of innocence and virtue and nasty with it.' He had this sort of a smirk on his jowl while he was saying it, the big man who'd had his own way with a little girl and made her Come and Come himself even if it was only in his kex. He'd had a bit of that there, something to chalk up. I had this kid on the bed, see, only a kid, lovely big tits though, all for it too.

'Get out,' I said. 'This is my room as long as my dad pays for it.'

'Ah, but he hasn't paid for it, has he?' smirked this bugger. 'He owes me, did you know that, no I can see you didn't. What's he doing with the money that's rightfully mine, that's what I want to know?' I felt my heart sink a bit when he said that. 'I'll tell you what he's doing,' he said, still with this smirk. 'He's spending it on that tart with the legs that go right up to her BTM. Took her to dinner last Sunday at the Metropole. Mrs Hendrick saw them there.'

'Who's Mrs Hendrick?'

'Her that takes the tickets on the pier. He'll get found out, you mark my words. I'm not having that fiddle player coming round here to make a row, I tell you straight. Anything like that and your dad's out and you with him. Messing about with a married woman, very dangerous that is, and it's not right either.'

I didn't know the word Hypocrite in those days. All I could say was: 'You're a right bloody bastard. You've got a lot of room to talk, you have. It's not true, I don't believe it. My dad wouldn't be such a fool. And it's none of your bloody business either.'

'Language, language,' he sort of grinned. 'This one with the fiddle suspects, I reckon, hotblooded he is like all fiddlers. Well, it's your dad that's doing the fiddling, and it's not right, specially with him not paying for his bed and breakfast.'

'Here,' I said, 'how much do we owe you?' And I went to my little box which I had in the top drawer of the dressing table. I had my wages and my tips in there, but I didn't think it would be enough. Still, I had to show willing. He said:

'Oh, fair's fair, give and take is what I say. I gave him a week to settle up and then we'll see. We'll say no more about it for now.'

'You mean,' I said, 'that I paid a bit of the rent just now. Which is making me out to be something I wouldn't dirty my mouth with saying what it is. Here,' I said, 'take it.' And I near threw it at him.

'Your dad'll pay,' he said. 'This business with this singing and dancing tart with the legs won't last. He'll get nowhere there, I can tell you. And that husband of hers will get him. It won't be with his bare hands, stands to reason, because he's got to keep his fingers nice, but he'll get him all right.'

'I don't believe it,' I said again. 'My dad wouldn't be such a fool.'

'You'd be surprised what people will do,' he said. 'When they think it's safe, that is.' I nodded at him very grim, to show he was one of those people himself. 'The Great Romanovsky or whatever he calls himself earns a bit extra on Sunday with the Palm Court Orchestra at the Grand while the regular fiddler's convalescing from his operation. Hernia, they said it was. But he'll find out and it won't be long, I can tell you.' Then he said, very perky and cheeky and like insolent, so you could tell the wells had filled up again, 'How about a bit more of that we had just then? It was lovely it was really, and you liked it too, can't deny it. And I do love you, I love you.' And he put his arms out just like Al Jolson in *The Jazz Singer*. I started to hit out at him with my wet towel and called him some filthy names very loud. He left then, grinning though, so I knew I hadn't had the last of the bugger.

Eight

I was worried about my dad, as you can imagine. I nearly ran out then and there to warn him, even seeing myself creeping behind his piano and putting my head round to say dad, dad, watch it dad, but of course my hair was not properly dry yet and I couldn't do a thing with it nor usually for days after it was washed. So what I did was to go to his room, which wasn't locked, he had nothing to pinch he used to say, and sit down on the rickety chair and wait. I was blazing not only about his like Infatuation over a pair of legs, for that's all it was, but about Flushing and what he'd done and I'd let him do. That wasn't going to happen again, that was one thing I was sure about. In future it was only going to happen when I wanted it to happen, and when it happened the man was going to know like the worth of it. So I sat there and waited, like brooding. Then I had a look in dad's drawers, which were full of things he hadn't bothered to send to the laundry yet, and then in the wardrobe, and there I saw the fiddle and bow in a case that he'd nicked that time, and I wondered why he'd never sold them when we were so hard up.

It wasn't till the pubs had closed, about half an hour after the end of the show, that dad came back, and he was a bit surprised to find me sitting up waiting for him, more like a wife than a daughter.

'What's up, girl?' he said. 'Everything all right? You look funny, different that is. Oh yes, you've been tubbing your crowning glory.' He'd picked up some of these like flowery expressions from Robbie Partridge, who always called himself a Great Reader. 'And very nice it'll look too when it dries.' Then he sat down on the bed, a bit weary.

'Everything's *not* all right, dad,' I said. 'And you know it as well as what I do. Everybody's talking about you and Maggie Paramour as she calls herself.' That took him a bit aback, as they say and you can guess, and he even like flushed. 'Flushing,' I said, 'he knows about it, and you taking her out to give her posh dinners and not paying for our bed and breakfast here. I was proper ashamed.'

'It's none of your business, lass,' he said, 'what a grown man does. You're only a little girl still and don't understand the world.' Oh don't I, I said to myself. I said to him:

'It's my business if Flushing gets nasty with me for you not paying the bill. I offered him my own money but then he started sneering about you throwing your money away on no good little bitches like Maggie Paramour.'

'Said that, did he? Well, I'll have the bugger on two counts. I gave the money straight and plain to Mrs Flushing before I went to the pier and got a receipt for it too which I asked for. So up his all the way. And the other thing is what right has he or anyone else to make nasty purgatory remarks about a poor girl who needs a bit of brightness in her life having been married ten miserable years to that bastard excuse my French of a gut scraper? What does he mean with his incinerations? I bought her this makeup outfit for her birthday and I took her out to late dinner while her husband was fiddling with the Palm Court Orchestra, and what's wrong with that?'

'You ask Ray Morgan what it's about,' I said. 'You do that. And then go downstairs and bash that Flushing for his nasty remarks to your own daughter.'

'I'll do what has to be done,' he said, 'and I'll have none of your cheek, girl. I'll go my own way, right or wrong.'

'Wrong is right,' I said, very witty. 'You know if there's a row, and there's going to be, no two ways about it, somebody's going to be out of a job, and it won't be Ray Romano Morgan with his four string fiddle.'

My father breathed like heavily and said, 'There's things a man can't help. There's feelings that can't be controlled.'

'All you mean is,' I said, 'that Maggie Morgan as her real name is has got these two very beautiful and long legs that go right up to her bottom and you're sort of fascinated like a rabbit by a snake. Why don't you start courting proper,' I said, 'with a view to getting married, for I shan't mind, dad, honest. It's not right for a man to be without Female Companionship, especially at your age. There, I've spoken straight, and if it was a bit out of turn I'm sorry, but I have my rights as a daughter, remember that.'

'Aye, you may be saying the truth,' he said, very weary. 'Arsing about like that and nowt to show for it. It's the fascination, you see, which you'll understand better when you're older. Like in the opera Samson and Delilah.'

'That's in the Bible,' I said.

'No, lass, it's in this opera by this French bugger, pardon my, the one that wrote The Dying Swan. Saint Something, I always forget his name. I'm knackered, girl, like Barney's bull, it's been a hard night, what with Ray Morgan wanting this thing of Paganini as an encore and I hadn't got the music and I had to fake bits of it. But he'll get what's coming to him, you mark my words. Saint Sawn was the man's name, that's why you thought it was in the Bible. So I'll say good night to you, girl, and gang awa tae ma wee bed which I'm on already.'

'And you'll play hell with Flushing tomorrow morning?'

'No point, lass, he just didn't know, that's all, he'd only have to apologise and what's the point in that? So I'll say good night.'

I gave him a peck on the head, just at the top where he was going bald. And I went to bed myself then, making sure to lock the door in case Mr Filthy Flushing got up to his tricks in the night. I hadn't heard his wife come in, perhaps she was staying the night in Bispham. Then I went to sleep though it wasn't easy. My intuition was telling me that something nasty was going to happen.

I saw Flushing on the street next morning. I was going to work and he had been sent out by his missis to do the shopping. He said 'The top of the morning to you, milady,' and I went up to him and said:

'Hallo, Mr Flushing, what have you been buying?' I was all smiles and sweetness and he was such a fool that he thought everything was all right between us, and he even made little kissing movements with his lips, the bloody idiot. 'Two dozen eggs,' I said, looking in his basket. 'For tomorrow's breakfast, how nice.' In those days eggs were put into paper bags not into plastic boxes with slots, so it was no trouble to pick a bag of a dozen out of his basket and drop them on the pavement. It was a nice hot day and they might even fry if left there. 'You should be more careful, Mr Flushing,' I said, 'spilling things like that.' Then I walked on and I could hear him growling and grinding his teeth behind me, and even some old woman coming out of a shop saying to him 'Ee, you've dropped all yer eggs.' I kept out of his way from then on.

What happened next was that not the following Sunday but the one after I went out in the evening with this Irish lad, Kevin Dempsey, just a walk by the sea almost to Cleveleys and back, him talking all the time about the wrongs done by England to the Irish so that I said to myself this is the last time, pity, because he's attractive in his redheaded way, and I came back to the digs to hear the wireless blaring away in the private sitting room of Flushing and his wife, and I went upstairs to my room. Now as I passed my dad's room I heard scuffling and whispering and panting and then this very high like silvery laugh of Maggie Paramour, it had to be her, nobody else I knew had a laugh like that, and I did a bold thing but I couldn't help it, blazing as I was that dad hadn't listened to my warning at all, I tried the door but it was locked, so I banged and banged on it, then they were quiet in there, then there was a bit of whispering, then I banged again and cried out 'What's going on in there?' and then my dad opened up. He looked a bit sheepish, just standing there with his shirt rumpled and his trousers with the braces dangling and in his socks, and I went in and there was Maggie sitting on the bed, complete with legs in gunmetal silk and all their glory. She wasn't a bit embarrassed. She was like unruffled in her turquoise jumper and black short skirt and not a hair out of place. She said in a common sort of Lancashire accent, not a bit of the oo la la in it:

'This your little girl then? Course it is, seen each other before, haven't we? How are you, love?'

'I've warned him,' I said. 'He knows I have. Don't encourage him, that's what I say.'

'Dear dear dear,' she said, grinning. 'Know it all, don't you, love?' And my dad said nothing, just standing there, biting his lip and looking first at me and then at her, very sheepish. What she said then was: 'Silly, be a good lad and go out and get me a packet of Players from a machine.' And she took a shilling out of her bag and threw it on the foot of the bed. I said:

'What did you call my dad then?'

'Silly. Short for Silly Billy. Billy being his name, okay?'

'Taking orders, are you?' I said to my dad.

'All right, girl,' he said. 'Don't take on so. I'll get your fags at the pub,' he said to her. 'They're still open.'

'Have a pint while you're at it,' she said. 'Me and your little girl ought to exchange the time of day, like. Girl talk, call it.' So my dad went out with his jacket on but no tie, this being bright and breezy take it easy Blackpool, Queen of the Irish Sea. Then Maggie said to me: 'Let's have a look at you, lassie. Hm, coming on nicely, aren't you, love? Break some men's hearts before you're finished. You break 'em, love, it's nice to hear them tinkle. Sit down beside me here, I won't chew you up.'

I sat down and we sort of compared legs. She said, as I expected her to:

'Not as long as mine, but you've not done growing yet. My best point or points, those are. Every girl's got her like speciality. Legs is mine. Drive some men mad, they do.'

'Driving my father mad, aren't they?' I said.

'That's right, and he loves it. Funny thing is Ray, that's my old man, you know, the Great Romano, he's never gone in much for legs. All right, he said to me when we were first courting, nice enough pins for walking on, he said. No more? I said. No more, he said. And then you know what he did, love?' She looked at me with these big black eyes and I shook my head to show I didn't know what he did. Then she grabbed my hand and put it on her Breast, the left one, very firm, still looking at me with these big black eyes. 'That's what he did,' she said, 'and that started him panting away like switching the ignition on.' She took my hand from her Breast but still held on to it as though she might want to use it again in a minute for some other purpose so to speak, and she said: 'Most men are bloody fools, they only want one thing. They don't know how to treat a woman or how to appreciate a woman's body, none of the buggers. They've rough, big heavy horny hot hands on them,' but she didn't pronounce all the haitches, 'and what I say is that only a woman can appreciate a woman.' I went hot and cold when she said that, I'd heard of that sort of thing at school in the cloakroom and there was a book which I'd always wanted to read but it was banned, and it was called *The Well of Loneliness*, but I never thought I'd meet that thing here in my dad's bedroom in a Boarding House in Blackpool. She looked me very full in the eyes then, and she said: 'Do you understand my meaning, love, do you see what it is I'm trying to tell you?'

'Yes, I think so.'

'Right, what's your name, love, what do I call you? You call me Maggie, because you and me's going to be pals. Ellen, is it? Well, it's a funny thing but I had a real pal once called Ellen, do anything for me she would. You can stroke them if you want to, love.' She meant the legs, God help us, and what she did then was to lie back on the bed with these great long legs in their gunmetal silk stockings spread out with her skirt up so you could see them right to the limit, and she had these very clean French knicks on. 'Go on,' she said, sort of excited, 'don't be frightened. We'll show those buggers of men, won't we, love, we'll show we don't need them with their hot hairy bloody paws,' and again she didn't pronounce the haitches. And what she got me to do to her was what Flushing had done to me, only I had to do it through the silk of the French knicks at first till she sort of half ripped them which sort of excited her, then it was 'Go on, love, quick, there isn't much time.' What she didn't say was Lock the Door, and I got the idea that there not being much time and the danger of someone just walking in and catching us at it was what sort of added to her excitement. I didn't like it, I didn't like it one bit, it sort of disgusted me, but there was a part of my brain that could sort of see the point, men being so rough and selfish with it. But I said:

'My dad'll be back. We'd better not.'

'Be quick, love, and I'll make it as soon as I hear him outside the door, go on, quick.' I didn't like this one little bit, it was sort of

Immoral, but I did what she said more out of curiosity than anything else, and then we heard heavy clumping feet coming up the stairs and then along the landing and she sort of howled and quivered all over and she bloody near choked me by bringing her legs together round my neck, strong legs they were, her being a dancer, and then she pushed me away so that I near fell on my arse on the floor, and she was sitting up real demure and looking in her bag for a cigarette I took it to be when the door opened. 'You've been a long time getting them fags,' she said without looking up, and then she looked up and I did too, and it wasn't my dad who'd come in, it was the Great Romano her husband, with his fiddle case in his hand and his eyes like blazing and his other hand ready to strike out at someone or other. She said: 'Oh, it's you, is it? Everything go all right?'

He didn't answer her, he turned on me instead and said in an accent more Yorkshire than Lancashire. 'What's she been making you do the dirty little bitch? You're Henshaw's girl, aren't you? Come on, out with it.'

'Just having a bit of a natter,' I said. And then I said the wrong thing, I said: 'Who told you to come barging into my dad's room without being given an invitation?'

'Aye, your dad's room,' he said. 'I knew all about it but I knew he'd get nowhere, poor stupid bugger. All take and no give, the dirty bloody selfish bloody little bitch.'

'Don't you call me names,' she said, 'I'm fed up with you calling me them names, selfish bastard as you are. Go on, get out, you're not wanted.' It was at this moment that my dad came into the room, the packet of Players he'd bought held out in his hand, and he was just in time to see the Great Romano put his fiddle case very carefully on the one chair and then make for his wife as if to strangle her, yelling:

'Unnatural and dirty bitch, teaching young innocent girls filth and dirtiness.'

Maggie started banging at him with her handbag, standing up now of course, and I didn't know whether it was proper for me to take sides, so I just stood there looking. Then when my dad saw the Great Romano give Maggie a right stinging backhander he waded in himself and grabbed the Great Romano by the collar and then these two started having a go at each other, but I could see that they were both scared of hurting their hands, this not being cowardice but their Art, and then of course Mr and Mrs Flushing start coming up the stairs and in a minute or so the little room was real packed out with people. Mrs Flushing, and it was funny really, it was she that had the Naturally Flushed Face, as though she'd married him for his name, said very loud: 'All right, all right, stop it.' And they did. Then she said to the Great Romano: 'I know who you are, you are the violin player, how did you get in this house, not by invitation I'll be bound, I'll have you for trespass.'

'Your front door is wide open,' he said, 'and the bell is broke. And I've come here to get my wife, which is lawful. And I knew my wife was here. And she and me are leaving now, and don't you worry missis, you won't see neither of us again. Come on, you,' he said to Maggie.

But you could see Mrs Flushing wanted a bit of scene, only right since there were these Theatricals here ready to do it, and she was probably bored to tears with what she'd been hearing on the Sunday evening wireless, so she stood guarding the way out and she said, with her arms folded, a big strongmade woman about ten years older than Flushing I reckoned:

'This has always been a respectable house, this has. I've had my eye on you,' she said to my dad, 'slow with your paying up and beer bottles in the room and never down to breakfast, not what we are used to here.'

'I pay for the breakfasts I don't have,' my dad said, 'so you're in pocket on it missis, besides it's no business of yours.'

'My dad's right,' I said, 'and I don't like what you said then about being slow paying up. I offered your husband there to pay out of my own wages but he said no hurry and wouldn't take it. I don't like that manner of talk,' I said.

'Nobody was addressing you to my knowledge,' said Mrs Flushing. 'Girls should be seen and not heard. And you're only a chit of a girl too, with your bit of lipstick on and making eyes at them who is old enough to be your father, and your father here might as well know it before I throw the pair of you out, because that is what

I have every intention of doing. Another man's wife in this room is something I will not have besmirching the good name of the house, so you might as well know it first as last.'

'All right,' I said, blazing now, 'get that husband of yours to keep his filthy hands off little chits of girls that are supposed to be seen and not heard, because he's a dirty bastard and I should have spoke up before.'

'What's this?' my dad said, and his underlip was very red. 'Is this true what my daughter here says?'

'She's talking through the hat she hasn't got,' said Flushing. 'A lot of nonsense, that. As though I'd touch anybody not my missis with the end of my walking stick.'

'Which you haven't got,' I couldn't help saying. 'But you've got filthy paws you can't keep to yourself and you take advantage that your missis as you call her knows nothing about your goings on when she goes to see her sister in Bispham. And that's the truth, and I was scared to speak up before because who'll take my word against his, me being only a chit of a girl as she there puts it.'

'I am not She,' said Mrs Flushing. 'I am Mrs Flushing so mind your manners,' and then she turned on her husband and said, 'What's all this, how does she know I've got a sister in Bispham, who's been telling her, if you haven't, what goes on here when I'm not here to keep an eye on things?'

'She said where's Mrs Flushing,' Flushing said, 'and I said she's gone to see her sister in Bispham. That's all. The time of day being passed, call it. And then that was it and so what's all the fuss about?'

'Come on, you,' said the Great Romano to his wife, 'this is none of us business.'

'I'd say it was the business of anybody decent,' Maggie said, 'when dirty old men like that one there can't keep their hands off young girls.'

'You keep out of it,' Mrs Flushing said. 'I've seen you on the pier showing your Limbs off and doing the oo la la, no better than you ought to be.'

'And what do you mean by that, if I may make so bold as to ask?' said Maggie. 'Here, you,' she said to the Great Romano, 'are you going to stand there and hear your wife insulted by the keeper of a common lodging house?'

'If it is common,' said Mrs Flushing, 'and which it is not, I ignore your vulgarity. It is people like you and this pianoplayer here that make it common. But it will be a common lodging house over my dead body, I can tell you that straight. Because I'm having you out of it toot sweet to use your own common language, so you will hear me out and then go.'

'Go is what we want to do, you stupid old faggot,' said the Great Romano. 'So stand out of my way before I lose my temper.'

'You heard?' said Mrs Flushing to her husband. 'Are you going to stand there and hear your wife called what this common fiddle player called her? Be a man,' she said, 'and stand up for your own flesh and blood.'

'You're not to call her what you called her then,' said Flushing, very unhappy.

'What I want to know is,' my dad said, 'is what my daughter said just now the truth, because she's been brought up to be truthful, and I've not known her tell a lie yet.'

'That's the truth,' I said, 'and therefore it has to be the truth what I said. He ought to be had up in court and put away,' and I pointed at him. Then my father bunched his fingers up and for some reason he tucked the thumbs inside, then he advanced with his lower lip sticking out and more red than ever on Flushing, but Mrs Flushing got in his way. But then the Great Romano chose this moment to say to my dad:

'It's no good, matey. You can't prove anything, not even if she gets pregnant you can't.' Mrs Flushing boiled over at that word Pregnant and said:

'How dare you say them things in my house?'

'Pregnant, Pregnant, Pregnant,' Romano said to her, and then to my dad: 'Me and her's going now, and I'll thank you to stop sniffing around. I know what goes on even if you think I don't, and you won't get anywhere, I know Madamerzel Maggie Paramour better than what you do. But just stay away and keep your eye on the music is my advice if you don't want duffing up, which I'm quite capable of doing, a violinist having a stronger arm than a pianoplayer. So now we're off, all, and I hope as how you revolve you little difficulties.'

'Don't you give me that load of offal,' said my dad, 'you unwashed gut rubber. Tomcats in pain is what you sound like. Your double stopping is bloody agony and if you don't know having no ear to speak of except the thick one you're going to get in a minute there's plenty as do and speak of it. Don't you tell me what to do or what not to do.'

And then the Great Romano put down carefully his violin case which he'd just picked up, and started having a set-to with my dad, but it was pretty feeble really. Maggie said 'Oh for Christ's sake stop it,' and then I said something I didn't mean to say, it just came out, but I knew it would settle matters one way or the other. I said very loud:

'Pregnant, does pregnant mean having a baby? Because that's what I think I'm going to have.' That stopped everybody, I can tell you, and it was funny to see my dad and the Great Romano sort of pausing to look at me with their fists out as if they were going to have their photo taken. Then Flushing, the bloody fool, called out:

'It's a lie. It's not me. I never went near her. Besides, it's too soon for her to know.'

'What do you mean?' said Maggie, sort of coming to like protect me, putting her arm round me and all. 'Too soon since what?' Then Flushing got very confused and he said:

'Since my wife here, Mrs Flushing that is, went to see her sister at Bispham, when she there says this happened, but she's a little liar.'

So then it was my turn to start hitting out. I had this quite big handbag with me, and I began bashing Flushing with it, which was a big satisfaction really, and I gave him and them the lot, crying out about him trying to grab me when I came out of the lavatory once and trying to get in my room with the duplicate key but I'd got my own key in the lock and he couldn't shift it and a lot of other things, some of them true. Mrs Flushing didn't know whether to hit me or hit her husband, but she kept saying: 'What happened that night I went to Bispham, something happened, somebody's not telling the truth here,' and then her bloody fool of a husband said:

'I didn't go as far as she says – ow.' That was me clonking him with my bag, but then Maggie stopped me doing it because she wanted to hear what he had to say. 'Nothing wrong with what I did, it was only natural, she's a liar making out I went the whole way with her, I only gave her a hug like she was the daughter which we haven't got, not your fault dear, and her own father's never around to look after her, so now she's just taking advantage of my natural affections and making out I did something only a bloody fool would dream of doing as it's against the law and there is heavy penalties.'

Mrs Flushing then breathed very deeply and said to him:

'You and me are going downstairs to have a talk about this on us own.' Then she turned to Mr and Mrs The Great Romano and said: 'Go, you two, and don't set foot near this place not ever again because I'll have the police near watching.'

'We don't need your permission, ducky,' said the Great Romano. 'It's a free country and we'll do as we like, which means going. Come on, you,' he said to his wife, who said to me:

'Don't stand no nonsense, love. They're all the same,' whatever that meant, and then they were both going down the stairs arguing. Mrs Flushing said to me and my dad:

'First thing in the morning you're out. It would not be Christian Charity to chuck you out now, which is what you deserve. But I don't want sight nor sound of either of you not ever no more.' And she made to go with Flushing very hangdog after her, but I said:

'We're going now, aren't we dad, we wouldn't stay another minute in your rotten stinking place where no young girl's safe when the landlady is seeing her sister at Bispham. Come on dad, we'll pack and we'll get out.'

Poor dad was very confused and upset about everything, and it was like a Robot that he got his old suitcase from under the bed. I pushed between Mr and Mrs Flushing, she really blazing but her lips very tight till she got him downstairs, and went to pack my own things. Then poor dad and poor me went out into the night and neither of us could get lodgings anywhere, what with Bolton and Bury Wakes Week, so we did what we never expected we'd have to do, we went to sleep on the sands. There was no law against it, and the police never came to stop it. It was a very warm night as a matter of fact and not a very long night either, it being midsummer nearly, but it was not all that comfortable and it was very gritty. I made up my mind that I'd make a better life than this for myself somehow. As for dad, it was too late for dad to be anything but what he was.

Nine

We had breakfast very early in a caffy full of lorry drivers and clean-
ers and such like, leathery fried eggs and very fat bacon and strong
stewed tea. My dad knew now of course that I wasn't pregnant but it
worried him that this Flushing had forced like sexual intimacy on me
and he was blazing and ready to get the police on to him, but I said
let it go, he didn't get anywhere really. And you could see at the same
time that he was still smitten with Mlle Paramour despite everything
and that he hadn't taken in that she was no more than a PT even with
her own husband. Dad was very tired and wanted more than anything else a proper lay down, so we started looking for new digs and
we found them at about eleven in the morning round by the Central
Railway Station, pretty grubby but not too dear, my room on one
floor, his on another, and most of the others staying there we learned
were people working at Amusements; especially those sideshows
they had on what was called the Golden Mile, dwarfs, the man who
looked after the sculpture by Einstein called Genesis, a clergyman
who had been defrocked for dirty things and was trying to cash in
on the scandal of the other one, and the Starving Man. The Starving
Man, who was called Magro but his real name was Joe Something,
was in a room quite near to mine, naturally a very thin man but he
had a good appetite and he was allowed to eat rump steak and plates
of cream horns up in his room where nobody could see him cheating. There was also the Manager of a lot of these shows not actually
staying in these digs but always hanging around. He was called Jerry
Fieldflow or some such name. Anyway, the landlady had actually

seen my dad performing or said she had, and she wanted to know why we were changing our lodgings, but I said that where we'd been staying was dirty, I wouldn't say where though, and she said: 'Well, it's not dirty here, love.' It was though, a bit.

Dad went to have a lie down. I'd dropped into Hargreave's caffy and told them I'd be a bit late this morning, and they said all right love, but I was there just in time for lunch, which today was

Soup
Plaice and Chips
Roast Lamb Cabbage Boiled Potatoes Gravy
Spotted Dick and Custard
Tea or Coffee
Minerals

Jim Birkenshaw was there, as usual, and he said how about tonight, and I said okay. Then he said:

'I still haven't seen the show on Central that your dad's in. How about us going to that?'

I looked at him, standing there with my empty tray and a man behind me saying Miss, Miss, and me ignoring him, always ignore the customer the first time is the rule, and I thought: Well, let's see if anything's starting to show in this show, let's say if like Personal Difficulties are coming out in the way they do things, so I said:

'Okay, we'll do that then.'

I'd seen my dad Disgrace himself at the showing that time in Manchester of the film on Our Lord, and now, though I didn't know it when I was serving the Spotted Dick and Custard, I was going to see him Disgrace himself on the stage and even get into the papers because of it. Only a little bit in the papers, though, and they left out his name, and the papers treated the thing as a joke, but it was still a Disgrace.

I went back to the digs when we'd finished serving lunch and I'd had mine (no plaice left so I had to have the other) and I had a bit of a job finding them. I hadn't taken down the address and I wandered a bit, and I even went into the wrong place first, where a sort of Indian came out of a room in a very dark corridor and said what you want missy. I looked into dad's room, which I found after going into the wrong one where there was a lot of very tiny dwarfs' underwear on a line dripping on to the floor, and it was a relief to find it was empty, so he must be doing the afternoon show as usual. But I was not pleased to find an empty half bottle of John Haig lying on the floor and his bag still unpacked and that stupid little violin case on the washstand. I sat on his bed and waited for him, and he came back just when I was ready to go off and serve teas. I said:

'How did it go, dad?'

'Bloody awful is the only way I can describe it, what with that bugger of a Morgan –'

'Pardon your French.'

'I don't give a bugger, I'll speak as I feel. This bugger Morgan got a very feeble hand on the Monti's Czardas, but he went ahead and said he'd do an encore, and these were the bastard's words: I'd like to play, he said, the most difficult piece in my repper toyr, which is a Cap richy o by the celebrated Paganini, but my pianist has unfortunately lost the piano part, so instead I'll oblige with Salute Damoor. And then he made this face at me and got a bit of a laugh, but I could do nothing about it, and when it was over I looked for him but he'd buggered off, but by the Lord Jesus I'll get the bugger tonight, you see if I don't.'

'I shall be there tonight,' I said, very calm. 'And you will do nothing but what you have to do. Do you want your daughter to be Ashamed of her own father?'

'It'll only be tit for tat, girl. All I want is the laugh on the bugger. And as for that other bitch,' he said and then just growled.

'Why other?' I said. 'There is only one bitch so far as I know, and I must say I'm very glad to hear you calling her a bitch because that means you have found out what she is. What did she do, then?'

'She showed me herself Naked.' And he hung his head as if it was him who'd done the showing.

'She what?'

'She had the door open to the ladies' dressing room, and she had everything off before getting into her stage gear, and she sort of grinned at me and then banged the door shut.' My father sort of ground his teeth at that, and then he sort of howled: 'Not a bloody stitch on, stark ballock if you'll forgive the expression. Not all the years your mother and me were married, girl, did I once see her in the altogether.'

'How did you do it then?'

'What do you mean, how did you do it? That's a very filthy thought. I know what's going on in your mind, it's that bloody Flushing, isn't it, I might have known there was something in it.' And then he kind of crumpled up and said: 'Oh, I've let everybody down, including my own flesh and blood. I'm no bloody good to man or flaming beast.'

'Did you eat anything?' I said.

'Bugger eating, girl. Eating's a waste of time.'

'I get what little bit of money I earn,' I said, 'out of people eating. You're coming with me to the caffy and get something inside you, that's what you're going to do, while I stand over you.'

'No. I'll have a bit of a lay down, and then I'll get something to eat on Central before the show. Don't worry about me, girl.'

'And think on,' I said, 'that I'll be in the audience tonight with a friend, and I want to see everything go proper. We don't want a repetition of that Jesus Christ lark.'

'Taking the Lord's name in vain, girl, that's going too far. All right, I'll be seeing you then.' And he lay down and went off almost at once, snoring like a grampus, whatever that is. So I went off to work a bit troubled in my mind, and when I'd finished I met Jim outside the Tower, and we went into the soda fountain and he had a Knickerbocker Glory and I had a Banana Split. No doubt about it, the ice cream in those days was better than anything you get now, chemicals and all sorts of muck. Then when it was time we went to Central Pier and I said who I was and they let us in Complimentary.

There was a chilly wind blowing in from the land, and the sky was very gloomy, so it was as well to be indoors, and as you might expect there was a very fair audience waiting chewing chocolates and puffing fags. In those days smoking had not yet become bad for the health, and so there was a lot of it. Chocolate too is bad for the health nowadays, when you come to think of it there doesn't seem to be anything that's good for the health except paying these very heavy taxes to the Government, a thing I've always avoided doing, and letting yourself get bashed by Hooligans, I always carry an ammonia spray in my handbag, but those were free and easy days when you could walk the streets without being mugged and smoke fifty fags a day and nobody said it was bad for you. The lights went dim, and then you could hear my dad playing a kind of Overture, in which he mixed up popular songs of the day in what he called a Fugato, too good for them, and then the lights went out except for the Spots and Floods, and then the curtain opened and off they went with their Cockadoodle doo chorus. Dad seemed all right, playing no wrong notes anybody would notice, and everything went smoothly and got laughs in the right places and plenty of applause. I noticed that there was a kind of smell of trouble though when it came to the Sign Please sketch, with Jack Rowbotham and Maggie Paramour embracing away, and my dad let out a kind of a big groan from the piano. This went down quite well as though it was intended and it got a bit of a laugh which Jack and Maggie didn't expect, because they looked kind of startled and then annoyed at my dad. It was after Maggie's own number, the oo la la one, that dad started going a bit too far. She said she had a laddair in her stockeeeeng and my dad, as I said before, had to run after her yelling that he was going to get up the ladder to clean her windows. This time he got to her before she ran off, and there he was on the stage in full view grabbing hold of her and trying to give her a smacker. You could see she was very angry, but the audience didn't think anything out of the ordinary was going on, even when she struggled with him blazing, and it was dad that got the big hand when he sort of tottered back to the piano.

Well then, there was nothing Untoward as they say until it was time for the Great Romano. Instead of him coming on, my dad picked up from near the footlights the fiddle he'd pinched that time, complete with bow, and you could hear a big banging a long way away behind the stage. My dad said: 'My esteemed friend and colleague the Great Romano seems to have got himself locked in the lavatory.' That got a laugh and some tut-tutting, because lavatory was a dirty word in those days. 'Till he manages to climb over the top of the door,' my dad said, 'I'll show you that there's nothing in fiddle playing, it's easy as pie. Why, I can play the fiddle with one hand and the old joanna with the other.' Then he sat down at the keyboard, tucked the fiddle under his chin, and started bowing on the open strings while he did big chords with his left hand. Of course, what he played was that Waltz which millions of kids in Japan now play and which I'm giving you as a free gift at the end of this story. The audience didn't wait for him to get to the end even of the first eight bars before they were giving him a big hand, and he didn't have a chance to finish the thing because the Great Romano walked on then blazing and near throttling the neck of his violin. My dad stood up and bowed at him and offered him the piano seat with outstretched hands, and this got a laugh. So the Great Romano, being used to the game after all, smiled back very toothily but still blazing and said to the audience: 'And now, for the first time in history, you will hear Monti's Czardas played on two fiddles. And it won't be me who plays second fiddle, I can tell you.' So my dad sort of slunk to the piano and said: 'Fiddle faddle,' and this got a laugh, once an audience starts they'll go on all night. So they played Monti's Czardas very seriously as usual, and everything went all right in the slow bit, except that some daft woman in the audience thought this was meant to be funny and started laughing and this started one or two others off. So my dad played up to them, doing big runs up and down the keyboard and swaying his body and lifting his hands up very high when the Great Romano had what they called a rubato bit. This made him frown and look daggers at my dad, but he couldn't do anything about it, not yet. Anyway, the fast part in D major went all right, except when they came to the end and the Great Romano like a bloody fool said 'Faster faster' and my dad said 'With the greatest possible animosity, maestro,' and he raced on so fast that he was finished first. He sat there with his hands on his lap, looking round sort of surprised that Romano hadn't finished yet, and Romano had to do the last two chords on his own, and his double stopping was lousy, even though the chords were D major and A seventh, easy chords for the violin. Of course, the audience thought this was very

funny, like a race or a contest of some kind, especially when my dad
shook hands with himself, standing up to do it, and getting as much
applause as if not more than the Great Romano. Jim next to me
thought it was very amusing and he said so. But when the interval
came I got up and excused myself and went backstage to see what
was going on there, though I could already guess well enough.

What was going on was a hell of a row, with Romano taking
swipes at my dad and my dad bunching his fists up, and Maggie
Paramour just standing there not sure whether to look pleased or
sorry till she saw me, then she said, grabbing my arm: 'Come in
here, what they call the dressing room, love,' but I broke free of her
because I knew what she was after, and the others were saying it's
not the pianoplayer's job to try and upstage the real Artistes and to
watch it boy and so on. Of course Robbie Partridge as boss of the
show, and his missis helping him, was trying to get order and love
and friendship and Cooperation and so on and saying to my dad if
there was any more of this nonsense he'd be out on his ear and his
own missis could take over on the keyboard, having got the RCM
cerstificate in pianoplaying and so on. And I told dad not to be such
a fool as well, but all he did was to swig from a pint bottle of Bass he
had there, still you could see he was a bit shook up.

Anyway, the second half went not too bad, dad being a lot quieter
and not playing too badly either, until it came to the last item, which
was the sketch in which everybody got shot and lay dead on the stage
waiting for the Last Trump, which was dad coming back to life first
and starting off the closing chorus. But this time dad refused to die.
What he did was sort of totter over to Maggie, who was lying on
the stage with her legs spread out, and by God my dad was on top
of her before she knew where she was, and then there was a hell of
a fight on the stage, what with the Great Romano having a go, and
everybody else trying to pull my dad and him apart, and Robbie
yelling Tabs, tabs, tabs, bloody tabs, and the curtain went down on
a scene of like Carnage. Then my dad must have struggled over to
the piano and you could hear Chopin's Funeral March played very
loud until somebody stopped it and you could hear a howl of pain,
which would be my dad's fingers being banged on by the piano lid

shutting. The audience liked it very much, except some said as it was not decent and so on, nothing to bring kids to, a disgrace it was. The curtain didn't go up again, and the lights came on in the theatre, and everybody went out sort of buzzing with talk, and I heard one man say it was like Pally Archie, whoever that was, and sort of singing Is Not the Actor a Man with a Heart like yoooooo till his wife told him to shut it, everybody was looking at him. I said to Jim that I'd better see to my dad, get him back to the digs and so on and even sort of hit him if need be, and he agreed, so we said good night then and there and he didn't even try to give me a peck, as if he knew what serious trouble my dad was in, being out of a job again.

As a matter of fact it was my dad who came looking for me, doing a thing that no Artiste was supposed to do, and that was coming into the theatre by way of the stage, through the curtains and down the steps at the side, calling: 'Where are you, girl? I'm sick of the bloody lot of them.' There was still some audience leaving, and some of them turned to look at him, and a woman tut-tutted at his language, but I sort of stalked up to him as he was coming down the aisle, and I said to him:

'You've done for yourself proper this time, what gets into you for the Lord's sake?'

'I was just sick of the bloody lot of them, girl. You sit there and play that junk, and you're dirt, just a Thing, something to be used, nothing more. It's going to be different, I can tell you.'

And as I and him walked along the pier to the way out, with this really cold night wind blowing away and the waves going whoosh at us, I said: 'In what way is it going to be different? You've always said your job was pianoplaying, being like the slave of a film or a fiddle player or somebody that thinks they can sing, that was your job you said, and now you've lost that job.' And he said:

'I had a long talk with that man Jerry Fireflaw or Feelflow or whatever his name is.'

This was the first time I'd heard about this man, so I said: 'Who's he when he's at home?'

'He was in the digs this morning and he told me he does these sideshows on the Prom. Then we had a couple of gills in the pub before the afternoon show, and he said there was a fortune to be made in what he calls a Piano Marathon. Playing the piano nonstop and people pay to come and see if you can do it.'

'You mean like a test of Endurance?'

'You can call it that, girl, but it means people are coming to hear you and not just some bloody stupid gut rubber or some bloody insolent girl that thinks she's the Queen of Sheba because her legs go right up to her arsehole, oh bugger apologising I can't be bothered saying sorry all the time, all right I'm sorry, I'm setting a bad example, I don't know what's coming over me these days, yes I do in a way, it's being fed up with the way I'm treated, that's what it is, anyway things are going to be different from now on.'

I said, 'You mean you have to play the piano nonstop, no food or going to the bathroom even? How long for? It sounds mad to me, it sounds dangerous even.' And I moved a bit away from my dad as we walked along to get a better look at him, as though to see if he was really all right in the head. He seemed okay, only a bit depressed and at the same time sort of excitable, and he was walking with quick short steps and his head down looking at the planks of the pier underneath him and his hands in his pockets. He said:

'We haven't fixed on how long yet, but this Flowflaw chap says he knew a man in San Francisco, that's in the States, that did it nonstop more or less for forty days and forty nights.'

That reminded me of something, and I remembered what it was, it was Our Lord in the desert. I said: 'But there had to be time off for him to go to the lav.' And then I said: 'That's ridiculous, that's impossible, what happened to him, no, it's not possible, nobody could do it, you're talking through your bloody hat.'

'Because I set you a bad example in matters of language, girl, there's no reason for you to follow it. He had two hours off a day, which was sufficient, and so he played twenty-two hours nonstop each day. Now the number of days Fourthfloor reckons is thirty. Can he do it? If it's under thirty it makes no difference, we get what money comes in, it's a kind of target for advertising. Can he do it? You see what I mean. Of course what the problem is is sleep, which I need a lot of, as you know, but Flawflow says a lot of sleeping is just a habit, and I can take tablets to cut down on the need for it. Can he do it?' he said again, as though he was talking about somebody else, but I could see that he was seeing a poster in his mind saying CAN HE DO IT?

'What sort of tablets?'

'Well, there's a kind called benza or bonza something, and there's caffeine tablets, and also you can suck coffee through a straw, which I rather like the idea of, cold coffee, although it brings on the Urine.'

'All this,' I said, 'sounds to me daft and not only plain daft but criminal daft and also mad daft. What do you get out of it? Money, I mean.'

'Well, Firefloor says we ought to go halves, him providing the piano, which he reckons he'll get on hire, a really good one, very cheap as we'll be advertising the make really, and he pays rent for the premises, which is this room where he used to have the Rat Man and the Crab Lady till they got married and went into catering, he reckons it holds a good hundred standing, and nobody will want to stand there all that long, except towards the end of the marathon, what Fireflue calls Coming In For The Kill. He says charge a bob, but also a half-dollar ticket for five visits, any time day or night, and of course he pays for the lighting.'

'"For the Kill", he says? He knows what he's talking about, this Fluefall. It'll kill you all right, it'll do for you once and for all.'

'And he sees to the advertising and taking the money at the door. He says the sooner we get started the better. You work it out, girl. We could end up with a hundred quid apiece, perhaps more. They'll be queuing up all day and night to get in when I get towards the end.'

'If you're alive at the end,' I said. 'And what do you mean to do with that money providing that you get it?'

We were on the Prom by now, and he stopped walking and turned to me; trying to look Impressive, and he said: 'We'll go to the States, that's what we'll do. We'll go to America, others have done it before us, as a matter of fact the States was made by people like you and me, not satisfied with the life back here. We'll go to the States and we'll make a fresh start.' I just stood and looked at him with my mouth open, not saying a word. 'I'll start a Violin School with this Method

I've been working on. I wrote some of the things down on manuscript paper. I wrote them in the Pier caffy while everybody was
having their tea and not taking a blind bit of notice of yours truly,
him being only the boy. I've got them in the suitcase in the digs, all
nicely written out in ink. There's plenty of rich people in the States
as will be delighted to have their kids playing the fiddle by a Method
that guarantees they'll be sawing away in a proper kids' concert
within a month of starting off. I've got it all worked out. I've shown
you how it works. In the States they're willing and eager to try out
new things, not like here. We'll make us fortune.'

'But I don't want to go to the States,' I said. 'I see enough of the
States at the pictures without having to go there. I mean, what is
there for me in the States?'

'A proper education first,' said my dad. 'And then we'll take it
from there. You might even marry somebody very rich, a pretty girl
like you are. But first of all we've got to earn our fares over.'

I said no more then, and we walked back towards the digs. When
we came near the Duke of Talbot which was not yet closed and full
of singing and noise, my dad sort of slavered and said: 'You go on
back, girl. Just one pint to help me sleep. I won't be getting all that
much sleep once we get started on the Marathon.' So I let him.

As I said earlier on, there was a bit in the papers, the *Blackpool
Mercury* it was and a bit too in the *Manchester Evening Chronicle*
about the to-do on the stage at Central Pier. What it said was something like this: Not since the opera Pagliacci (that's it, not Pally
Archie) has there been seen on the stage such a display of personal
feeling as animated a performance on the Central Pier at Blackpool
last night. Evident differences of an amorous nature caused the
final item to turn into a free fight on which the curtain had to be
rung down with speed and dispatch. The audience seemed to think
this a refreshing change from the normal tenor of good troupers'
behaviour. The father of the troupe and low comedian, Mr Robbie
Partridge, would make no comment except that there would be a
change of pianist for tonight's and all subsequent performances and
that Madame Estrella de la Roche, the internationally known singer,
would be demonstrating her keyboard talent. Madame de la Roche,

who in private life is Mrs Partridge, holds many degrees from musical colleges at home and abroad and numbers many successful professional pianists among her former pupils.

My dad read this out to me in bed, where he stayed for three days and nights getting ready for his Piano Marathon. And then he got up and had seven pints of Bass, most of which came up again, and then he was ready, as he put it, for the Fray. And a right Fray it turned out to be.

Ten

It was one of these places on the sea front which had once been a tobacconist's shop, as you could see if you looked behind, where there was a filthy old empty stockroom with dusty old cutout signs advertising Craven A and Kensitas and Black Cat and a very strong smell of the wood of Swan Vestas. There was also behind a very dirty lavatory with a cracked washbasin, and this Jerry Flyblow had had the water turned on again by the Corporation. The big shop window had all been blacked out so that nobody could see in and they'd got a signpainter to paint a sign saying BILLY HENSHAW THE MARATHON MAN NONSTOP PIANO PLAYING FOR THIRTY DAYS AND NIGHTS CAN HE DO IT? At the entrance there was a blackboard and easel but very small, more like a kid's toy, and there was chalked up every day which day it was. There was a raised sort of platform in the middle inside all covered over with a cheap bit of carpeting and on this was my dad and the piano. There were little lights all trained on him which kept going out because the wiring was Deficient until they brought a young lad in to put that right. There was also a battered old armchair for my dad to rest in. I can see him now in the middle of the night on DAY TWO, just starting his two hours sleep in this chair at 2 a.m., and nobody there except a man who can't sleep sort of looking enviously at my dad who is snoring like a grampus and a young couple who came in on the last train and haven't got a room to go to. And there's me, and there's the Manager, as he calls himself, Jerry Fieldflow (that can't be his real name, it doesn't sound like a real name, there's something fishy about it).

These are some of the things my dad played during his first two days and nights: Avalon, Mountain Greenery, California Here I Come, Carolina In The Morning, Happy Days and Lonely Nights, Chopin's Nockturne in E Flat, Beethoven's Mignonette in G, Paderooski's Mignonette simplified, O Shinanacky Da He Play De Guitar Outside De Bazaar Haha Haha, You Were Meant For Me, Sonny Boy, Für Elise, the slow movement of Tchaikowsky's (thank you Rolf) Fifth Symphony, a piece by my dad made up as he went along for the left hand only, the same piece shoved up for the right hand only, Handel's Lager, Mendelssohn's Spring Song, In A Monastery Garden with whistling obbligato, In A Persian Market, The Sanctuary Of The Heart, Handel's Water Music (selection), bits of Eine Kleine Something (Mozart), the Intermezzo from cavalry Rusticano, On With The Motley from Pagliacci not Pally Archie, One Fine Day from Madam Butterfly, the Pilgrim's Chorus from Tan Houser, Tortoises from the Carnival of the Animals (a very good piece when you're tired, it is the Can Can from Refuse in the Underground played as slow as you like), a selection of Favourite Protestant Hymn Tunes, a selection of Not So Favourite Catholic Hymn Tunes, When It's Nighttime In Italy It's Wednesday Over Here, Rule Britannia Two Tanners Make A Bob, the Marsellayse, Over There Over There For The Yanks Are Coming, Keep The Home Fires Burning, There's A Long Long Trail A-Winding, funeral march for the left hand only, chirpy little tune for right hand only (made up by my dad), If You Were The Only Girl In the World, Let The Great Big World Keep Turning, Yes We Have No Bananas, I Lift Up My Finger And I Say Tweet Tweet Hush Hush Now Now Come Come, Never Be Cruel To A Vegitubel, Bye Bye Blackbird, Me And Jane In A Plane, Poor Papa (He Ain't Got Nothing At All), My Hero from the Chocolate Soldier, Old Man River and Only Make Believe and Can't Help Lovin' Dat Man, all from Show Boat, Rose Marie I Love You (Ma belle Rose Marie. La vache de la prairie), Indian Love Call (when I'm calling Yew ew ew ew Ew ew ew Ewwwww), The Man Who Broke The Bank At Monte Carlo, Daisy Daisy, She Was A Sweet Little Dicky Bird, The Peer Gynt Suite (selection), Beethoven's Pathetic (slow movement), Here's Another One Off To America, Philadelphia In The Morning, Finnegan's Ball, Phil The Fluter's Ball, After The Ball Is Over, Balls To Mr Bangelstein, Over The Waves, The Blue Danube (hard bits left out), Voices of Spring, Tales From The Vienna Woods, The Skater's Waltz, They Call Me The Belle of New York, Selections from Gilbert and Sullivan, slow bits from Borodin's Polovsky Dances, Mammy Mammy (I'd walk a million miles for one of your smiles, a bit exaggerated I've always thought), Lady Be Good, The Girl With The Flaxen Hair (mostly right hand, left hand seizing up a bit), Great Dirty Songs (Cock of the North, The Ash Grove, Colonel Bogey, Samuel Hall), Loch Lomond, Ye Banks and Braes, Mother Macree, The Harp That Once, The Mountains of Mourne, John Brown's Body, Softly Awakes My Heart, Wayward Is Womankind As Feather In The Wind Varying Ever And Constant Never, Jealousy, The Bach Gounod Ave Maria, the other Ave Maria, My Little Grey Home In The West, Smilin' Through; Somewhere in Sahara, Shepherd Of The Hills I Hear You Calling, Because You Come To Me With Naught Save Love, Song Of Songs, Pale Hands I Loved, All Through The Night There's A Little Brown Bird Singing, Little Brown Jug Don't I Love Thee, Beer Beer Glorious Beer, Dear Old Pals, Come To Your Nabob On Next Patrick's Day Be Mrs Mumbo Jumbo Jitterboo Jay O'Shea, Just A Song At Twilight, The End Of A Perfect Day, The Rosary, Slow Tune for Two Fingers, Twinkle Twinkle Little Star, Alice Where Art Thou, The Sunshine Of Your Smile, You Wore A Tulip, and a hell of a lot more.

You'll want to know first how he managed about going to the lavatory. Well, for what he called The Major Operation it was a matter of waiting for his two hour breaks – the one at lunchtime when things were a bit slack. For the other thing, they'd attached a rubber tube to his Thing, and this was fixed to an empty petrol can under the piano that was covered with cloth to make it like a kind of decoration, but he found he could hold it in well, having had a lot of practice playing in picture houses with a belly full of beer. He fed himself as he went along, mostly cold rice pudding which I got cheap from the caffy where I worked, bananas already peeled for him, pieces of plum cake and ham sandwiches. He got more and more constipated as time went on, as you can imagine. He took caffeine tablets but these turned him off coffee, and his nourishment of a liquid nature was cold tea from a big bottle, plenty of sugar in it. He found it better to sleep sitting up than lying down and he slept with his hands soaking in soapy water. There had to be somebody on duty all the time. If it wasn't Jerry Flyflaw it was a dark thin man always chewing a match who was called the Assistant. I was there as often as I could be, and sometimes Jim or some other lad came along with me. The first day's takings were only twenty-five shillings, and the second about thirty bob, but then the takings got a bit bigger because dad was starting to suffer, and people will always pay to see people suffer. Jerry Fieldflow put the money in the bank every day and showed dad the receipt to convince him that there was no funny business going on.

Dad wore just trousers and socks and his old bedroom slippers and a flannel shirt. The piano wasn't all that good, an old Mittelberg grand, but the action was very easy, so dad didn't have to over-exert himself. At the end of the second day he said he felt a bit light headed and his muscles were sore and there were calluses coming on his thumbs and the edges of his little fingers, but otherwise he said he felt like he could go on for a long time yet. The real trouble, he said, was that the business was making him start to not like music any more. It wasn't long before he got me to get him some cotton wool to shove in his earholes. He had a shave every day, and the Assistant gave it him while he was asleep, with a big cut throat razor that he had all the time in his pocket for some reason. He would strop it on the sole of his boot. My sleeping dad never felt a thing. I would give him a catlick with a wet flannel when I was around and comb what bit of hair he had left. When he woke up he was ready to fall from one chair to the other. The chair he sat on to play the piano had cushions on it.

The crowds started to come in when he got to DAY FOUR. Jerry Freeflow had by this time put soft blue and green spotlights on the floor trained up on him, and when the people came in they were very hushed, some of them, as though dad was something on an Altar, very holy or very dead, and this became more so when an old lady, Mrs Haggerty her name I discovered later was, started like to worship my dad and brought flowers in, lilies and white carnations. She was an Eccentric old lady that lived alone and never slept or ate; and it was as if my dad suddenly became a Meaning in Life for her, she was there nearly all the time. Some of the young bloods that wandered in when the pubs were closed, going huh huh and so on, would shout out things for him to play and Swing it, but the Assistant would come up to them and just look at them, he had these horrible eyes, and that would usually quieten them down. One night between eleven and twelve, when there was quite a fair crowd, a man who had what is called Religious Mania got in and he started to preach a sermon:

'Be mindful of the justice of the Lord God and the righteous anger thereof, for is Blackpool not the black pool of all iniquity and one of the Cities of the Plain where fornication and adultery is rife and like to be smitten down with fire and brimstone,' and all the rest of it, like in the Protestant Bible. He was soon thrown out, but it wasn't so easy to throw out a Communist who came in with four toughs who had all paid their money at the door good as gold and went on about Comrades and the wickedness of the Capitalists, and there was even a man in a black shirt who said that my dad was a victim of a Jewish Conspiracy and the only solution to England's Problems was to see off the Jews. The police came in once or twice to see Jerry Feelflo's Showman's Licence and there was a visit from someone in the Musicians' Union that wanted to know if dad was a paid up Member, which he wasn't, but the Unions didn't have the Power in those days they have now. The things that dad played in addition to what I mentioned before were these:

Happy Days Are Here Again, The Sunny Side Of The Street, Prelude and Fugue by Bach in E flat minor (first book of 48, I didn't know what that meant at the time but I did later), When The Sun Goes Down, Another Little Drink Wouldn't Do Us Any Harm, The Frothblower's Anthem, Daddy Wouldn't Buy Me A Bow Wow (Bow Wow), the slow movement of Beethoven's Seventh Symphony, A Bachelor Guy Am I, Love Will Find A Way (both from The Maid of the Mountains), Little Nelly Jelly, I'm A Yankee Doodle Dandy, Will Ye No' Come Back Again, Musetta's Song from La Bohème,

Ma He's Making Eyes At Me, Am I Blue, Body And Soul, big tune
from Raspberry in Blue Jars, big tune from Rachmaninoff's Piano
Concerto No. 2 last movement, big tune from Greig's the same first
movement, Blaze Away, The Stein Song, The Birth Of The Blues,
Chloe, Invention for right hand thumb with loud pedal down, Duet
for little fingers, The Nose Song (dad dropping off and his nose
banging the middle C, but that was just before knocking off time
in the night of DAY FIVE), selection from Wagner's The Master
Singers, Prelude to Third Act of Tristan and Whatshername (all right
hand and nobody could say he was cheating), Invention for right
hand in triads (dad's left hand being out of action with paralytics
and his right hand seized up in triad position like a claw), Music for
Monsters (dad's fists going like mad in a like feeble way all over the
keys), I Love Little Pussy Her Coat Is So Warm, Memories of Last
Christmas (popular carols), In A Chinese Temple Garden, Pomp
and Circumference March (the one with Land of Hope and Glory),
tune from Jupiter in The Planets by Gustav Holst, St Louis Blues,
Last Spring by Greig, I'll Sing You One Oh Green Grow the Rushes
Oh What Is Your One Oh and a hell of a lot more, and all from
memory, not one note of music in front of him.

On DAY SIX, when it was time for dad to knock off playing for
his two hours rest, he found he couldn't sleep. He was horrified
and he looked horrible too, all grey and haggard and about twenty
years older than he really was. This old lady Mrs Haggerty had some
sleeping tablets in her bag, but dad said if he took any of those he'd
never wake up again. The Assistant offered to knock him out, but
that was thought to be cruel, though it was meant kindly. What was
done was to fill him with bottled Bass, the pubs being open, this
being lunchtime, and then he dropped off for a bit, but he woke up
before his time was up and said (so they told me, I was serving lunch
in the caffy at the time): 'I can't make it, I've had enough, it's killing
me, I Hate that bloody piano, I Hate music, how much have we
taken so far?' Jerry Fallfly said:

'About thirty quid all told, less what we've paid out in grub and
booze and that and then there's the rent and lighting. A lot of them
that come in come in on the cheap ticket. Next week we put the price

up. You'll have no trouble, Billy, if you just keep at it nice and steady and don't give too much of a bugger. You've got to make them thirty days and you will if you go about it the right way, not giving too much of a bugger.'

'I can't do it, I can't.'

'Listen, all you have to do is, sit there at the joanna and put your elbows on the keys and bang. Read a book or the morning paper if you like and just sort of let your fingers wander up and down. You're being too much of an Artist, that's your trouble.'

But dad *was* an Artist in his way. He couldn't help wanting to play properly, as if the people that came in to gawp knew the difference between D sharp and Allegretto non troppissimo. It hurt him to play a wrong note when he knew he was sort of the focus of attention, and not just a Thing accompanying something else. In a way he was turning into what he thought he never could be, not a Pianoplayer but a Pianist, God help him. One lunchtime, or just before, before I'd started serving in the caffy, I went round to see how he was getting on, sitting very old and grey and haggard in his chair, and he said: 'Girl, I want you to get me some music. Use your own money, you'll get paid back later, there's bound to be a music shop that has what I want.'

'I don't like the look of those hands of yours,' I said. They were very swollen and there was blood coming from his right thumb where the edge of the nail had got pushed in.

'Get,' he said, 'all of Beethoven's sonatas and all Bach's 48 and the vocal scores of all Wagner if you can. I've got to give my brain something to do as well as my fingers or I'll go bloody mad.' Well, I went round to the music shops on the Prom, and it was all Lawrence Wright latest hits by Horatio Nichols, and they said: 'Batch, love? No, we don't 'ave im, we only 'ave the latest 'ere.' But there was a big piano store, Kemp's, where they dug out some tattered old stuff, with Beethoven and one volume of the 48, making it the 24, and there was a vocal score of The Rhine Gold and another of The Twilight of the Gods ('not never bin axed for them afore, love,' said a very old man who smelled of peppermints), and I dashed back with them to my dad, who sat at the piano in like a daze and his fingers just going up and down like a machine, playing chords. His hands were better, though, having been soaked in soapy water and the nails having been cut by the Assistant, who carried a very sharp pair of scissors in his pocket along with his cut throat razor.

So my dad got the Bach and played that book from beginning to end, not giving a damn about whether anybody liked it or not. Then he got down to the Beethoven, making a mess of a lot of it but nobody noticed, and then he was on to the Wagner (which is pronounced like Vaaagner because it is German), which didn't make much sense to anybody who couldn't see the words, which were in German anyway. On DAY EIGHT, Jerry Flayflea said: 'You'll have to go easy on the highclass stuff, Billy, because the customers don't like it too well. If it's sheet music you want I can get hold of popular selections like The Desert Song and The Student Prince and that for you, no trouble, don't mention it, but lay off the heavy stuff, there's a good lad.'

There's no doubt about it, dad's Marathon was drawing them in, but it was the horror of it that was fascinating a lot of them, dad looked awful, and there was a doctor who had a look in, very good of him because nobody had asked him, and tested dad's heart with the earphones and had a look at his hands and recommended rubbing them with violin rosin to toughen them up (that was while he was snoring away, real exhausted), but he said that he didn't think dad would last out. That was on DAY TEN, only a third of the way, and dad swore when he woke up that it must be at least DAY TWENTY, they were kidding him, and he cried because they were having an old sick tired man on, and I didn't know what to do or say. Another thing was that Jerry Flowflaw was getting a bit vague about how much money had come in, and he said it was not near enough yet, and I told him that a hundred quid for us was all that was wanted, but he just sort of sniggered and said not nearly enough yet.

Dad was back on odd easy pieces now, whimpering sometimes and sort of muttering threats and prayers as he played, his back and arms very stiff but his wrists and fingers bearing up, hard as iron at the tips the fingers were now. He played again all the stuff he'd already played, and he also played The Dying Swan, How Beautiful They Are The Lordly Ones, There Are Fairies At The Bottom

Of Our Garden, I Love The Moon, what was to be known later as the Strippers' Anthem (Hair on the G String), The Golliwog's Cakewalk, Darktown Strutters' Ball, Demande et Réponse, Tosti's Goodbye, bits of Swan Lake and the Coppelia Ballet, the Poet and Peasant Overture, Call Call Vienna Mine, Down In The Forest Something Stirred, Where The Bee Sucks There Suck I, The Death of Nelson, Asleep In The Deep, Hush Hush Who The Hell Cares Christopher Robin Has Fallen Downstairs, Three Green Bonnets, The Intermezzo to Guy Domville, Mighty Lak A Rose, Loola Loola Loola Loola Byebye, Mr Flanagan and Mr Sheen, Give My Regards to Broadway, first movement of the Moonlight Sonata done like a very long slow foxtrot, Purcell's Trumpet Voluntary, Fairest Isle All Isles Excelling, When I Am Laid In Earth, the Ode to Joy of Beethoven with Free Variations, Chopin's Waltzes in E flat, A flat, D flat and C sharp minor, Popular Selection of Themes from the Four Symphonies of Brahms, Lager from the New World, and God knows what else. Felix Kept On Walking, Horsey Cock Your Tail Up, Valencia Land Of Orange Groves And Sweet Content I Saw You From Afar. No limit, my memory just gives out on me.

The night of DAY FIFTEEN was a terrible experience to begin with like a Nightmare. There was another Communist, much better educated than the other one, and he gave a speech about my dad being a horrible example of Exploitation by the Ruling Classes, you consider this a fair way of making a living, he would not have to do it if the Means of Production had been Properly Distributed. My dad said 'Thanks I was at my wit's ends for a tune,' and started to play The Red Flag and even to sing it:

The people's flag all dripping red
Reminds us of our comrades dead.
The rich have bloody joints to carve
While bloody workers bloody starve.
But underneath the Russian star
The workers all get caviar,
And if they say it makes them sick
They beat them with a bloody stick.

Of course, he was making up all these words, and it was perhaps a good thing nobody really heard him, what with all these Bloodies. Nobody really heard him because Maggie Paramour had come in, complete with legs, the show just having finished, and she yelled out:

'Stop, stop, make him stop, he's killing himself, it's all for me he's doing it, stop, Billy, stop, please, PLEASE.' Dad hardly seemed to know who the hell she was, but he sort of snarled at her and banged out some nasty chords in a very feeble way. The man who was making the speech tried to drown her, crying out:

'There we are, a typical Bourgeois Assumption, as though personal Epiphenomena like what she calls Love have anything to do with the real issues which are the class struggle and the wrestling for the Possession of the Means of Production.' (Thank you, Rolf.)

'I,' she said, very loud but quite ladylike, 'am Maggie Paramour currently appearing in the Cockadoodledoos on the Central Pier every night except Sunday, matinées daily, and I do not know who you are, young man, but you are clearly ignorant or else you would know that Love is a Common Phenomenon and not what you said. So keep your ugly big nose out of it, this is a matter between Artistes with Feeling. Stop, Billy,' she went then. 'It's not worth it, killing yourself like that for me. I know you're desperately in love with me, but I belong to Another and it's not worth it, Billy.' Then Mrs Haggerty shouted at Maggie, crying out: 'How dare you flaunt your vulgar body and your vulgar emotions in the presence of this Crucified Man, you vulgar creature.' This was all ridiculous, I was there to see and hear it, this young a bit pimply man going on about the Workers of the World include Pianoplayers even though they do not produce anything, the real workers are the Pianomakers, but Music is part of the Super Structure (thanks, Rolf) and will be allowed in the Workers' State, and the old lady and Mlle Jambes Paramour sort of scratching at each other, and the crowd taking it all in, and Jerry Fallflea not interfering, it was all Show Business, and the Assistant looking for orders whether to get his razor or his scissors out. And my dad was playing away there, just sort of feeble chords as an Accompaniment to his groans and moans, and then he collapsed with a terrible noise and slid out of his chair and his head fell on the keys in a horrible discord and he was Out, Out. A man in the crowd cried:

'He's finished, he's not made it, his Marathon's done.' But another man with a very Educated voice said:

'No, no, no, that's a Genuine discord, an inversion of the mystic chord in the Poem of Ecstasy by Scriabin with a few notes added. If he can hold it he's still in.'

What Jerry Fellfloor and the Assistant did then, and I didn't know whether to help them or not, was to grab dad and beat him about a bit and he sort of came to, going Who What Where, and they got him upright on his chair and dad seemed to know what was going on, because he put his hands on the keyboard and made a real chord and then he passed out till the chord had nearly faded away and then he banged the chord again and once again he passed out. Now there was shouting of all kinds going on, about he's finished stop it it's bloody cruelty and keep on at it and get a doctor and fetch the police in and blame it on the Capitalist System Comrades and Oh Billy Billy you're breaking my heart. And then, as if all he'd needed was just a couple of seconds in Never Never Land and was refreshed and ready for the Fray again, dad came to, sat upright, smiled at everybody including Maggie though it didn't seem as if he knew who the hell she was, and then banged a lot of very clear and like crisp very modern chords and said:

'Ladies and gentlemen, for the first time in history I present with no extra charge an Opera made up as it goes along. We will call the Opera – ah ah aha – we will decide on the name after the Overture, and here it is, off we go, silence all.' And then by God he dived into a fine loud piece with menacing chords and nice tinkly melodies and then a march and Coda, something absolutely new, nobody had ever heard it before, and everybody listened with their mouths open. 'And the name of the Opera is,' said my dad, and you could tell that he still didn't know what he was going to say even when he'd got as far as Is, '*The Destroyers*. Prelude before the curtain goes up.' And he was playing away there, rolling in the bass and doing runs in the treble. 'The curtain goes up,' he said, 'on a street

in a modern city full of men and women on the dole and they sing
a Chorus about it.' Then dad started making up this Chorus, words
and all:

> How can we live?
> No one will give
> Us work.
> You and I
> And our children die
> Without work.

My brain will not allow me to remember it all, but it looked as if dad
was coming back to life again because his brain was doing something
at last. He pulled the bits of cotton wool out of his ears while the
policemen on horseback who had just come in sang a bar without
any accompaniment about

> Break it up
> It's the Law
> What's all this in aid of?
> What do you think we're made of?
> Straw?

Then there was this Duet for the two young lovers on the dole who
were going to have a kid, and what sort of a world was it going to
be for this poor kid. Dad did the high voice without any effort, as
though he'd been taught it specially in his couple of seconds passing out. Then towards the end of what I have to call the First Act
the workers make up their minds to burn down the house of a mill
owner, but then a man comes on with a beard and long hair and you
can tell it is really Our Lord, and he sings to them about Peace, and
ask your Heavenly Father, and Love your Enemies. The chorus
won't have this and tell him to bugger off, but he stands in front of
them and says You are hungry, well here is a Miracle, and there is
kind of cross-singing between him and the workers, who think he
said Mackerel:

Mackerel mackerel I could eat a mackerel.
Miracle miracle I repeat a miracle.

And it is actually mackerels that fall from the sky along with loaves of freshly baked bread, but one of the Workers yells out It's a Capitalist Trick Comrades, but the others kneel down munching away and they sing:

We trust in Him
He will put everything right
Our eyes are dim
In the brightness of heavenly light
We trust
Because we must
His heavenly might.

Then the curtain was supposed to come down.

Did you ever in all your born puff hear of anything more mad than this, certainly I never did. Dad even got a round of applause after the First Act, and nobody minded him taking a minute off after it, he said: 'You get a half-hour interval in a real Opera, so has anybody any complaints?' but nobody had any. Then he got on with Act Two, with the leaders of the Bosses and of the Communists trying to get Our Lord on their side, but he says Love is the answer not Politics. Then both lots hate him, the Communists because he is teaching the unemployed workers Peace and Love and the Bosses because he is saying there is no need of Factories and Industry, nobody needs much of anything except Peace and Love and a bit of bread and a drop of water and perhaps the odd heavenly mackerel. Then at the end of the Second Act it is announced that War is coming and that there will be plenty of jobs now building ships and making tanks and planes, so the workers cheer and will not listen to Our Lord when he says Peace and Love.

Peace and Love
You can shove

Peace and Love
Up your

But dad didn't sing the word, he just made it into kind of a growl and a discord. And at the very end of the Act the kid is born to the two lovers, and Our Lord is very bitter about him being born into a world of Hate and Destruction, and that's the end of that.

In the Last Act there's a War on, and everybody's happy, but Our Lord says Love your Enemies. Then an old Jew comes on and sings:

I am a Jew
Just like you
And my people are being destroyed
How can I avoid
Hating the swine?
Are you trying to undermine
The justness of this fight?
You are, you unnatural Jew?
Right right right
You'll get what's coming to you.

Of course it is really Judas, and he goes to the authorities and reports Our Lord, and Our Lord is arrested for spreading Disaffection, but it's really Affection of course, and he is put on trial with a judge and a jury and the verdict is that he's an Enemy himself and has to be put to death, and it all ends up with him being marched off to be hanged, crucified really. But at the moment of dying he calls out about Loving your Enemies. Dad did all this out of his head, doing the characters in different voices, and making the old Joanna sound like a real orchestra. And at the end of it, which was about four in the morning, with quite a lot of people still there sort of fascinated, he was bright and cheerful and ready to do another Opera if anybody wanted it. He had not moved from being a pianoplayer to being a pianist, he had moved from being a pianoplayer to being a Composer, but none of the words and music he made up could be written down and in those days there was no such thing as this thing I'm talking into one summer afternoon in Callian, Var, France.

What he said he was going to do next was to make up ten Symphonies. Beethoven had only done nine, and he was going to go one better. It was five in the morning, and he reckoned he could get all ten done by midday, when he had his two hours kip. It was at this point that I went back to the digs, being very tired, and I would not go to work tomorrow morning for Morning Coffee, and I had my own door key to let myself in. It was dad's key really, and yet dad wasn't there any more. He'd given up his room and his luggage was in mine. This made me shiver a bit: it was as if dad didn't exist any more as a real person being someone who has a bed to fall into, as I fell into mine. The funny thing was that when I woke up quite refreshed at eight, as though my dad was sort of working miracles on me, and I called in on him on my way to work, and there he was on his Seventh Symphony, doing a passage for cellos and double basses with his left hand while he had a sup of tea and a bite at an Eccles Cake with his right. He was very chirpy but looked very old and was very thin and he seemed to have lost most of his hair, which was all absolutely grey now anyway. Jerry Fieldflaw was there with copies of newspapers, not just the locals but the big ones like the *Mail* and the *Express*, and there was a bit in all of them, not much, and all in a kind of joke, about dad's Marathon. But Jerry Flowflaw shook his head and smiled in a queer sort of way, and the Assistant chewed his match and didn't show any expression. It was as if they knew that dad couldn't last for thirty days.

I tried not to think about dad at all for the rest of the day, it upset me too much, and though I was only a kid really it seemed to me I had a right good time and my own life, and I went out with Jim that evening. We went to see *Broadway Melody* again, it looked as though it was going to run in Blackpool all that summer and when we walked back to my digs afterwards, after eating some fish and chips from greaseproof paper and the *News of the World* wrapped around, plenty of salt and vinegar on them, me wiping my hands clean on Jim's big white handkerchief, we sang to each other:

You was meant for me
I were meant for you
Nature fashioned you and when she was done
You were all the sweet things rolled up in one

I said: 'We'll have to be very quiet going in.'

He said: 'Like two teeny weeny little mouses.' And then we were up in my bedroom on the bed, a risky thing to do, and he said: 'I love you.' I didn't say anything, but the funny thing was that I was able to fancy him now in that way, which I'd never expected. He kissed me gently and then a bit fiercer and his hand was going under my skirt to stroke the part of my leg where the stocking came to an end when I sat right up and said:

'Something's happened.'

'Nothing's happened,' he said, a bit annoyed. And then, as I was getting off the bed and into my shoes 'What do you mean, something's happened?'

'It's dad,' I said. 'I just got this feeling then. I've got to go to him.'

'Your dad will be all right,' but you could see he was a bit doubtful, women usually being right when they feel something's going to happen.

'He may be and he may not be. But I just got this feeling. Come on, get up from there.' He was a bit grumpy about it like all men are who think they're going to get their Oats and then don't get them, but he got up and went down with me, and I had this feeling that I'd better hurry.

I was right. There was a big crowd outside the place where dad played, but I could hear no sound of dad playing. What I saw was dad being carried out on a stretcher by two men in white coats, and then when the Corporation Gondola Tramcar that had just stopped there had gone by (and the passengers and the driver and the conductor had a good gawp), I saw an ambulance was there, and they were putting dad in it. I got through the crowd, and I nearly hit one middle-aged woman in a flowery hat who was saying he should never have been such a fool, there's one born every minute, and I yelled: 'I'm his daughter, how is he?' They shook their heads and then there was Jerry Foldflaw shaking his head too and the Assistant just chewing on his match and neither shaking nor nodding.

Eleven

I was heartbroken of course when the doctor came to me and Jim in the hospital waiting room and just sort of said with his long face that nothing could be done. Then it was: 'Cardiac failure. Total exhaustion. He should not have done it.'

'What else could he do?' I said. 'He needed the money. Me and him were going to go to the United States.' And then I cried, which was only natural. Jim sort of very awkwardly tried to put his arm round me, but the doctor looked stern as if he knew, which he did in a way, that I was really too young for that sort of thing. While I cried I was also very angry, because here I was an orphan, and dad should have had the sense to realise what he was letting me in for. Then Jerry Fieldflow (his real name was Jeremiah Feldfloh, as I found out later that day, it being already after midnight) came on his own in a taxi and he heard the sad news too and he said:

'He could never have made it. It must be the British record, but it wasn't what we had in mind. Poor old bugger, he was a great man in his way. Well, there's money enough for his funeral so long as you do it on the cheap,' very cold and heartless.

'More than enough, I should have thought,' I said. It was terrible going on about money when my Father was lying dead a few yards away, but that's human nature. When people die or are dying, the big thought in everybody's mind is always money; how much they're going to get, how much they're going to have to shell out, the loss of the Bread Winner, and all the rest of it, life having to go on, human nature like I say.

'There might well be more than enough,' said Jerry Fieldflea, 'but I can't let you have it, if that's what you have in mind. You're under age, and any money has to be held till you're twenty-one, but I think you'll find when the funeral's been paid for there won't be anything left worth talking about. He should have got himself insured, but it might have been a hell of a big premium. It's all a great pity, and now what's going to happen to You?'

'I've got this aunt,' I said, 'and two cousins. They're in Manchester. I'll have to go there I suppose.'

'And where is he to be buried?'

'In Moston Cemetery, I suppose, along with my mother.'

'Send me the bill, then.' Which I did, but the letter came back address unknown. 'Poor kid. But you've got guts, I can see that. You'll be all right.'

As it turned out, I was all right and still am. The rest of this book is my own story, and you may be wondering what it has to do with the title, but it has a lot to do with it in a way for people who will use their imaginations. I said goodbye to Jim and everybody else in Blackpool, but when I thought I was going to say goodbye to Mrs Haggerty, who came to have lunch in the caffy and also to see me because she knew I worked there, she said: 'I have my responsibilities, my dear. I shall travel with you and your poor father's body on the train to Manchester, and I will make all arrangements, you poor orphaned child. I shall deposit you with your aunt. I shall stay at the Midland Hotel and make sure the funeral is conducted with proper ceremony as is only right for a Great Man.' And on the train she told me what it had been like, my poor dad's last piece of music before he collapsed for good. She said:

'Your father began to play a piece of music that I was sure was his own and that I was equally sure we were all hearing for the first and last time. I am also quite sure that the music, if you understand me, came from a source which may have been divine and may have been diabolic but was certainly not of this world. Those who listened were spellbound and somewhat frightened. There was a man present who said he was a professional musician and had been adjudicating at the Blackpool Musical Festival. He said the music was wholly original.

It was wholly modern, he said, and yet it had hints of what the future might hold. He said it was also very deeply in the past, but not a past recorded by history. He said it was a crying shame that there was no device for recording the music there and then, for he knew that, once played, it would be lost for ever. It was altogether remarkable. It was ethereal, yet there was nothing feeble or moribund about it. It was the Music of the Spheres.' I asked Mrs Haggerty if she would write that down for me, because I wouldn't remember it otherwise. She did, and here it is, and I had to interrupt this taking down of my story to go to my apartment in Cannes to get it.

My aunt was not pleased to see me, and I was not pleased to be put back into that old room again, which had not changed in over ten years, where I'd had the nightmares and there was a picture called Beware on the wall. I was sent back to school, a day girl at the Convent of the Sacred Heart, and I'd no idea what I'd do when I reached fourteen and left. But I was just a week off my fourteenth birthday, the middle of February and real brass monkey weather, when we had this Visiting Nun. She was Belgian and very tall and beautiful and she was called Sister Marthe. She said her Convent outside Brussels was willing to take on girls who were interested in Completing their Education in Belgium. They would learn French and be very Well Equipped Indeed for the Great Battle of Life. She spoke the most lovely English and she had this very sweet and beautiful face. She said that every girl interested in going must obtain permission from their parents or parent or guardian or guardians and present this permission in writing along with a personal Letter of Application and a recent photograph. This could be given to our class teacher and the Application would be Forwarded. Then the successful Applicants would be hearing what to do next. And now we will have a little prayer.

I wrote off and sent a photo, and the reply said that I must be Furnished with a Valid Passport and that a party would leave from London on May 1. Girls must report to Mme Giroux at the Hotel Armorica on Southampton Row, WC1 the day before, ready to depart from Victoria Station the following morning early. As you will understand, my aunt could hardly wait to get hold of a Form of

Application for a British Passport. She got me on the earliest train she could from London Road Station to Euston, and I ended up at this hotel before any of the rest of the girls. The girls were about twenty in number, nobody else from our school and only two others from Manchester, the rest being from all over the country. I got the idea that there were these parties going off every month, so it must be a pretty big convent, I thought. There was one very ugly girl with glasses and a horrible skin disease and one leg a bit shorter than the other, and it turned out she had sent a photo of Miss Walthamstow, the girl that had won first prize in a beauty contest and lived next door to her. Mme Giroux, who turned out to be Sister Marthe's London Agent as she was called, was quite nice with this girl but told her to go back home, here was her fare both ways, they were sorry that she was not Really Suitable. This Mme Giroux spoke the most lovely English. So the girl went off crying back to Walthamstow, and that was the end of that.

The rest of us stayed the night in the hotel, four girls to a room, and in the morning we knew each other fairly well, all good Catholic girls from fourteen to sixteen or thereabouts, some of them very pretty, as we'd had dinner the night before together, and breakfast in the morning very early, and in between had a chance to talk and giggle a bit. Then we went by bus to Victoria Station and got the boat train to Dover, where we found Sister Marthe waiting for us with two more girls, last minute ones, and then we were on the boat and over to Ostend. We all had to show our brand new passports there, and we giggled a bit at being addressed in French. Then there was the train to Brussels, a lovely big town full of chocolate chamber pots and the Mannequin Piss, which is now the capital of the Common Market. We were in the Convent in the suburbs of Brussels in time for a real English tea, with sandwiches and little cakes, and after tea we were shown to our dormitory. In the evening we had a talk from Mother Superior, a most beautiful woman who spoke lovely English. She also wore high heels, which I had always thought nuns were not allowed to do, but perhaps here in Belgium it was different. She said:

'My dear children, there are many ways of serving Our Lord God. Some serve him by denying the world and others by embracing the world. When we hear of the World, the Flesh and the Devil, we are not to suppose that they are all one and the same thing. The World is God's World, not the Devil's, and the Flesh is of God's own creation. The World and the Flesh alike have pleasures that draw us away from God, but they have also pleasures that draw us closer to Him. There are certain experiences we may have in the Flesh that are a Figure of the Ecstasy we shall know Eternally in Heaven. I refer to the beauties of Art and Music, I refer to the Embraces of Lawful Love.' When she said that some of the girls went red and others wanted to giggle, but she was so calm and beautiful and serious that it would have been like giggling at Holy Mass. 'I say all this to you, my dear children,' she went on, 'so that you will know in advance what kind of Christian Philosophy you are to learn here. Many are called, so said Our Blessed Lord, but few are chosen. And of the many that are called to us here, only a few will be chosen for the Special and Holy Work that waits in the World outside these Walls. So some will leave us after but a short time to begin that work, while others will leave us to return to whence they came, and none with regret, for all will have learned something. Now let us pray for guidance and for the blessing of Our Blessed Lord upon our Enterprise.' She turned then toward the altar, for it was in the Convent Chapel that she was talking to us, and we all knelt down on our new stockings.

There was a lot of talk that night in the dorm after dinner, which was very good and very French with Wine, all about what Mother Superior meant, but we started to learn what it was all about the next morning after our Continental Breakfast, when we had these Interviews. I was Interviewed not by a nun but by a very smart and beautifully dressed lady who said she came from Anvers or Antwerp, and she spoke English very well but with a sort of ooo la la accent like what Maggie Paramour put on. She said:

'Do you have very strong family relations back in England?'

'No, miss.'

'You may say No, Madame.'

'No, Madame. If you mean does anybody need me or love me or want me back in England, then the answer is no. I am an orphan and have only an aunt and two cousins who do not like me and regard me as a Nuisance.'

'So if work can be found for you in Belgium or in France you would be willing to undertake it?'

'What sort of work, Madame?'

She sort of sighed and put her hands together, and she had the most lovely and expensive rings on her fingers. 'It is good work and interesting work for girls who are truly suited to it. We may call it Entertainment. Do you know anything of Entertainment?'

'You mean singing and dancing and suchlike? Well, my mother was a singer and dancer and my poor father was a pianoplayer –'

'You mean pianist?'

'No, Madame, a pianoplayer. But I don't have any gift that way.'

'Well, there are other ways of Entertaining. For instance, there is talking over dinner with gentlemen of good family. There is being kind to lonely gentlemen. There is the gift of your Youth and Beauty to gentlemen who have need of it. Do I make myself clear?'

'Do you mean being a Prostitute?'

She was sort of horrified by me using that word, and her rings went flash flash in the electric light that was on because it was a very dark morning for early in May, rain being on its way, She said: 'That is a terrible, terrible thing to say, and you must drive out of your head any memory of your having used that most terrible, terrible, terrible of words. No, no, the word refers to the most degraded of creatures, walking the streets and selling her body to any who will pay the money. Never, never, never must you think that that is what I meant. Tell me, mon enfant, are you a Virgin?'

I knew the word, as I said earlier on, being brought up a Catholic, but I'd only heard it used in Conversation once before, and you will remember when that was. I said: 'Well, if you mean have I been with a man that Did It To Me, I say yes, but it wasn't my idea. He just went too far, and I wouldn't have let him go even a bit of the way if it hadn't been that my father was out of a job, Madame.'

She made a little note then on her paper and said: 'So you took money in payment for sexual favours granted and you were, of course, at that time under the legal age of consent. I see. You were very fond of your father?' She made it sound a bit like farthair.

'Oh yes, Madame.'

'There is a very charming establishment owned by a certain Madame Recamier, that is not a true name but an assumed one, she has her private reasons for the substitution, Madame Recamier was a very beautiful and important lady in French History. This establishment is in the beautiful town of Rouen in France. You would have your room and your clothes and such money as you might need to spend, although you will truly need to spend very little. Your task will be to be friendly to gentlemen and to Entertain them. The work will be interesting. Many of the men will be men perhaps old enough to be your own farthair, and they will all be in great need of a daughter. You would, you will, be a daughter to them.'

'You mean a father doing it to his own daughter? There's a word for that but I can't remember it Madame.'

She made her rings go flash flash again in like horror. 'You must not employ such locutions. You are not to think in such a degraded manner. That is vulgaire.' And I could see Mrs Haggerty hitting out at Maggie Paramour and using that word, though with a very English accent. 'We must be most careful of words. Many words are like devils tempting us to the wrong road. Perhaps Mother Superior has already said that to you.'

'Not yet, Madame.'

'I see. Well, you will think of this thing for a few days. Today you will start your Instruction, and soon we will talk again. You may go now, Hélène.' It was queer hearing my name in French for the first time, it was as though I had already turned into a new person.

The lessons we were given were given some by nuns and some by not nuns. We were taught some French, but only Phrases that we had to say and say over and over till we got them right with a Perfect Accent, not Grammar but things like 'Je suis tout à fait ravie monsieur de faire votre connaissance' and 'vous pourrez faire ce que vous désirez cher monsieur ce m'est tout à fait égal' and so on. We had history lessons, but they weren't about kings and battles and Acts of Parliament but about Great Ladies and Kings' Mistresses and so on.

And we were taught about different kinds of wine and even taught how to drink them so that we wouldn't get drunk easily, like taking a pint of milk first or a spoonful of olive oil, because that Prevented the Quick Absorbing of the Alcohol. We had meals that were like lessons, because we had to learn to eat things that seemed horrible to us English girls at first, snails and a lot of garlic and things cooked in Burgundy. But while these lessons were going on, we all got the idea that they weren't the most important part of us being there, because every day some girl would go off all smiles and excited with her bag packed, saying 'Au revoir mes chères,' she was going to a job in Aries or Antibes or somewhere. One girl said the place was really like a Depot, and later on I got to see what she meant. But all the lessons were interesting and useful, it was not like being in school at all. For instance the lessons on Personal Hygiene and the Use of the Douche and the Bidet were very good, and so were the Lectures we had on Dress Sense. And there was a man who came up from the town of Grasse, very handsome and with a beautiful trimmed moustache, who taught us about Perfumes. But every day I waited for my next Interview, and then one day I got it. It was the same lady as before, with another ring added to those she already had, and she said:

'Ma Chère Hélène; Madame Recamier expects you the day after tomorrow. She has at last a vacancy. Are you prepared to go?'

'I haven't really much Alternative, have I, Madame?'

'That is one possible reply, but it is a Negative one. What I require is a Positive Response. I have told you that it is an Admirable Establishment and that Madame Recamier is eager to have you. You are a fortunate girl to have the Opportunity. So now what do you say? You may say it in French if you wish.'

'Je vous remercie Madame de votre gentillesse. Je suis sûre que je serai heureuse chez Madame Recamier.'

'Bien, ma petite. Alors, après demain.'

So that's how my Profession started. I was with Madame Recamier, who was a nice old thing and very kind to her girls, until 1934, when I told her I wished to change. She understood perfectly, she said, a changement was a good thing always, the nature of life is change, ma petite, is there any fashion in which I may aid you in your procuring

of a changement? You have now seventeen years, is it not, and without doubt grow a little too aged for our clientèle. My cousine, who
appelates herself Madame Pompadour, a name famous, my cabbage,
governs an establishment very refined at Paris herself, no less, truly
outside the city boundaries; for convenience at Malmaison. To her I
will write tout de suite.

So I worked at Malmaison, which is where the house of Josephine
was when Napoleon kicked her out for not giving him an Heir to
the Imperial Throne. The house is still there, of course, and I often
thought when I visited it what a nice Establishment it would make.
The difference between Madame Recamier's house and Madame
Pompadour's was that the first was for old men who wanted daughters, and the second was more general, with a few specialities on the
side. It was in Madame Recamier's that I sometimes got a kind of
dirty feeling when these smartly dressed and beautifully mannered
elderly men came along, it was too much like my own father was
doing it, and this was worst when one man came along who was a
Famous Pianist and his hands were just like my dad's, very hard at
the finger tips. In Madame Pompadour's Establishment the clientèle
was of all ages, and some men were very young and shy and had to
be taught a bit what to do. I only had the normal stuff, and I had a
lot of regulars who were really friends, considerate and sometimes
humorous, and they liked to give pleasure as well as take it. One of
the girls, a German blonde named Brigitte, specialised in the queer
stuff called Necro. She would have to lie like a corpse for one man,
surrounded by lilies and candles, and for another she had to be nailed
into a coffin, though this had a trapdoor at the bottom. Another girl,
a big tough Swede called Ingrid, did the beating up of men dressed
as ladies' maids and so on. But, as I said, it was mostly ordinary
routines for me, with a bit of fais moi le pompier ma petite and so on.

I was happy enough there until 1938, when the Munich business
came and the French got very excitable and talked about finishing
off the foul Boche, il faut en finir and so on. I could smell the way
things were going. We had a party of Germans one night and I had
one of them who was Impotent until he started talking about steel
whips and this got him excited enough to do the job, but not very

well. You had to admire these damned Germans all the time and let them talk about what they were going to do when they took over the whole of Europe, and by God they meant it. So I went back to England with a nice little pile, and I settled in this private hotel in West Kensington, waiting to see what was going to happen. Of course, that was when Chamberlain, or J'aime Berlin as they called him in France, said It Is Our Peace In Our Time, but nobody in his or her right mind believed it. There was trouble coming all right, and Chamberlain was just putting it off. In that year I was twenty-one but had had the key of the door a long time, and I was too young to be wasting my Lovely Beauty in a private hotel. When I was walking in Chiswick one day, I had been to have lunch at the Doves on the river, I passed a house and saw a young housewife taking her kids out all nicely got up for a bit of a blow on Chiswick Mall, and it struck me that perhaps I was missing something.

I met Albert Ross (a silly name he always said at first, like the bird in Coleman's or Selfridge's poem, but I didn't understand, that was one of my Charms he said, not always understanding things) on Piccadilly Underground where it gives you The Time All Round The World. That used to make me smile a bit because I'd given Round the Worlds to Yank clients plenty of times. I had bought some wine at King Bomba in Soho and the bag broke and a bottle of Frascati smashed and he said what a shame and we got talking. I was quite ready to be asked out by a man of Mature Years, and Albert was Mature all right, he had been living with a woman who worked at Broadcasting House in his nicely appointed flat off the King's Road, and they had just broken up. He ran his own Estate Agency and was not at all badly off, he had nice manners and always a nice smell on him, like new mown hay mixed up with alcohol, as though somebody had been getting boozed up in a field. When we'd been going round together for a bit and he'd learned that I'd been working as a Secretary in Paris but had come home in preparation for the War, he said:

'Who knows what's going to happen? The time's past for mucking around. I've got this Territorial Commission and want somebody to come home to. Because it won't be long now.' This meant that he was proposing marriage. I don't think I'd have said yes right at that time if we hadn't been a bit careless in his flat, but now I thought: well, yes, we may all get seen off by German Bombs, and I ought to have the experience of Married Motherhood. So Robert was born six months after our wedding at Caxton Hall. I had no trouble giving birth to him in the London Clinic, and he was a sweet child, but I don't know what it was, I didn't have a real motherly feeling towards him, perhaps I was not cut out to be a mother, and I liked him only as I liked the kid of the lady living next door. Still, I looked after him properly, though he was brought up on a bottle, and having him to look after I was not called up for War Service, but you can imagine it was a dull job after what I'd been used to, with the bombs coming down too every night on London. When the Battle of Britain was over, Albert's twin sisters, who lived together in Horsham and were both exempt from call up because of Thyroid Deficiency, agreed to free me for War Work, because after all I was dead bored and had been used to an Active Life, whatever they tell you about the Profession being just lying quietly on your back or your front, according to the tastes of the client. I got a sort of Liaison job with the Free French, once meeting General de Gaulle, oui, mon général, non, mon général, who was a great man for trying to get his hand up your skirt for all his talk about the Glory of la Belle France. I did my bit for the Free French, giving some of them service beyond the call of duty, while Philippa and Calinda, silly names but nice girls though a bit dim what with the Thyroid Deficiency, looked after young Robert in Horsham.

Albert my husband was a captain in the infantry over in North Africa, and he was sent home on what was called a Staff Course without giving me any warning. He came into the flat while I was in bed with a Free French adjutant, and he actually found us when the adjutant was just coming, which was very embarrassing. He tried to beat up the adjutant, which the adjutant thought was very reasonable, saying 'Vous avez absolument raison, mon capitaine, vous avez les droits du mari,' and he went out saluting. Then Albert turned on me and I turned on him back.

'What's this war done to people?' he said. 'You were the sweetest girl in the world, and now you've turned into a common prostitute. If it wasn't that the madness of the war has got into you I'd tear you to pieces with my bare hands.' The funny thing was that he still had his gloves on, as it was a cold winter's night outside.

'What do you mean, common prostitute?' I said. 'What's common about it? It's a skilled profession like anything else of a professional nature.'

'Oh yes,' he sort of sneered, 'you know all about it now, of course. Taken it up as war work, haven't you? I'm disgusted to my very stomach.'

'If you want the truth,' I said, 'which you don't, you can have the truth whether you like it or not.' I told him, and he listened with his mouth open. 'What you've had for the cost of a marriage licence,' I told him, 'adds up to a fair sum of money at the rate I'm entitled to. So stick that up your jaxy and about turn and bugger off.'

'I'm reporting to the Staff College now,' he said, 'and that's the last you'll ever see of me, you scheming lying little bitch. I Married A Prostitute,' and he said it as though it was the name of a film. 'Oh my God, my God, my dear God.' And then he said: 'There's one thing, you'll never lay eyes or hands on my son again, not that I know whether he's my son or not, you evil creature that you are.'

'Oh, he's yours all right,' I said. 'I'd laid off while we were together, and he's got your nose.' And then a very strange idea struck me, and it was if my poor dad was sort of prodding me from Purgatory. 'But,' I said, 'he's still partly mine, and I had the trouble of giving birth to him and feeding him with a bottle, so you'll make bloody sure when he's old enough that he gets decent piano lessons and is given the chance my poor dad never had.'

So he drops his jaw again and looks at me, still with his gloves and peaked cap on, and he said: 'Are you mad as well as a common prostitute? Have you been knocked on the head by a bit of flak? I may not survive this bloody war to be a proper father, and the kid's only a baby still, and you talk of his being given blasted piano lessons.'

'Piano lessons,' I said, very fiercely.

We didn't get our divorce till the end of the war, when there were a lot of divorces and a lot of murdering of wives too for unfaithlessness, but, of course, being a good Catholic I couldn't take the divorce seriously because I couldn't take the registry office wedding seriously. But it irked me a bit about my own child being taken away from me like that on the grounds that I was not good enough to be his mother, though I'd been good enough to have him in the first place, which was more than the law people who went on and on about the Custody of the Child could do. I was glad to get out of England again when it was possible, a very hypocritical country with Sir Stafford Cripps and rations getting smaller all the time but plenty of everything if you had the money.

When it was possible for me to get back to France I did so, and I got a nice little flat on the rue Abelard, being glad to be free again and used to independence after all and working on my own. Then one night, lying under this panting Yank, I sort of saw the light. The sort of Rhythm of what was going on brought back, and this was very strange, my poor dad's Marathon to me. I could hear him playing all those tunes, beat, thin, grey, old, doing his bloody best. I Scream You Scream We All Scream For Ice Cream, Pink Elephants On Parade, Begin The Beguine, That Old Black Magic Has Me In Its Spell. I was sort of horrified to realise that some of these songs had not been written yet at the time of his Marathon, and yet I could hear that piano in Blackpool and see his hands coaxing the tunes out of the keys. If I went on listening I'd start hearing my dad play tunes that hadn't even been written yet. The Scar On Your Nose, Give It Me In Small Doses, Grasslands Of The Moon, Yer Gorra Gerrout Babah. I twitched myself and thrust up and I said:

'Go on, get out, bugger off.'

'Wozzat?'

'Yer gorra gerrout, sport.'

'I ain't finished.'

'Off, out, I've had enough.'

'I've paid, ain't I?'

'It's still there on the mantelpiece. Take it and get out.'

He snarled some nasty American things at me, but he did what I said. I don't think he liked the look in my eyes. And he must have known that any girl on the job in Paris in those days who didn't have a ponce had a gun tucked away, I had a Mauser, and life was cheap always, as the War had kindly Demonstrated. When he'd gone and I'd sat astride the bidet and dressed, I went out to see a friend of mine, Lollo Camoens, a very well made dark girl, half Portuguese, who was free that night. She gave me a glass of white port and I tried to say what had come into my mind. I said:

'A woman's not a thing for a man to do what he wants with.'

'She turns herself into a thing when she takes money.' She spoke this very nice sort of upper class English, having kept this British officer in hiding in Lyons for a good part of the War until he got picked up pretending to be a French agricultural worker and not making too good a job of it. She got no bloody thanks for this from the Glorious Allies of the British, because just after the Liberation she came to Paris and was walking near Les Halles when some men started yelling 'Let's shave the bitch's head, she has been sleeping with the foul Boche.' though that wasn't true and this was her first time in Paris. Of course the men who started this head shaving lark had all been on the black market and were covering themselves up by getting at the Innocent, a lot of that in Paris, the French are a bloody bad lot, just like everybody else. 'It is she who makes the choice, after all.'

I heard my dad playing again, very loud and clear, and I could even hear his groaning and sighing. I said: 'A woman is like a musical instrument.'

'I know, I know, darling. Play me like a violin, make beautiful music out of me. Old stuff, my sweet, vieux chapeau as Rodney used to say. Have some more porto.'

'More like a piano that a fiddle,' I said.

'No,' she said, when she'd poured again. 'You don't keep a violin around, fiddle yes, many years since I hear the word, just for any sort of a son of a bitch to scrape at. It's in a case, something with a little key. A piano's there for anybody to hammer at.'

'No,' I said, sort of inspired. 'The piano belongs to him that can play it.'

'There aren't many pianists about,' Lollo said.

'Well,' I said, 'they've got to be taught, they've got to be trained.

Not everybody can play the piano, as you say, and a man that can't play it isn't such a bloody fool as to say that he can. But every man thinks he can do Sex.'

'What do you have in mind,' she said, a bit sarky, 'a School for Lovers?'

'Why not?' I said. 'I know nobody would want to go at first, thinking they know all about it already, bloody idiots, but the more sensible ones would see it was a good idea. And then there are very young men who know nothing at all about it and are shy, and curing shyness could be part of the teaching. I tell you, it's a waste of opportunity not many knowing about it and just learning the hard way. It's more difficult than trying to learn how to play Beethoven and the others. With a piano you've only got the same twelve notes repeated up and down. With a woman you've more than that. Some stupid bastards play a woman as though their hands had been chopped off at the wrist.'

'You're cracked,' Lollo said. 'You need a vacation, ma petite.'

Twelve

It was in 1956, when I was getting on for forty, that the chance came. It came as chances usually do, by chance, and that's why it is called chance. I'd gone over to Singapore, having got fed up with Europe and especially France, and I was running a little house off Orchard Road, getting to the age of organising more than doing the job myself, though I was always available for special clients who liked Maturity. The rent of the place was very steep, Chinese landlords being worse even than French ones, but we had ten working rooms as well as the Usual Offices, and a big waiting room with an American organ in it. This had been a small hotel first run by Chinese and really a *hôtel de passe* for opium smokers, then it became a Baptist Mission, and somehow the American organ had got left behind when the Mission refused to cooperate with the Singapore police. I remember an unfrocked priest, as he called himself, from Kowloon who used to play hymns and so on on the American organ and sing in a singsong but very gloomy way while waiting for Dorothy Lim, a very pretty little girl from Georgetown. He was singing and playing Nearer My God To Thee one day, and that struck me in a way I couldn't explain but I'll tell you about later. He saw me looking a bit preoccupied, and he thought I was thinking it was wrong to be playing hymns in a place like this. But he said:

'Not blasphemy, Madame Hélène, ah no. One is nearer to God in a woman than in a church or chapel.' That was a bit vulgar, but English was not his first language, although he spoke it beautifully. He knew some French too, having been in Indochina, so I told him the story of the young French priest who could resist no more the temptation of the flesh so he went to see the P'tites Sœurs des Cœurs, or one of them rather. I knew the story by heart practically:

'Tout se passe le mieux du monde mais au moment stratégique, dans l'impossibilité de dominer son émotion, notre abbé s'écrie: Ah! ma fille! Le bon Dieu est avec nous! Bon d'accord, rétorque la môme, mais dans ce cas, c'est tarif double!'

I had little Dorothy Lim and a Malay girl called Aminah, voluptuous but a very lazy girl who chewed sireh all the time, a Eurasian beauty called Betty da Silva, two Russian sisters, twins but not identical, which was a pity, called respectively respectfully respectably Olga and Natasha Solzhenitsnaya, I may have got that a bit wrong. There were also one or two British housewives who were like Belles du Jour, doing the job for a bit of spending money while their husbands were at work in banks. And there was this very fat Tamil girl, absolutely purple in colour, called Chelvanajaky, very popular with the Chinese clients. The chance I was beginning to tell you about happened when a Mr Shaw, a Chinese in spite of his name or perhaps because of it, came to see me about his son.

'Madame,' he said, in this very beautiful English which he'd learned at Eton or Harrow College or some place like them, 'I am a wealthy man, indeed I am what is called a Straits dollar multimillionaire, which is the same as saying a sterling millionaire, and I refer only to my cash flow not my real estate and holdings in stock, but I have learned in my long life that money cannot always buy happiness.' He thought of himself as old, but he was only about fifty, with very smooth skin and beautifully turned out. I knew that most of his money had come from tin and rubber and the building of big office blocks on Singapore Island as well as in Johore over the border. 'My son, for example,' he said, 'Robert.' I felt my heart come up in my chest when he said that name, Robert being the name of my own son. 'Robert is a young married man, but his wife is already talking of leaving him. She is an American lady from Topeka whom he met when they were fellow students at the university called UCLA in California, but their marriage is breaking up because of certain difficulties he is shy of expressing to myself, although his wife is becoming somewhat loud and vulgar about them. She had a little too much to drink the other night at the Rotary dinner and she said some things of a very intimate nature. I think there is some problem in himself which no doctor would be able to diagnose. I should be grateful if you could talk to him and perhaps more than talk. I have, as you must know, heard from some of my senior employees the best possible reports of your contribution to Human Happiness.'

'*Hsieh hsieh*,' I said. If he had taken the trouble to learn to speak such beautiful English, it was only right that I should thank him in his own language. 'This may seem a daft question,' I said, 'but does he play a musical instrument of any kind?'

Mr Shaw looked a bit startled, but he said: 'He has blown a saxophone, I believe, in the band at his college. The saxophone I consider to be a most barbarous instrument, but I suppose it would be termed a musical one.'

'Send him to me, Mr Shaw,' I said, and he did.

This Robert Shaw was the first one I ever had who was able to be taught seriously and slowly and in Great Detail about the music that was lying waiting in a woman to be drawn out by a man willing to learn as a man who wants to play the piano is willing to learn. He was a handsome lad, very neat and polite, and every morning for two months he came to my house off Orchard Road, and I would explain to him that a woman is a very sensitive instrument that has to be Approached with love and respect and knowledge. The use of the two hands and the eight fingers and the two thumbs, of the mouth, of rhythm and what my dad called Counterpoint and what he called the most difficult bloody thing in the world, far worse than three against two in slow time, namely five against four, all these things and other things, I taught to him. My girls, who he went to for the Practical Parts, said he was a slow but Thorough learner. He went out with his like invisible Diploma, and I heard soon after that his marriage was saved and his wife hung round his neck like a flower lei you get in Honolulu, not a nice town really. His father was very pleased. Apart from the fee I charged, which was $5000 (Straits not US), he gave me a camphorwood chest filled with Shantung silk and made me a guest of honour at a big twenty course Chinese dinner, complete with snake wine and hard boiled hundred year old eggs, at the Lotus House. They kill the snakes at the table and you have to drink the blood, which is good for Potency, but I didn't see how Potency applied to a woman so I didn't have any. There was Mrs Shaw hanging like a lei round the neck of her husband so that he could hardly get his chopsticks working.

After a lot of talk and discussion – Mr Shaw was a careful man with his money, that's why he was a multimillionaire – it was agreed that the money should be put down for starting the School of Love, of which there were to be five to begin with, in Singapore, Jakarta, Seoul, Bangkok and Bali resp. The Singapore house, which he bought freehold for not too much money, using some of the strong men of one of the musical Gong Societies on the owner, who had been my very grasping landlord, was like the Headquarters, and it was here that the courses were held for those that would run the other places.

I was not much good at giving lectures, my English being always too Uneducated, like my poor dad's, but I was good at Organising and Discipline. I laid down what had to be taught and I supervised the Practicals about Woman as a Keyboard, bringing in Volunteers, very young men that knew nothing though they thought they knew a lot at the start and were surprised to find how much they paid to learn, for Demonstrations. More than anything, I laid very strong emphasis on Time, pointing out that my father had played the piano continuously for fifteen days, and that Sex was not like a quick nosh in a snack bar but a very Leisurely Banquet. Mr Shaw was very pleased with the progress of the School of Love in the East, and he started talking of going into Europe and even America. But I knew America would be useless, being too Neurotic, as they say, and I knew also we would have great difficulties with the Law, which would think a School of Love to be a kind of Brothel. That is a ter-rible word and yet also a funny word, kind of domestic in a way, it always brings back my aunt saying when I was a kid living with her: Drink it all up now, that broth'll stick to your ribs.

We managed to get nicely settled in Hamburg but in Paris the police thought they ought to get their bit of a cut, which wasn't right, we were, as Mr Shaw said, a Serious Educational Establishment. In

London we knew there would be Hypocrisy, and I went into it in London with my eyes open very wide. The trouble began with the adverts in the papers, the better class papers would not take them, not even when they were worded very carefully by the publicity expert that we hired. Like this:

Love is an art, like music. Like music, it has to be learned. A woman is a sensitive instrument. Properly treated, she can discourse the most heavenly harmony. Ellen Henshaw's School of Love offers to all male aspirants the opportunity to learn. Play the piano of love with the skill of a Horowitz or an Oscar Peterson. Write to Box – for further details.

The London School of Love was off Queensway, and it was Mr Shaw of Singapore who was paying the rent, which was pretty high. It was Mr Shaw too who had the bright idea, being Chinese and very clear headed, that we ought to remember that Love meant more than the Sexual Act, it meant what Our Lord preached too, though of course he got crucified for it and if he came back to preach Love they'd crucify him again. But there was nothing that the Law could find fault with if the School of Love invited well known clergymen like Lord Soper and the Bishop of London and the Archbishop of Birmingham, who I'd met once as a kid in Manchester in his mother and father's greengrocer's shop, to give like sermons on Christian Love and especially Married Love. None of them came, they were too busy with religion they said, but at least they were asked. And we were able to put a letter on file from Lord Soper wishing us well in our endeavours to promote the idea of Love. If there was ever to be any trouble we could always bring that out.

Anyway, the police were watching us but they had no warrant to enter. This was a private place and no money changed hands: all payments were to Shaw Enterprises and were by cheque. They could not get us on running a Disorderly House. There were a lot of Serious Applicants for the course, and I saw we had a big future if only the Law would mind its own business and not go looking for Loop Holes. I got a chance to tell the world what we were up to when BBC Television rang up, I was staying at the Dorchester which was not run by the Arabs in those days (I have nothing against the Arabs, though, they have always been helpful and grateful because some of their princes and emirs and what not have been among our students), and invited me to come for an interview on a programme called 'Tonight and Every Night'. I knew that I'd do the thing very badly, me with my Uneducated English, so I got my second in command at the London end to do the job for me. Her name was Petulia Grigson, and she was a very lovely girl, about thirty, with an education at London University in what was called Social Sciences, and she appeared under my name, which was perhaps cheating but nobody seemed to bother. This is what they called the Transcript of the interview:

Bob Tarson: Ellen Henshaw, what precisely is the purpose of the so-called School of Love?

Petulia: You are the so-called Mr Tarson?

Bob Tarson: I *am* Bob Tarson.

Petulia: All right, let's cut out the so-called nonsense. Our School is seriously concerned with teaching Love in all its aspects – Christian Love, Marital Love, Universal Love – because we believe that Love is the answer to the world's problems.

Bob Tarson: You teach what you call the art of love?

Petulia: That is correct.

Bob Tarson: Meaning the art of sex?

Petulia: That is a somewhat crude way of putting it. Love contains sex, but sex does not contain love. A woman is not a mere object to be used for the sexual release of the male, she is a complex psychosomatic organism whose sexual needs are inseparable from her spiritual needs. Many men are too selfish to realise this.

Bob Tarson: I see. One of the slogans of your, er, institute is this: A woman is like a piano. Could you explain that?

Petulia: Certainly. A pianoforte, if expertly played, can give out music whose meaning is more spiritual than physical, though the physical appeal of sheer sound is not, of course, to be discounted. No man considers himself capable of playing the instrument unless he has been trained to do so and is willing to practise regularly and rigorously, whereas most men consider themselves capable of engaging in the act of Love with nothing to guide them but appetite and instinct. The purpose of the School of Love, or Schola Amoris as it has been suggested we call it, to give it both intellectual dignity and the patina of classical values, is, as it were, to turn men into sensitive and skilled discoursers of the Music of Love.

Bob Tarson: A piano is a material object, isn't it, a mere thing? Are you suggesting that a woman is no more? The forces of Female Liberation will not thank you for that.

Petulia: A piano unplayed or played ineptly is a mere thing. A piano expertly played communicates on the aesthetic or, indeed, the spiritual level. It is not, of course, an analogy that must be carried too far. Analogies are necessary in discourse, but all analogies are fundamentally mendacious. We merely say that, as complex skill of a high order must be brought to the art of pianism, so similar if not greater skill is essential if the act of Love should become, as it should, an experience of supreme spiritual import.

Bob Tarson: Is the act of love taught, er, practically in your Schola Amoris as you term it?

Petulia: Of course. We are not mere theorists.

Bob Tarson: There is a name for such an establishment.

Petulia: Indeed. A School of Love.

Bob Tarson: No, there is another name. Are you not perhaps breaking the law of the realm?

Petulia: In what manner? No, don't answer. Let us attempt to be serious. One of the tragedies of our age, indeed of most ages, has lain in the failure of the human male to comprehend the erotic aspects of the marital relationship. And yet our traditional educational systems have done nothing to inculcate even the barest notion of how to encompass that psychoneural satisfaction which, apart from the religious experiences of the mystic, is one of the greatest potential gifts that our Creator has bestowed on his higher creation. Oh, I know that in our State Comprehensive Schools a little human biology is taught, but there is no attempt to take the true issues seriously, the issues which are comprehended in the term Love. There is a conspicuous and shameful gap. Our School seeks to close it.

Bob Tarson: Thank you, Mrs Henshaw.

Petulia: Miss.

Bob Tarson: I'm sorry. I was using the, er, honorific to signify also a profession. Mrs is short for Mistress (leers).

Petulia: You see, ladies and gentlemen, how much the School of Love is needed. Mr Tarson's expression, as you can see, is appropriate to a warbler of Rugger Club songs or a furtive voyeur in a pornographic cinema. If the pundits of a great public communication enterprise will not treat Love in an adult manner, they had best enrol in one of our elementary courses. Englishmen, grow up. Englishwomen, help them.

Bob Tarson: Good night, *Miss* Henshaw.

Petulia: I accept your apology.

Petulia did us a lot of good with her combination of Beauty and Intelligence. The School has been doing well, though with no support from clergymen or politicians, as you might expect. The police are still chewing their helmet straps. But, in the name of the song that my poor dad played more than once during his Marathon, Love Will Find a Way. Poor dad. It might be no satisfaction for him to look out of the fires of Purgatory and see his daughter doing well in a profession that has really nothing to do with Entertainment, but there's been another reward for him, and that's the last thing I'll tell you about.

Twelve and a half

Because I am superstitious.

My husband Albert Ross got married again to an actress, a pretty little thing so I heard but not much good, she came to his agency looking for a flat and that's how they became acquainted. She'd been told by a doctor that she couldn't have children, something to do with her Salopian Tubes or something, a woman's inside is very complicated, and she didn't mind having a young son already provided. The funny thing about the bringing up of young Robert was that it was she who insisted on him having piano lessons and not Albert, who had turned against me very nastily and, when his son was old enough, told him very nasty stories about me and said that he had to consider his stepmother his real mother. And yet later on, when his stepmother, who was very short sighted but would not wear glasses owing to her vanity, got knocked down and killed by a Bugatti when she was crossing a street in Haywards Heath, and when Robert was already a married man, he stuck an advertisement in the papers asking his real mother to make contact with him. My Mother Was A Prostitute. That was a thing to be more proud of than ashamed about in the Age of Permission, showing how everything has gone to the dogs these days. Petulia, who read the high class newspapers, saw the advertisement and I got in touch with him. He told me the queer story of his marriage, and I'm going to tell it you now.

But first I have to say that Robert became very good on the piano and, unlike my dad, he had real ambitions to be a pianist and not just a pianoplayer or joannathumper. He had a good teacher and he was put to the proper playing of scales and Beethoven's sonatas and Chopin. But his teacher told him to put out of his head any idea of being a Great Pianist, because he just didn't have that extra something that was needed. This was a disappointment to Robert, but he would give a Recital and everybody would rave about how good he was and then his name would be made and he'd be one of the Great Ones. By 1960 he was working in Sassoon's, the big chemical firm, and not doing too badly at it either, but he was still playing away at his Chopin and Bach on the Bechstein upright he'd been given as a twenty-first present and dreaming of great success some day, because teachers, however good they are, don't know everything.

It was in 1963 that he married a girl called Edna, who let on to like music a great deal and would go to concerts with him (in London this was) and say how beautiful Chopin was, he is like the moonlight and the starlight playing on the waters of an Italian lake (she'd picked that up from some sloppy women's serial). She was ten years older than him and still is, of course, though she looked a good deal younger. It was as though it ran in her family to get married older than the average and to a younger man, because her mother, Mrs Aldridge, had done the same thing. Edna's mother was seventy-two in the year of Robert's marriage to Edna, so she must have been getting on for forty when she had Edna, who was the only child.

Now Edna's father had been the temperature tester in a brewery, and the doctor pad always warned him that the Occupational Hazards would get his liver some day. It wasn't his liver that got him, though, but his heart, he was carrying too much weight like Mrs Aldridge herself, and the horrible thing is that he collapsed and died of a heart attack during the speeches at the wedding reception. He was due to make a speech himself as the Bride's Father, and he'd written it all down what he was going to say, but when he got up the couple of bits of paper he had fluttered from his fingers and he cried out: 'I've had it,' and put his hand to his throat. Everybody thought this was meant to be humorous, but then he went all purple and collapsed on to the wedding cake. So the honeymoon that had been planned for Bognor Regis had to be cancelled, and when Robert and Edna moved in to the little terraced house in Hammersmith that they had on mortgage Mrs Aldridge moved in with them. Robert had always liked Mr Aldridge but he had no time at all for Mrs Aldridge, who he would never call mother-in-law or ma but always Mrs Aldridge. I'd better add that Robert's father, my former husband, had gone to Spain to get into the real estate racket there, he said also his blood had gone thin in North Africa and he needed the sun. Robert said that his father did not approve of his son marrying beneath him (don't do what I did, boy, marry on your own level or a bit above it) but Robert said he was in love and would go his own way.

Edna insisted that her mother moved in with them, after all they had the spare room, and mother couldn't be expected to keep up the house she'd lived in with her husband, the rent was a disgrace and she only had her widow's pension. Robert tried to put his foot down at first, but Edna showed a side of her he hadn't seen before. She screamed about him being a heartless beast and the neighbours started to bang on the wall so he gave in, he had a lot of his grandfather in him. So Mrs Aldridge moved in, bringing all her furniture and thousands of ornaments, little china dogs and so on, horrible stuff, and then there was a row about the piano. Mrs Aldridge couldn't stand him playing it, she said, it gave her a Piercing Headache, specially after all she'd been through. He tried playing pppp with the soft pedal down, but that was no good. She said that they ought to get rid of it to give her furniture and little china dogs more breathing space as she put it, but Robert said no and put his foot down, this time not on the soft pedal.

'You,' he said, 'Edna, what have you to say about all this? You know music is my pride and joy and with things as they are it's the only comfort I've got.' By Things As They Are he meant that with Mrs Aldridge in the spare room they hadn't properly got down to doing what husbands and wives have to do, the creaking of that bed gives me a Piercing Headache. In fact, and Robert was able to speak to me very frankly about this, he'd not even managed to get it in yet, to put it very simply, and this was very frustrating.

'Music's all right in its place, I suppose,' said Edna, 'but it's a thing we have to sacrifice for the sake of mother's health and wellbeing.'

'You say that,' said Robert, 'and you were always going on about how much you like Chopin and the rest of it. There's been a bit of a change going on here, and I don't much like it, Edna.'

'Well, to be honest,' she said, 'music's something I can take or leave. It was all right when we were courting, but now we have the television I need something that'll take me out of myself a bit more than music does. And mother feels that too. As you won't be able to play that much more except when mother and me are out at the pictures or at Mrs Ellis's or something, well, I think mother's right, it only clutters the place up.'

'You,' sort of spluttered Robert, 'you who were always going on about Beethoven giving you visions of bloody Paradise and all that bloody guff.'

'Don't you speak to my daughter in that manner of tone.'

'Oh, to hell with it,' and he went out to get a drink while Edna and her mother watched Emergency Ward Ten on the television.

One day when he got home from work he found two surprises. The first was a car outside the front gate, a secondhand Fiat but in good nick, and he went inside where his wife and mother-in-law were watching the telly, and he said: 'Whose is that small green job outside?'

'Ours,' said Edna. 'Isn't mother good? She bought it for us out of dad's insurance money. Now we can all get around a bit.' And then Robert got his second surprise, and that was to find that his piano wasn't there any more.

'Where is it, what have you done with it, come on, speak up, you pair of bitches.'

Of course there was shouting and screaming about him calling my daughter and my mother names, but then the story came out that the piano had been carted off by Headingley's the Removers to a lady who Mrs Aldridge had met in a caffy when she called in for her morning coffee and ten cream cakes to keep her widow's strength up and who said she wanted a piano for her little girl. Got just the thing for you we have, said Mrs Aldridge, come round and see it, but not in the evenings because my son-in-law's home then and he's a terrible shouter and swearer. Anyway, there was the money on the mantelpiece, what was left of it, because mother's bit of money from the insurance had not been quite enough to cover the price of the car, it had been in Hadow's Showrooms on the Broadway and one of Hadow's men had driven it round. 'I never asked for a bloody car,' Robert yelled at them, 'my licence is out of date anyway, bugger it.'

'Get it renewed and stop that swearing, it's disgusting, the neighbours'll start knocking on the wall again.'

And so the row went on, even when they sat down to their tea, kippers or herrings or sardines or something, the place always smelled of fish, and Robert began to think up a way of driving them both mad. It was typical of him, and of my dad too in a way, to cut off his nose to spite his face. Instead of fighting to get his piano back and insisting on his rights, which he had every right to do, he went out to Barlow's the carpenter's and got them to cut him a piece of bird's eye maple that should be the length and width of a piano keyboard. You'll remember my dad had one of those dummies too that time when he tried to teach me. Robert went a bit further than dad, he had the whole lot from bottom A to top C and he got the thing painted properly in black and white by a young lad that was learning Commercial Art and was glad of the odd couple of quid for doing the job, and a lovely job it was Robert told me. He spoke about it as though it was better even than his own real piano, which again was typical

He was very quiet about things from now on, and this worried Edna and her mother more than his shouting and raving and calling them a pair of bitches. What he did while they were watching television was to sit in such a way that they couldn't avoid seeing his fingers flashing up and down the dummy keyboard. He did about an hour and a half of practice on this every evening after their fish tea, with the music his silent hands were playing very clear in his mind, and he told me it was a real pleasure and in a way he got more out of it than doing the real thing, because he knew the neighbours wouldn't complain. Now neither his wife nor his mother-in-law could really complain either, except that one or the other would say why don't you do that in the bedroom or the lavatory, it gets on our nerves you fiddling about like that, but he'd just sort of smile and carry on. Then of course one day Mrs Aldridge said it gave her a Piercing Headache, and then he roared at her like a lion, so they thought he was Mad. He didn't make them mad themselves really, but he Disturbed them, and that was the main thing. And all this time he hadn't yet put it in, and this was driving him round the bend in a way they couldn't appreciate, not being men.

In the spring of 1964 it was time to start thinking of their summer holidays, and Robert had like visions of himself and Edna Naked in bed, but it wasn't really Edna of course, it was just some beautiful Naked woman, in the heat of the afternoon with the blue sea beneath, and this time, poor lad, he would get it in and do a lot more things besides, because Robert, unlike his mother, was a great book reader. Robert thought the surest way of not having Mrs Aldridge with them getting Piercing Headaches when she heard the bed springs ten rooms away was to have a holiday Abroad, women of her age and position in life not caring much for Abroad. But she said what a good idea, I have never been Abroad, and we've got the car and perhaps we can tour about a bit and see quite a bit of Abroad, only right I should see what I can before I go, because I've not got long (oh don't talk like that mother), your father was always one for Clacton every year and it was a Big Adventure when we went as far as Hastings St Leonards. Robert said:

'To start off with, Mrs Aldridge, Edna and I are going Abroad because we see it as a sort of a honeymoon, which we haven't yet had, and a honeymoon couple ought to be on their own, because there are things they have to do which you once did yourself, Mrs Aldridge, because without them you would not have given birth to this charming daughter of yours.' Oh, that's rude, that is, such things are like the Lavatory and are not to be spoken of. 'And there's another thing, and that is that you will not like Abroad, Mrs Aldridge. You won't like the food, which is all garlic, and you have to drink bottled water because the tap water gives you Typhus, Typhoid, Cholera, Dysentery and all manner of deadly diseases. And another thing is the Heat. You get more Heat Abroad than you get in England, that stands to reason because England's an island and has these cooling sea breezes playing all over it. Now I don't want to be Personal, but you're carrying a lot of weight, and that and the Heat combined and the rich feeding are not going to be much good to your health. I reckon you ought to go off quietly to a seaside boarding house or even a hotel as you used to and you'll be all the better for it.'

'Ah no,' she said, 'I'm not having that. And I'm not having you being Personal about my Appearance neither, did you hear what he said Edna, it's natural to put on flesh when you are a Mature Woman.'

'It is *not* Natural at your age,' Robert said, 'to stuff cream buns into your face at all hours of the day and night too for all I know of, and pouring the hot fat over your bacon and eggs, it makes me sick to see it. I tell you your Heart won't stand it, Abroad will about do for your ticker, you mark my words.'

'That's right, deprive me of my Lawful Rights, do you hear him, Edna?'

'No, mother-in-law or ma or whatever I'm to call you,' he said, 'I'm thinking of your health, no more. I want you to be spared for many many more years to sit there and stuff and have Piercing Headaches when I play my dummy keyboard and gawp at bloody nonsense on the telly. And while we're on about rights, what about my rights as a bloody musician?' And then he was back very unexpected on to the selling of his piano, but it was mostly to make both angry and not because he really cared much any more. If he cared for Edna still it was as a Naked Female Body that he had not yet had, and that was a dangerous thing. If anybody had taken a close look at him they might have seen that he was on the way to a nervous breakdown. I mean, he worked hard at Sassoon's, but Edna never wanted to hear about his hard day or discuss things with him, always the flaming telly and her fat mother, and no sex, what with Mrs Aldridge being a Very Light Sleeper despite her loud snoring and complaining about the creaking of the bed and she couldn't get a wink of sleep and so on. Another thing they might have noticed, and very interesting too because he got it from my dad, was that he had started to read about murderers, having books from the public library and fair eating up the *News Of The World* on Sundays. He told me later on that he'd first got interested in murderers because of

music, and it wasn't the Brides in the Bath man Smith, who played
Nearer My God To Thee while his wives were drowning in the bath,
not all at the same time of course, but a man called where's the name
got it written down somewhere ah yes Gesualdo, who was a great
musician and a great murderer.

Mrs Aldridge had got it into her head that the one place Abroad
she wanted to go to was Italy. Why Italy, mother? Because Mr
Roderick at the brewery had married an Italian lady and though she
did smell a bit of that garlic that him here referred to she had lovely
like raven hair which she touched up as she got older and she had a
lovely creamy skin and was very well built as is right for a Mature
Woman and I loved to hear her speak this broken English that she
used to speak, being a foreigner. So Robert said:

'So I'm to drive all the way across France to Italy, am I, a couple
of women telling me how to do it, not much of a flaming holiday the
way I look at it, Mrs Aldridge.'

'So it's Mrs Aldridge is it like it was no more than as if I was no
more than a Visitor, do you hear him Edna, not one ounce of Respect
or Love or Feeling in his whole personality. I am your mother-in-
law and ask a mother-in-law's rights to Affection and Respect and
not to be treated as a Stranger in my own daughter's house.'

'And another thing is that Italy's really Hot in August and the
Heat will surprise you, Mrs A. But if that's the way it's to be that's
the way it's to be and I'll say no more about it except that we had
all better hurry up and get our passports, so your first job Mrs A
is to get some little photos of yourself taken at Ashburn's on the
Broadway and I'll see about getting the forms.'

Anyway, when August came they packed their bags and put
them in the boot of the car and set off for Dover, Robert having,
he thought, enough money in travellers' cheques and Mrs Aldridge
having stuffed five-pound notes in her corset. Mrs Aldridge also
travelled down to Dover with a carton of Dimbleby's cream horns,
which she ate on the way, spitting crumbs on the back of Robert's
neck when she said Look at the man crossing the road Edna, doesn't
he look like your Uncle Edward, and that's a nice little house over
there that one painted white, oh I'd love to live in the country. It was

a bit of a rough Channel crossing, but she wasn't sick, oh no. It was poor Robert who was sick and he'd eaten hardly anything to be sick on. It is sometimes a very unfair world.

So they travelled down through France, staying at motels and eating in little restaurants and spending less than a day in Paris, which Mrs Aldridge said was a Haunt of Sin. It got to be very warm as they moved south, and Mrs Aldridge kept fanning herself all the time with a little fan with like blue duck down on it which she said she had been left by her Mother and was Very Old. She ate heartily of lunch and dinner, as well as an English breakfast and a light meat supper, she drank Perrier water and said it brought the wind up lovely. She said Abroad was very nice and very quaint but very Hot and there were too many foreigners. Robert bore all this very bravely but he did not get much Compensation in the way of Sex. Edna said once oh if you want to do it do it but be quick about it and I am not removing my nightdress, enough to put any man off. When he thought he was going to get it in she yelled out at him that he was Hurting, so he gave up. So it wasn't much of a holiday for poor Robert, except that he got a bit of sun and fresh air and a change of diet, Mrs Aldridge not liking the fish, too many tentacles on it and you can't beat a bit of Cod. He drank his fair share of wine too, so the time wasn't completely wasted.

They got down to Nice and to Monte Carlo and then they crossed the border at Ventimiglia and they were in Italy. Mrs Aldridge said well so this is Italy and very nice it looks, look at that sort of priest there Edna in a black skirt. She was looking very fit but very red like a Lobster and she still kept fanning herself all the time. She ate heartily of the spaghetti and bits of veal and drank Sangemini mineral water but said it didn't bring the wind up as nicely as that French water they'd had. Robert said he was sorry about that, you stay here and I'll rush back over the border and buy you a couple of crates. Do you hear him, Edna, with his sarky isms. And then the trouble started and very nasty it was.

What happened was that the car broke down one evening when they were in open country, some miles inland from Albenga I think it was. It started to cough and then to jump and then it stopped. Robert opened the bonnet and looked inside, but of course he couldn't see anything wrong. A stopped car is like a dead body, it looks the same except that it's not breathing. Edna said:

'What's the matter with it, Bob?'

'How the hell do I know?' he said. 'I filled her up with petrol at that place ten miles back and there's oil and water. I'll have to get a garage to have a look at it.'

'But how can you when we're miles from anywhere?'

'That's very good,' Robert said. 'That's just what I'd say myself if I felt like saying anything other than damn and blast and sod it.'

'I will not have such language,' said Mrs Aldridge. 'And another thing, I will be wanting my dinner soon.'

'You had lunch enough for twenty,' Robert said. 'You'll just have to let your great big belly rumble, Mrs A.'

So then they both went on at him about him being coarse and bad tempered and what he was going to Do except just sit there and insult people? By now the night had started to come on and of course it had to start raining, and very heavy too as it can in Italy. Robert could do nothing except close up the bonnet and get back into the car, and they all just sat there while the rain pelted and teemed down. 'This,' said Mrs Aldridge, 'is not my idea at all of going Abroad for a holiday.'

There she was sitting in like state at the back, and Robert turned from his driver's seat to look back at her as though very surprised at her words and he said:

'Really? Really? Isn't it, Mrs A? I should have thought it was precisely everybody's idea of a holiday, sitting here with the rain peeing down, and it's even coming inside, you'll be sitting in a real big pool of it soon, Mrs A, miles from anywhere, or perhaps I should say kilometres since we are Abroad, with nowhere to stay the night and not one word of the language between us except the musical phrases I was familiar with a hundred years ago it sometimes seems when I was permitted to play my flaming piano. I'm really enjoying this, even if you're not, Mrs A. Perhaps we ought to sing a song, no, of course, anything like music gives you a Piercing Headache and that wouldn't do, would it, Mrs A?'

'Don't you talk to my mother like that.'

'Oh let him, Edna, it flows off me like water off a duck's back, there's no doing any good with some men, as I have learned in my time.' It was not the best chosen of things to say, so Robert told me, that about the duck's back, because the water was really coming in and her little fan with the duck down on it was getting soaked. 'I'm not staying here anyway,' she said. 'I'm not going to get drowned in my own car and catch my death, he'll have to find us somewhere to shelter.'

As it happened, there was a big building fairly near that Robert could just about see through the dark, not really a building, more of a barn, and Robert was made to get out and run sploshing through the rain to see what it was, it might after all be a slaughterhouse. It was a real barn, he found out, full of straw and hay, and he told them that they'd better go and shelter there, not what they were used to, no telly and not even any light, and as for something to eat, ha ha ha, but Mrs Aldridge could eat anything couldn't she, so long as it was not too refined, so let her chomp at a bit of straw like a flaming nannygoat. Don't you speak to my mother in that manner of voice. Let him, Edna, I'm above his type of personality. So they got out of the car, and Mrs Aldridge sort of waddled to this barn, Robert having run there again ahead and being ready to give a sort of welcome, saying:

'Come on, hot water bottles in all the beds and the sheets ready turned down for the night. Shall I bring you a nice hot cup of cocoa?'

So the idea was that they should kip down there for the night and early in the morning Robert would thumb a lift from somebody to a garage and somebody would come and look at the car. All the Italian Robert knew, as he'd said, was like Allegro Moderato and Lento ma non troppo and he remembered that that thing in music like a half moon with a dot inside is called a Fermata, so he would say something like Fiat fermata, but he wouldn't get much further than that. Mrs Aldridge complained about the Pangs of Hunger, but then she found some French lemon lozenges in her handbag and ate them all, crunching away, and later she complained about the Acidity. The rain still teemed down, but it was dry where they were, though Edna complained of insects, and soon they all settled down for the night in the straw and slept. Robert woke up at one point and saw that the rain had stopped and the moon was coming up, and Mrs Aldridge was snoring like a grampus and Edna was just honking gently in a very ladylike manner, and he went back to sleep again.

What happened after that was very strange. Robert woke up to hear very loud sounds. The moon had gone under a cloud so he couldn't see at first what was causing the noise, but he could see very dimly what looked like Mrs Aldridge seeming to be dancing around and around with somebody very big and hulking and he could recognise the voice of Edna going ow! ow! ow! and thought he could see her shape sort of cowering against the wall of the barn.

'What in the name of God,' said Robert. 'What the hell does she think she's doing?'

'Ow! ow! ow!' And Mrs Aldridge sounded like she was snuffing it, but still she went on dancing round and round in a kind of waltz, and Robert couldn't see who the hell she was dancing with, but he seemed to have a very rough fur coat on, which was strange because this was August and in Italy too. Now Robert had got my father's bravery, it takes courage to do a Marathon, and he was brave enough to go up towards this fur-coated figure to ask it what the hell it was doing with Mrs Aldridge, and then he tripped over something on the way and fell in the straw and he found that what he'd tripped over was a man laying there sleeping, but he woke up and started to fight when Robert fell on him, but then the sort of very dim sight of Mrs Aldridge dancing around got all his attention and he began to shout. He cried out:

'Bruno! Bruno! Vieni qua Bruno,' or some such words. (We had a girl for about two days in Singapore who said she came from Sicily and was called Maria la Sporca, a filthy girl, she had to be thrown out but I picked up one or two words from her.) Then Mrs Aldridge was let go, and she dropped really fatigued on to the hay and straw, and this Bruno then came lumbering sort of panting towards this man, and the moon came out big and strong like a spotlight, and this Bruno turned out to be a big brown bear. He was made to sit down quiet and not disturb anybody any more, so he turned his big brown bottom on everybody and curled up and was soon snoring like a human being. Mrs Aldridge just lay there, really Out, but she was still living anyway despite all the Exertion, being a big strong sort of a woman, fortified by good feeding and not taking much exercise of any kind except with her jaws. What this man, a fat man and very unshaven and stinking terribly of garlic, said now to Robert was that this Bruno was an *urso ballante*, and Robert got the meaning of that, a dancing bear, and this man took him round the towns and villages for money, but he'd got caught in the rain coming from a little place called Acquarossa or something and the bear had played hell about getting his fur all wet, and they'd come here for shelter, both a bit tight, because the bear Bruno could knock back the vino like any Christian, and he must have got woken up by Mrs Aldridge getting up to go and pisciare, and he thought he had to start dancing with her. When Mrs Aldridge was able to speak she said she reckoned the dance must have been going on for over ten minutes, round and round and round and no reverse turns, and might have gone on for ever if this man hadn't woken up and called the horrible brute off.

Well, the dawn came up on a fine hot Italian day, and this man, who said his name was Alessandro Grosso, had food in a bag, sausage made of horse and goat and a stale chunk of bread, and a squashed bunch of grapes, and there was still some vino left in a bottle he had, Mrs Aldridge ate some bread and sausage and drank some of the rainwater that had fallen into a big empty oil can outside the barn, and she said nothing except 'Well', over and over, but with big intervals in between, and she kept looking at the bear Bruno, who sat quite quiet on his hunkers, eating grapes like a human being but sometimes looking over at her kind of interested in a mild way, met that woman before somewhere. In the strong sunlight it was possible to see the fleas jumping up and down all over him, as if rejoicing in the fine Italian morning. Alessandro Grosso felt a kind of responsibility for what had happened, as was only natural, and he said he'd have a look at the car, a Fiat, Italiano he said, and he rummaged round inside the bonnet while Bruno the bear sort of lumbered about on all fours, snorting at the butterflies. It was the candles, Alessandro Grosso said, meaning the plugs. He held up one of these and said Sporco, and he cleaned them up with his handkerchief and soon the car started, Robert said, sweet as a bird.

Well, Mrs Aldridge got in the back, very quiet and looking like she'd seen a Holy Vision, the back was drying up nicely in the sun, and Edna and Robert got in the front, and Robert said: 'Right ladies, we're on the road to the Leaning Tower of Pisa.' Edna sort of sniffed, as though she'd like to say that the dancing bear was all Robert's fault but couldn't in all honesty, and Mrs Aldridge said: 'Well.' Alessandro Grosso was smiling all over his unshaven face, waving goodbye and making Bruno do the same, but Bruno seemed to get the idea that it was time to start dancing with Mrs Aldridge again and he lumbered towards the car with his paws out, sort of going huh huh huh to Establish the Waltz Rhythm, so Mrs Aldridge let out like a stifled scream, and the car went on its way towards the south.

The car went quite nicely, and they stopped for lunch, more of a big mid-morning breakfast really, at a little town, and Mrs Aldridge felt a lot better when she'd had some *zuppa di verdura* and a double portion of *spaghetti alle vongole* and then a *bella bistecca* (a beef steak always has to be bella in Italy, just as a cup of tea always has to be nice in England) and a big bottle of mineral water to bring up the wind. 'Pity you can't get a nice strong cup of tea and some fancy cakes,' she said, so Robert knew she was all right again, big strong woman as she was, like a big flabby old Cow. So on they went through the blazing Italian summer day, and Mrs Aldridge's fan had dried out nicely and she was fanning herself with it in the back in solitary state, saying nothing, still sort of Visualising what had happened to her in the night. Robert guessed she was Visualising that, and he Visualised it himself and couldn't stop himself laughing. Edna said:

'It's downright rotten to laugh like that after what poor mother has been through, you heartless beast.'

'He doesn't worry me, Edna. I'm past worrying about his manner of behaviour.' And then there were no words, just a kind of choky gargling and a sort of distant rattling noise, and Mrs Aldridge had slumped over head first on to Robert's back, so that he was nearly driven into the steering wheel. Edna saw her and let out a little scream and then a bigger one. 'Stop the car, stop it, mother's col-lapsed.' So Robert stopped the car by the side of the road. It was one of the side roads, not the autostrada, which Mrs Aldridge said she couldn't stand because of the fumes of the petrol and everybody going fast enough to break their necks. Mrs Aldridge was dead all right, and at first Edna wouldn't take it in, trying to get her to wake up, wake up mother it's me it's Edna, by slapping her cheeks and punching her on her back. But Robert said:

'She's had it, no doubt about it, poor old bitch.' Of course that made him heartless and a beast but Edna didn't help by screaming at him as if her dying was all his fault. Robert kept very calm and said: 'Listen, Edna, take it easy, she can't be brought back again, she's dead and that's it, and it's also the end of our holiday, but she's been Abroad and she's even died Abroad, and that's something for her to be thankful for, wherever she is.' Now if Robert had been brought up a Catholic, which he wasn't, he would have meant Purgatory, but he really meant nothing since he believed nothing. Edna had been brought up Church of England, which meant she believed nothing too, but she thought Robert meant Hell just to be nasty, Hell and Heaven meaning to people like her a kind of fairy tale, not much use in real life, a bit like music. Still she said:

'She's gone straight to Heaven, she's looking down on us now, she hears every word you say,' though she didn't believe in Heaven any more than Hell and the other places that only Catholics believe in. It was just that if there was a Heaven, then her mother ought to be there. Robert said:

'We'll have to get her buried pretty quick, she won't keep long in this Heat,' and that was a horrible thing to say too according to Edna. And even to say We'll Have To Get Her Buried was all wrong too, because Edna, though she was pig ignorant, knew that Italy was an RC country and her mother would come back to haunt her every night if she was given an RC burial. Protestants always say RC or Roman Catholic as though that made English Catholics sort of for-eigners and not worthy to live in Good Old Protestant England. 'All right,' said Robert, 'cremation then,' and that started Edna off about how dare he suggest burning poor mother oh mother mother come back to me he's saying horrible things, the silly little bitch, all right that's Defaming her Character but I'll cut that out later when we find a publisher if we ever do. And then Robert said, very reasonable: 'No, there's no cremation here anyway, I'd forgotten, the Church of Rome doesn't believe in cremation because of the Resurrection of the Body.' And then he got on the right track by saying: 'We should by rights have her buried on English Soil, which means getting her Refrigerated and carted back, it'll cost a packet, but it has to be done,' and of course to stupid Edna that was the wrong thing to say, except about the English Soil. 'In other words,' said Robert, very calm, 'we have to get her to the nearest British Consul, and to my way of thinking the nearest British Consul will be in Genoa, and so it's to Genoa that we have to go. It won't be decent having her body at the back there gaping at all the world, so we'd better cover her up with that raincoat of hers that's in the boot.' Even Edna could see that was reasonable, so that was done right away.

Now, as you might expect, the car broke down again and Robert had to laugh as they pushed it towards the nearest garage. Edna had no breath to say how dare he laugh. They were lucky, because the nearest garage was only about a kilometre away. A lot of cars went by, but nobody offered any help, they just waved and sort of Jeered, and that made poor Robert laugh all the more. A Fiat like theirs is a very light car, but the weight of dead Mrs Aldridge inside didn't make it any lighter. They got to a little AGIP garage that said APERTO, meaning open, and Robert started off by trying to think what might be the Italian for My Mother-in-law Is Dead And That Is Her See In The Back, but it wasn't easy. He felt it had to be said though because the garage people might be suspicious and superstitious if they just saw that lump there with the raincoat over it and ring up the police, and if there was one thing that would put Edna into Hysterics it was the idea of bringing foreign policemen in with Guns, all she wanted to do was get her poor dead mother on English Soil, meaning the Consulate at Genoa. Well, what Robert got out of his musical Italian was Morendo, which means Dying and is at the end of some of the pieces by Chopin. He couldn't think of anything else, so he shut up about it. The garage men, a man and his son really, had a look at the bundle in the back but they seemed to think it was just a big pile of dirty laundry, because after the one look they took no more notice. They fiddled about inside the bonnet of the car and then the son got into the driver's seat and played about with the gears and the choke and tried to start the engine, then he began to sniff nff nff. And then he said: 'Formaggio?' but Robert didn't understand the word, which means cheese, like the French fromage, but he understood from the sniffing that the smell had started and he got it himself when he put his nose in.

Anyway, what was the matter with the car was about every damned thing in the world, it was such an old car, it had done over ninety thousand miles, the gears were working badly and the brake discs were worn out, and Robert couldn't help muttering: 'Your fault, you old bitch, but you're nicely out of it now,' but Edna didn't hear him, she just sat on a chair they gave her because she'd sort of sign languaged that she felt very faint. The two mechanics did something that had to do with bits of wire, and they sign languaged that he ought to scrap the car and get a new one, and then the body in the back of the car gave a kind of groan and tried to sort of heel over, and the two men didn't know whether to run away or make the Sign of the Cross. Then Robert had to try and explain what had happened, saying: 'Her madre cardiaco molto old, fine fine tutto finito.' They just stared at him and then they tried to get the car started, and then they succeeded. Robert paid them and then he and Edna got away as sharpish as they could because even Edna could see that the father and son were looking at each other as if something very fishy had been going on, the old woman murdered for her money. But really sharpish was out of the question, because the old Fiat would only crawl in second gear, and it was going to take them a hell of a time to get to Genoa.

It was evening when they came to Vado Ligure, and Robert insisted on going inland where nobody could see what they had in the car, Vado Ligure being on the coast, as I know well having been there, and plenty of people about for the summer. He said:

'We'll have to sleep in this car tonight, you know that, we can't afford to have people sniffing round it.' It was a pity he'd chosen that word, the right word really, but it wasn't very kind to Edna's mother's corpse, it ought by rights to be smelling as sweet as violets to Edna's way of thinking. She saw Robert was right, but she said:

'Mother's there, though, and there's not room for sleeping two in the front. Besides,' and Robert knew what she wanted to say though she didn't say it, you couldn't sleep with a corpse and the corpse was getting a bit high, even though it ought to smell of attar of roses. So he said:

'Let's get on this side road, if the bloody crate will take us that far, and then we'll have to heave her on to the roof. I mean, there's that luggage rack and she's only like a bit of luggage now, I mean your Real mother's up there in Heaven, isn't she. Isn't She?' And Edna had to admit that her dear mother was up and away among the Angels, and this body that was left was really only a bit of, a lot of, old rubbish. But she started crying and beating her fists at Robert when he said: 'Oh, we'd better get that money she has stashed away in her corset, you do it, love, it's only decent.' But Edna said she couldn't and she wouldn't. So Robert pulled up Mrs Aldridge's skirts and found a fair number of five-pound notes tucked inside where her corset began, all nice and safe, and he put these in his pocket, still warm they were, and Edna wanted to cry but couldn't, but she *did* say: 'Give that money to me to put in my bag, it's Mother's money not yours, you heartless beast.' He didn't see the reasoning in that, but he handed the fivers over.

Getting Mrs Aldridge on top of the car was a hell of a job, and Edna wasn't much help. Robert had some rope for towing in the boot, and there was also a piece of tarpaulin he saw he should have used before when the rain started teeming down. 'Need a bloody crane,' he told Edna. She was a dead weight, Mrs Aldridge, which was only right and proper. He tried knotting the rope under her armpits and getting on to top of the car and pulling her with Edna pretending to push, but it was no good. Then they saw an old oak tree with a big branch sticking out, so he pushed the car over to it, since it wouldn't start, and then he dragged Mrs Aldridge along the grass to just under the branch of this tree. So now he was able to sort of derrick Mrs Aldridge up so that she was swinging from the branch, and he anchored the end of the rope to a branch lower down and then he was able to swing Mrs Aldridge on to the luggage rack. He was sweating cobs and had a hell of a thirst on him by the time he'd got her roped round twice with the tarpaulin over her, and she made the roof sag; but at least she seemed pretty firm up there, all right till they got her to Genoa. Then Robert tramped a long way till he found a grocery store that was also a drinking place where old men played cards, and he bought two big bottles of vino and a loaf and some cheese (it was there he found out what formaggio meant) and a can of Israeli corned beef that would I should think be kosher, and some Swiss milk chocolate and even a knife, and they had their supper in the car, with Mrs Aldridge on top of them. After that they slept, Edna stretched out as far as she could in the back, and once in the night she woke up to yell: 'It's the crows, they've come to peck at Mother,' but it was only the branches of the oak tree crashing and banging.

They had a hell of a job getting off next morning, the car just wouldn't do more than imitate Mrs Aldridge, being just a heavy lump with no life in it, and Robert said: 'Well, as I hope we're going to the British Consulate, I'd better have a dig in the grave,' meaning a shave, but Edna thought that he was having another go at her poor Mother. There was no water around, so he wet his face with what was left of the vino and scraped it while looking in the car mirror. That seemed to work like magic on the car, as if all it wanted was for someone to shave in it, and it agreed to start. And off they went in second gear towards Genoa or Genova as the Italians prefer to call it. But then they heard a terrible crash, and Edna went 'Oh oh, it's poor Mother,' and so it was. The knots of the rope had not been tight enough or something, or the Substances coming out of Mrs Aldridge's dead body had been eating through the rope like Acid or something, but anyway she went crashing off the roof of the car on to the dusty Italian road. Poor Robert found that the car would not go into reverse, so he had to walk several yards to where Mrs Aldridge lay in the dust of old Italy, and he had to drag her by the feet towards where the car was. Edna kept on at him all the time for his Irreverence, but he just snarled like a Savage Beast and sweated cobs till he got her into her old position in the back of the car. She still looked like Mrs Aldridge, but a Mrs Aldridge that had been dead for a couple of days in the heat of a Foreign Country. As there was the smell of formaggio in the car from the supper they had had in it, and there was a hot wind blowing that smelt of garlic and thyme and rosemary, Robert felt that he could cope with decaying Mrs Aldridge till they got to Genoa, and Edna's nose was so bunged up with her crying over her Poor Mother that she could sniff nothing.

Now, as it happened, they never got to Genoa. One thing about Italy is that though it is a very civilised country and a very old one, there is a lot of violence in it, also a lot of kidnapping and robbery. Some people say that this is because it is an RC country that doesn't have the advantages of Protestant Law and Order and others say that Italy is so old that it is still sort of living in the time of Julius Caesar throwing people to the lions and Lucretia Borgia that I saw once in a TV series poisoning everybody within reach. And other people say that the police are no good and are underpaid and are always in League with the Criminal Classes and so are an encouragement to crime. Whatever the reason, Robert and Edna and dead Mrs Aldridge soon found out about Italian criminality. As they were hobbling along the road in second gear they got sort of caught in a sort of crossfire.

There was a big car speeding along in the opposite direction to Genoa raising dust, and there was another car with POLIZIA written on it chasing this first car. There were men in uniform leaning out of the police car firing away with pistols and, Robert said later on, a kind of sub-machine gun. They were not very good shots, not having had the advantage of good weapon training like in good old peaceful England, where the police are unarmed but are all very good shots when they are told to be, and where you have 007 setting an example to everybody that is against the Queen's Enemies. What happened was that these Italian police managed to shoot a hole in the tyre of one of the rear wheels of the car in front, and this made it skid and then the police were on to it. The other thing that happened was that a police bullet got Mrs Aldridge, going through the windscreen and shattering it and just missing Robert and Edna. Edna fainted, as she

had to, and Robert was pretty well trembling like a leaf, starting off
a lot of trembling that he became subject to, as I shall tell later. He
could tell that something had knocked Mrs Aldridge over, for she
flopped down on to the floor of the back of the car, not that there
was enough room for the whole of her body.

It turned out that the car the police were chasing was doing a
kidnapping job. There is a lot of kidnapping in Italy, where they will
kidnap anything or anybody they can lay their hands on. There are
the Red Brigades and the Black Brigades that will kidnap politicians
for the sake of Social Justice, and there is the Mafia, and just ordinary
kidnappers in the way of it as private business. There was even a
film called Casanova by Fellini or Fellazione or whatever his name
is or was, and that got kidnapped. These kidnappers that were being
fired on and missed by a bullet that got Mrs Aldridge instead were
in a small way of business. They had picked up a kid on the road
coming home from school in a little town just outside Genoa and
they thought he was the son of a newspaper proprietor. Actually he
was one of nine kids of a butcher. Their common sense ought to have
told them that the son of a newspaper proprietor would not go to the
same school as the son of a common butcher, but they were not very
bright kidnappers. Anyway, they got picked up by the police, and
the kid went back to his dad and mamma complaining, because he
had been in the middle of a nice little adventure like on the films, and
here he was having to go back to school again the following morning.

But now there was the question of Mrs Aldridge. A police inspector inspected the smashed windscreen, this being his job or else he
would not be called an inspector, and then he inspected the body of
Mrs Aldridge, which, and nobody could blame him, he did not like
the look of. The body was loaded on to a police van and taken to the
Questura in Genoa, and Robert and Edna, who kept going Well and
Oh, just like her mother at the time of the dancing bear, were taken
to this same Questura in a different vehicle and shown into an office
where the police got ready first to bully Robert for being in the line
of fire, the police always begin by bullying you even when you're
innocent, and then to be apologetic. Mrs Aldridge had been cooled
down in a kind of morgue, and a kind of police doctor's assistant got

down to digging the bullet out of Mrs Aldridge's layers of blubber. It was a police bullet all right, but whether it had killed Mrs Aldridge or she had merely died of shock was not a thing to be argued about, because nobody could really tell.

Edna was in her own state of shock and had to be given an injection and shoved into a hospital. Later on she would be put into one of the cheaper hotels in Genoa, as it was at the police's expense and they would not put her up in one of the more expensive ones. They brought in to talk to Robert a police superintendent who knew some American English, because he had once had a holiday on Mulberry Street in New York with his brother who made religious statues. Robert kept on saying:

'Your responsibility. Burial and all. Compensation. Otherwise big trouble between your government and ours.'

'How much a compensation you tink you a gonna get?' said the superintendent.

'A new car for a start.'

This was where the superintendent and the inspector and what other policemen were sitting around this office under a crucifix on the wall looked very sad and also shifty. The car had been left on the road with its shattered windscreen, and the local vultures had hauled it off and Robert would see that car no more. They were willing to give Robert a few thousand lire, and they were ready to see that Mrs Aldridge got buried in one of the local cemeteries – a Catholic one, because there weren't any Protestant cemeteries available except for great dead Protestant poets, and there was a lot of arranging to be done before you got a place in one of those. A lot of arguing and forms to fill in, the superintendent said. Robert said: 'I want a proper tombstone for her. It needn't be too expensive, because my mother-in-law was not one for luxury, but I want an inscription on her grave. Just this: HERE SHE LIES, THE OLD COW.'

The Superintendent knew enough American English to know that that was not a very reverend or reverent epitaph, if that is the right word, but Robert said: 'You don't seem to realise that the cow is a very precious object among us people. The cow is a sacred object to the Indians, and India was part of our great Empire until the

Labour Government gave it away. With us too, in the green fields of England. Mrs Aldridge was a cow to me, and she was also old. So OLD COW is just about right. It is what her daughter would want.'

Robert was given a few thousand lire, and he went and got drunk on it before going back to the cheap hotel where a twin bed was waiting till such time as Edna should come out of her Sedation. He was given assurances that the stone would be cut, and he wrote out the inscription in big block letters so that the stonemason would get it right. Edna, who was howling a lot but was otherwise all right, saw the grave before the cutting, which she was told was to be THE BEST MOTHER THAT THERE EVER WAS, and she put a few Italian flowers on it. Then the police paid for their flight back to England – tourist class, of course.

On the plane going back Robert kept laughing and then falling into a very gloomy silence, and then trembling like a leaf, like a rhythm, but Edna was just white and peaky and shivery all the time. Just before they landed at Heathrow, Robert said, very loud:

'There's some corner of a foreign field
That is for ever Mrs Aldridge,'

and he laughed and laughed all the way towards where the taxis were. In the taxi to Hammersmith, though, Robert went very gloomy and Edna didn't help much when she kept on saying: 'I dread going back, I dread it. All Mother's things there. Mother in the house still in a way of speaking. And at the same time she's dead. In an RC cemetery in a foreign country. Owwwwww.' So Robert got nasty and said:

'Ah, shut it, do you hear, put a sock in it or I'll put my fist in your face, do you hear?'

As you can imagine, life for both of them wasn't very pleasant. The house had been shut up, and it was a warm summer even in England, and there was a smell of Mrs Aldridge everywhere. Then Robert started to have nightmares with Mrs Aldridge coming into the bedroom and just looking at him with a kind of blue light coming out of her earholes and a voice like the voice of God saying This Is The Light That Comes Off Blue Cheese, and he'd start waking up and screaming. Edna wouldn't stay in the same room with him, and started sleeping in her mother's old room. One day Robert said:

'Well, there's one thing anyway. With the insurance money for the car when it comes through if it comes through perhaps I could buy a secondhand piano. I won't be giving anyone a Piercing Headache any more.' But Edna screamed and beat at him and said:

'No no no no, never. I'll honour the memory of my dear mother till I'm dead myself, and the money will go to buying a plot in the cemetery and a stone with her name on it and when the time comes I'll lie there myself.' And she beat at him some more. Robert said:

'On a point of information, what is to be the Nature of our Married Life together? I mean, are we to have Sex any more, for instance, not that we've really had it yet?' That made matters worse. Filth and dirt and blasphemiousness and how dare he even mention that horrible thing Sex. So Robert shut up about Sex and went his own way.

But Robert was not well, and no wonder. At Sassoon's where he worked he did something terribly wrong. He put the wrong chemical or something into the first Experimental Batch as it was called of Sassafodder for Farm Animals and the first Experimental Feeding killed six or seven bull calfs on the Experimental Farm in Hampshire. The Management had him in and said he was a good man and a fine worker but there was obviously something Terribly Wrong with him and they advised him and then they as good as ordered him to see a doctor. The doctor said he was run down and needed rest, and he was sent home on half pay till such times as he was better and had a doctor's certificate to prove it. So there they were, he and Edna, at home all day, and Robert played all the time on his dummy keyboard and it drove Edna near mad, gave her the screaming abdabs as she put it. She said she was going to get a job and she did, working on the accounts in the Goodgrub Supermarket on Chiswick High Street, she having been in an accountant's office before she got married. But it was Agony for her she said having to come home in the evenings to see Robert playing away on his dummy keyboard and she Immersing herself in the telly till it was bedtime.

Then one day Robert was walking by himself in the sun off Hammersmith Broadway and he came to a secondhand shop, full of horrible junk, and among the junk was what is called an American Organ. I had one of these, as you already know, in the Establishment in Singapore. You sit down at it and you pump air in with two pedals left foot right foot, like riding a bike. It is the sort of instrument that always made my dad shudder, it reminded him of horrible hymns like All Things Bright and Beautiful and Let Us Gather At The River, a Protestant sort of musical instrument really. Now Robert went in and asked the man if he could try it, and the man said yes, so Robert played bits of Wagner and Tchaikowsky (thanks, Rolf) so that the man said:

'You can really play that thing.' Then he belched and said: 'Five quid and it's yours.'

'I can give you Things,' Robert said, 'worth more than five quid. You wait. Don't sell that to anybody else. I'll be back.' And he went home and got out of the kitchen two of these big blue plastic bags they used for putting the rubbish in, and he began to fill them with Mrs Aldridge's ornaments – china dogs and little girls with the wind blowing their skirts up and showing their china knickers and figurines of what Mrs Aldridge had used to call Pagan Godices, also some very good plates, Sèvres I think they were, that Mrs Aldridge had got at an auction and said were Too Good to Use, and a complete Constable tea set, also an electroplated coffee pot that was never used because they preferred Camp Coffee, and he ended up with a fistful of Mrs Aldridge's jewels and trinkets, some of them with real gold in them, and off he went to the junk shop again. The man was having his midday dinner and came out chewing, and he was a bit suspicious when he saw all this stuff. 'It's my mother's,' Robert said, and I feel like something walking over my grave and sending the shudders through me when I repeat that, 'she's just died poor old lady.' Well, the upshot or outcome was that the man said okay but you'll have to make your arrangements for moving that there American Organ. So Robert went along the street and he was lucky enough to find a coal merchant just loading up his cart and he was just going to deliver coal round the corner from where Robert lived, and he agreed to deliver the organ to Robert's place for a quid. Robert got on the back with the coal sacks and the organ, and he even played the Wedding March from Low and Grin as they drove through the streets of Hammersmith, a sure sign that he wasn't well.

Robert had to slip the coal merchant's assistant five bob to help him move the American Organ up the stairs on to the landing near the bathroom, because that was where Robert insisted on having it put. Of course the instrument was all covered with coal dust, and Robert cleaned it very carefully with one of Mrs Aldridge's lace afternoon tea cloths, but he didn't bother to clean himself up, because he was very keen to get down to playing again, real playing that is, with real sounds. He would much rather have had a piano, of course, but this was better than nothing, and besides it fitted in with what he thought he had to do when Edna came home.

When Edna let herself in with her key she heard like Solemn Music corning from upstairs, and she ran upstairs and played hell and howled and tried to beat him, and he grabbed hold of her to stop her beating him and she got all coal dust over her. When she found out what Robert had done to get the American Organ, all her mother's nice Special things gone, she howled even worse and hit out stronger and got more coal dust over herself. Then Robert let on to be very sorry, and he'd take the thing back tomorrow and recover all Mrs Aldridge's Lovely Things, let's kiss and make up, but she said get away you horrible filthy pig.

She only quietened down because she saw how filthy she was, all over her hair too, and she said she had to have a bath and she'd really have a go at him when she'd had it.

'You do that, dear,' Robert said. 'I've put the water heater on. I knew somehow you'd want a bath.'

'You mean you knew *you* wanted a bath,' she said. 'You're Filthy. You can have a bath when I've had one.'

'We can have one together, dear,' Robert said, nice as pie. And then of course that was filthy and horrible, and when she went up to the bathroom she locked herself in. Robert went up very quietly and stood outside the door listening to the water being drawn. And then he said very loud through the door:

'I'm going to play you some music, dear.' She made some kind of a noise through the sound of the water which Robert took to mean that she didn't want any music, it would give her a Piercing Headache. He sort of smiled, so he told me, and he sat down on the Boudoir chair he'd taken from Edna's bedroom that used to be her mother's, and he started to play the hymn Nearer My God To Thee. He called out to her in the bathroom: 'Can you hear what I'm playing, Edna dear? It's a hymn that they sang on the Titanic when it was going down, and it means what it says. Nearer Your God To Him. I'm coming in there now. And when I come out again I'm going to play this hymn again, but you'll not hear it.' Then he tried to force the door open but he couldn't. So he went downstairs and got the hammer from the tool drawer and came up again and started to bash the door with that. This time, Edna was screaming away fit to kill. Funny expression when you think it was really the other way round. The hammer was taking too long, so he went down again and got the axe they used for chopping wood to start the fire with, and this got through one of the panels of the door nicely, and he was able to put his hand in and unlock the door.

Of course, Edna was no longer in the bath, which put him off a bit, having had this very clear picture in his mind of her waiting in the water sort of cowering ready to be thrust under and drowned. There she was all naked and wet and slippery, and when Robert got near to her in his clothes, all dusty with the coal, he got the idea that was wrong somehow, so he started to tear his clothes off. Then he said when he was near naked:

'You and me are going back in that bath, Edna, and this is It, so get ready for it,' his idea being to get on top of her and keep her held under. Well, you can imagine the splashing as he started to push her into it, all arms and legs, and you can guess what happened. There was no killing that night. She howled and yelled and beat at him at first, but she couldn't very well say it was dirty and filthy this time. Robert blushed and hesitated a bit when it came to this part of the story, but I told him he couldn't shock Me, get on with it, and so he gave me the whole lot. It was the first time they'd either of them got anything out of Sex, he said, and from then on they had the water heater on all the time. Edna, as you might expect, couldn't get enough of it now, and they were the cleanest

couple in Hammersmith. Robert went back to work cured, and
when he got home from work there would be Edna waiting for
him, all ready, it wasn't necessary to do it in the bath all the time
and there was the price of the electricity, the rug in front of the
fire would do as well. It wasn't long before they had a piano in the
house again, a Jap one, but Edna didn't give him much time for
practice. All this shows you the importance of Sex in people's lives,
which I've never doubted and have spent a lot of my time trying
to make people see.

And now I come to the name you'll know, even though you don't
know much about music. Little William Ross, son of Robert and
Edna and named after my poor dad, was the Child Wonder when
he was seven and Richard Rodney Bennett wrote this Concerto for
him, without any octaves because of the smallness of his hands. The
kid had a natural instinct which his father did his utmost to help
come out, and it was really the Family Gift at last. It had been trying
to get through for a long time, failing with my dad and succeeding
in a twisted sort of way with his daughter (A Metaphorical Sort of
Way, says Petulia), failing again with Robert and then bursting like
a flower with little Billy. Not so little now, a young man of twenty
in this year 1984, handsome and with a bit of a look of his great
grandfather, making money for himself and Robert, who acts as his
manager, and giving beautiful music to the world.

If only my poor dad could have foreseen this when he was banging away at his Marathon. It might have made things easier for him,
but perhaps not. But nothing had really been wasted. Out of the
blood of a pianoplayer, so to speak, a Pianist came at last.

I think I ought to cut out those Thank You Rolfs, but I meant
them at the time. Rolf said that the typing of this stuff helped him
to break his Block, and he showed me the first few pages of his own
thing that he'd started. But there were about twenty FUCKS on the
first page alone, and people screwing under drugs and men giving it
each other in the arse, and I said: 'Oh no, I won't have this sort of
Filth in my house, even if it is only my country one, so pack your
rucksack and get out.' Which he did, quite happily, taking two of my
rings with him and a necklace and my little radio. Easy come easy

go, as they say. M. Belfond who plays the cello in the orchestra in
Nice wrote down the piece of music I promised you early on, and
here it is.

Mr Yamasaki borrowed my dad's Method from me in Singapore, but I never saw it again and I can prove nothing. This piece comes at the beginning of the Method, and it has different names – Waltz On The Open Strings, Look Mom No Hand, GADEway to Heaven and so on, but it is best known as Fingers Off. My dad believed that with his Method any kid could be playing Mozart in a month. It was the only thing he was ever optimistic about.

Appendix 1: Anthony Burgess, 'An American Organ'

From *Splinters*, ed. by Alex Hamilton (London: Hutchinson, 1968), pp. 76–82.

There was no room for a piano in our new (and very small) house, but my fingers itched for a keyboard of some kind. 'Why,' suggested my wife, 'don't you get a piece of wood and plane it smooth and then paint it with black and white keys? You could practise on that.' Practise, yes, but practise for what? Practise for the time when we should have a piano again? There wasn't room, you see: it was a very small house, stiflingly small but all that we could get. And afford. There might have been room, of course, if we weren't so cluttered up with all my wife's mother's furniture and knick-knacks. When I walked through the house it rang with jolting china dogs. 'Throw some of these things away,' I advised. 'Sell them. Then we could have money enough for a second-hand piano. Also, indeed, space.' But I had uttered blasphemy. Sell the precious things which had belonged to her dear, dead mother: How could I be so heartless?

But one day, when my wife was out at work (I wasn't allowed to work, you see, because I was considered unstable. There was something wrong, said the doctors, but they couldn't say what.) As I say, when my wife was out at work, I took a big bag and in it placed several china dogs, some china pigs at a china trough, an ebony elephant or so and some genuine Sèvres, then caught the bus to Chipping Wellwater. There was a filthy antique shop there, filthy, one that no self-respecting American tourist (and all American tourists are self-respecting) would dream of entering. For that matter, I never saw anyone go in. But, this grey filthy day, I went in and encountered a strong dusty smell of antiquity. There was, I could see at once, nothing of either value or beauty in the outer room of the shop – gilt-framed Holman Hunts, a huge anonymous engraving of a highwayman in the stocks and a pretty serving-wench stealing keys to free him from a snoring bellied beadle, a tray or two, hideous Victorian vases, copies of *An Illustrated History of England*, a broken bellows, a tarnished brass fire-screen, unknown decaying filthy wrack of the nineteenth-century sea hiding behind the above, and other just presentable things.

The shop's owner came out from a sort of den, shambling like a den-living animal. He was chewing bread and wore a dirty waistcoat, was unwashed and so myopic that he had to come straight up to me, as though we were television actors about to start a long scene together. 'These,' I said, opening the bag. He grumbled, handling them myopically, bringing them up to his face as though he were testing their usefulness as disguises. He belched at the china pigs, a sweet strong tea belch. He said:

'Can't give you no money because I've got no money. Not one penny in till or pocket I haven't got. Not that any of these is worth all that much.'

'Oh, come,' I said. 'The Sèvres, for instance ...'

He held a dinner plate to his face as though draining gravy from it. 'You can take your choice of the shop. Whatever takes your fancy to the value, no more. I know what these is worth.' I went into the inner room of the shop. There I saw an American organ. I treadled the pedals, feeding it wind, as I lifted the lid. Yellow keys. Hungrily I fingered them. I played the Pilgrims' Chorus from *Tannhauser*. The shopman came in, suspicious. 'You can play that all right,' he said grudgingly.

'Could I have it, do you think?' I said. 'That Sèvres is worth far, far more.'

'Nice bit of stuff, that is,' he said, as if it were a girl. 'Had many an offer for that, I have.'

'I don't believe it,' I said. 'Who would want an American organ nowadays?'

'Religious people,' said the man. 'You,' he added, coming close and examining my face as if for a particular minute scar he'd been told about, 'don't look religious to me.' That seemed, somehow, to decide matters for him. 'You can have it,' he said. 'Take it away.'

This man had a nephew who ran a small coal business. This nephew expressed himself willing, when I crossed the road to see him, to take both me and the organ back to our little house. He had, he said, to deliver a ton or so beyond my village. He would do the job for five bob. He did it for five bob. There we were, the organ and I, sitting on the coal sacks under the drizzle, bumping home proudly. I even played a bumping tune – to the astonishment of odd cyclists and pedestrians – as we went: the big tune from the Prelude to Act III of *Lohengrin*, the bridal tune.

The coalman helped me hump the organ into the house. We scratched the walls a bit and sent a china dog flying (there were still plenty of china dogs). The organ wouldn't go anywhere, that was the trouble. We tried the little dining-room, but it looked silly sitting in the middle of the carpet. Besides, *she* wouldn't have it, I knew she wouldn't. The sitting-room, bunged up with her mother's massive lounge suite, that wouldn't do either. The coalman had a cleft palate. 'Ghe ghlanghin,' he suggested, several times. 'The what?' I said. 'Ghe ghlanghin.' That seemed the only place, the landing. So we heaved the organ up the stairs, scratching and tearing the wallpaper. We got it up, though, yes we did. Panting, we stood and surveyed it, standing on the landing outside the tiny bathroom. Passing it to get into the bathroom was difficult, and the spare room was blocked for ever. As for a stool to sit on to play the organ, that was simple: my wife's dressing-table stool did fine. 'Ghray uh homehing,' snorted the coalman. I played him something. I played the melody from the slow movement of Beethoven's *Pathétique*. He called for more, a most musical coalman, but I wanted to clean the organ up and provide a little surprise for my wife when she came home. So I sent him away with half-a-crown for his help in humping the thing.

My wife was home at five. 'A surprise,' I said. 'Come upstairs and see the little surprise.'

'You're filthy,' said my wife. 'What on earth have you been doing?' With her sharp woman's eyes she saw that the wallpaper of the little hallway had been torn in places. Suspicious, she looked farther, but could find only further tears and scratches. The house was so full of china, especially china dogs, that it would be many days, perhaps weeks, before she would find that anything was missing. Still, she railed at me for a time, but did not go on too long, for she knew I was not well. She just went into the kitchen for a while for a little cry. 'Come on up,' I invited. 'Come and see what I've got.' Then I thought that it would be an even bigger surprise if she just heard the music, strange music coming from the upper part of the house, before she actually saw the source of the music. Up I went, then, sat on her dressing-table stool, and, in the autumn twilight, began to play. I played the Andante Cantabile horn tune from Tchaikovsky's Fifth Symphony. Diddidy DA daaaaaa, diddidy DOO daaaaaa … It sounded well. It drew my wife running upstairs.

'What?' she said. 'OH.' She knew I was happy, something for my fingers to do. She was perhaps not pleased, but she knew I was happy. 'Very hard,' she said, 'to get in and out of the bathroom.'

'You can squeeze past,' I said. 'You better than me. You're very slim.' She had, indeed, a lovely slim figure.

'Now,' she said. 'Just listen to me. Wouldn't it be far nicer if you could sit and play that organ *clean*? Clean and tidy, ummm? You're covered with coal and fluff and dust and things.'

'It was the coalman,' I said. Diddidy DA daaaaaa…

'Stoke up the boiler,' she said. 'Have a nice hot bath. Put on some clean clothes. Then you can give me a lovely organ recital, clean.'

'Yes,' I said. Full of love and gratitude, I rose from the stool and embraced her, filthy as I was.

'Oh,' she said, 'don't. Oh, you're covered with dust. It's all over me now.'

I went down to the kitchen stove and filled it full of coke. I opened and shut things and soon had a great draught lashing the flames. The water began to sing and bubble. 'When you've finished,' she said, 'I'll have a bath too. There's going to be plenty of hot water.'

'You have it first,' I said.

'No, you first. Then you can play the organ to me while I'm having mine.'

I had a good hot bath, then I changed my clothes. I found a clean shirt with a stiff collar. Downstairs my wife was putting something in the oven for our evening meal. She was a good wife and there would never be another like her. I dressed myself very formally, in a dark suit with black shoes. I was to give an organ recital. 'Come up now,' I called down to my wife. 'I've cleaned the bath and there's still plenty of lovely hot water.'

After a few minutes she came upstairs. Meanwhile I sat at the organ, stiff in my stiff clothes. I tried to imagine that a forest of pipes proliferated above the keyboard, rising like trees into the high air, invisible at the crown. My wife went into the bedroom and took off her clothes. She came out naked, ready for her bath. There had never been any shame between us, no nonsense about dressing-gowns. She edged past me, finding it, for all her slimness, a difficult squeeze. 'Whoops,' she said. Then she was in the bathroom, drawing water. 'What shall I play?' I asked. 'What?' she shouted. The noise of the two taps was very loud. I waited till she had turned them off, then I asked, 'What shall I play?' She was in the bath now, splashing. 'Oh,' she said, 'anything.' I remembered my triumphal journey of that morning, playing Wagner to the drizzly country sky, jolting on top of the coal lorry. I smiled and then laughed aloud. Then I started the *Lohengrin* Act III Prelude, bridal music. She splashed away happily. Myself, I had not felt so happy for a long time. Bridal music. I stopped playing and went into the bathroom, squeezing past my lovely new organ with difficulty. I kissed the hot wet nape of her neck. 'A bride in the bath,' I said. 'Who was that man?'

'Oh, that? Smith, I think.' Like most women, she liked to read of murders.

I sat on the lavatory seat, smiling. She smiled back, glad to see me so happy, so much better, having got something I'd wanted. 'He played the organ while she was dying,' I said. 'What was the tune?'

'*Nearer, my God, to Thee,*' said my wife, sponging herself soapy.
I got up off the lavatory seat. 'How did he do it?' I asked.

'He hit her head on the bath and made her unconscious. Then he lowered her into the water and left her to drown.'

'Why did he do that?'

'The usual reason,' said my wife. 'Money. Pass me the towel. I've got soap in my eyes.'

I picked up the towel from the rail but I didn't pass it to her. Instead I took her head in both my hands. She was surprised and said, 'Don't play about. I can't see. Give me that towel.' Then, holding it firm, I cracked her head quite hard against the head of the bath. This wasn't enough, so I cracked it again. Then I let her slide into the water so that her head was covered. She was not a very tall woman and, even in that small bath, there was plenty of room. While she was bubbling away I quickly edged round my organ, sat down on the stool, treadled air into the organ's lungs, and then started to play *Nearer, my God, to Thee*. But, damn it, I couldn't think of the tune. I tried humming. I one-fingered something I thought was it, but I knew it wasn't right. And, of course, no other tune would do. It had to be that, or else the whole thing was wasted. I could have cried with vexation, not knowing the tune. I went back into the bathroom, but it was obviously all too late. Everything had been wasted. I didn't know any hymns at all. That shopman had been right, saying, 'You don't look religious to me.' Anyway, what was done couldn't be undone, so I started to play, with great expression, that piece of Tchaikovsky, then some Beethoven, then various odds and ends of more modern composers. I played till the bathwater was quite cold and the food in the oven was burnt.

Appendix 2: Reviews

Erica Jong, 'Anthony Burgess and the Music of Love', *Washington Post*, 'Book World', 16 November 1986, p. 1 and p. 6.

I have never understood why there is not general literary rejoicing in this country every time Anthony Burgess publishes a new book. If he had given us no more than *Earthly Powers, Nothing Like the Sun, A Clockwork Orange*, he would be in a different solar system from most sublunary writers, both because of the importance of his concerns and because of the music of his language. But there are also *ReJoyce*, an extraordinary study of the author of *Ulysses*; two other excellent books about Joyce, enormously perceptive studies of Shakespeare, of Hemingway, of D.H. Lawrence; translations, children's books and some of the most astute literary essays ever published under the guise of occasional journalism.

As if to confuse and confound us, there is also Burgess the composer, Burgess the screenwriter, Burgess the public pundit and Burgess the literary educator. In America Burgess's literary reputation has suffered not only because, like Joyce Carol Oates, he is so prolific, but also because he refuses to do that quintessentially American thing: choose a major in the great graduate school of life. We require of our artists that they make things easy for our categorizers and declare themselves for poetry, for fiction or for literary criticism. We tend to feel uncomfortable with the sort of Renaissance man or woman who ranges generally over the fields of art and science, stopping to graze wherever fancy leads.

Our parochialism is more than a pity: it tends to belittle our most ambitious artists and to aggrandize narrower ones. Other cultures celebrate men and women of letters without penalizing the possessors of such global talents. Neruda poured out astounding quantities of first-rate poetry while also producing prose and serving as a diplomat. Robert Graves supported his poetry habit with some of the most arresting fiction and nonfiction of our time. Simone de Beauvoir and Jean-Paul Sartre exploited their talents in imaginative fiction, philosophical nonfiction and drama. Neither Spanish nor English nor French literary cultures discriminate against the generalist the way Americans do. The ideal of the Renaissance man or woman is still very much alive in Europe and Latin America. We should revive it here if only to celebrate Burgess's extraordinary oeuvre while he is alive to enjoy it.

The Pianoplayers, Anthony Burgess's 29th novel, is a delicious little book – a novel that masquerades as the not quite literate (let alone literary) first-person account of her life by a retired courtesan/ call girl, the unsinkable Ellen Henshaw (who, in our day, might have become the Mayflower Madam). Ellen Henshaw rises from humble beginnings to complete happiness because she recognises – in a direct, uncomplicated, Wife-of-Bathish sort of way – the power of lust in our lives and how it relates to pianoplaying. The daughter of a piano player who, when he works, accompanies silent movies, Ellen is raised in seedy rooming houses and what the British call 'bed-sitters' by her loving, drunken, brawling dad. Though he is no 'Paderooski', as he himself would be the first to admit, he loves music as perhaps only a third-rate musician can: he knows and admires what he cannot do. He tries to pass this gift on to his daughter, who is pretty hopeless as a pianist but finds another application for his lessons and dedicates her life to teaching men to play the keyboard of a woman's body.

So much for the rudimentary plotline. The happy ending I will not divulge; suffice it to say that *The Pianoplayers* is, among other things, a spoof of what publishers like to call a 'generational saga', and it takes us through four generations of 'pianoplaying' of various sorts. The analogy between sex and music is elaborated in a variety of ways, both satirical and touching.

Among the many delights of this novel are its literary music lessons and the colloquial voice of its narrator-heroine, who is dictating to and simultaneously arguing with a young man, a writer, whom she has captured to play Horatio to her Hamlet. A kind of generational war goes on between Ellen and her amanuensis Rolf Marcus, and through its skirmishes we come to see the worlds of the '20s, '30s, and '40s and how they differed from our own both in style and content. I know of no other modern writer, except Joyce, who has used the metaphor of music so successfully and wittily in fiction. There is one whole chapter here dedicated to the rudiments of the piano, and it is a tribute to Burgess's humor and sense of language that this chapter is as amusing as the chapters on Ellen's adventures in high-class brothels.

As we already know from *A Clockwork Orange*, the Enderby books, *Earthly Powers*, and that extraordinary early novel of Shakespeare's love life, *Nothing Like The Sun*, Burgess can manipulate the English language with Joycean virtuosity. No wonder his heroes are Joyce and Shakespeare, two of the deftest prestidigitators of language-as-music. In an age when the most successful novelists have not tin but leaden ears, when love of language (the wooing of Dame Philology, as Auden called it) has become almost vestigial, Burgess's gifts should make us giddy with rejoicing.

If you have read none of his novels, *The Pianoplayers* is as good a place to start as any. It is breezy, entertaining, funny with a center of considerable substance. It also contains some of the most delightful comic characters to lurch through recent fiction, characters worthy of Smollett or Dickens.

If I have any quibble with *The Pianoplayers* it is the same minor quibble I have with certain classics like *Moll Flanders*, in which a male writer impersonates a female heroine yet inadvertently glosses over some of the most wrenching passages of a woman's life: maternity and child-rearing. Picaros both, Ellen and Moll are rather flippant about maternity – flippant in ways I imagine only a male writer could suppose women to be. Only in novels do women drop babies with never a backward remorseful glance. Obviously Burgess intends Ellen to be the male ideal of a lusty woman, determined to live like a

man despite her biological predisposition to loyalty, Angst and longing. Bored by babies, Ellen nevertheless has strong dynastic feelings,
and eventually she must triumph as the unconventional matriarch of
an unconventional clan. Like most women of great strength and *joie
de vivre*, her life comes to exemplify the proverb 'living well is the
best revenge.' The details of this good living I leave for the delighted
reader to discover.

Anthony Burgess is not only one of the most versatile artists of
the English language but he is truly wise about the ways in which sex
and music bind and harmonise our lives. This new novel should be
both a cause for celebration and an excuse to go back over his amazing oeuvre and trace the evolution that brought him to this ebullient
display of his extraordinary gifts.

John Banville, 'Burgess and His Mess of Pottage', *Independent on
Sunday*, 7 September 1986, p. 16.

The jacket of this latest in a very long line of books by Mr. Burgess
tells us that it is 'one of his most unusual novels to date'. How dis-
creetly, with what tact, does the blurb-writer reveal his unease.

The Pianoplayers (Hutchinson £8.95 sterling) is unusual, all right,
in that it is a shamefully slapdash, ramshackle piece of work by a
novelist whose musical sense, if nothing else, should have prevented
him from publishing in its present form, or, more correctly, in its
present state of formlessness.

Where is the Burgess of *Napoleon Symphony*, of *ABBA ABBA*,
even of the more recent *Enderby's Dark Lady*? Where is the sensibility that produced those and many other shaped and rounded works
of art? Sold, it seems, pawned, at least, for that mess of pottage which
is 'popular appeal'.

The story is narrated by Ellen Henshaw, who is living in retirement in the South of France. Born in Manchester before the First

World War, Ellen grew up in a seedy world of small-time entertainers. Her father, Billy, earned a precarious living by playing the piano accompaniments to silent films, and providing musical background for a seaside theatre troupe.

In this remembered world of dingy boarding houses and fish-and-chip dinners, almost everyone has a heart of gold hidden somewhere about his or her person. The portrait of Billy Henshaw, the 'piano-player', is fond, sometimes moving, and almost convincing.

He is in his way a sort of genius, who achieves his apotheosis in a pianoplaying marathon, when, after days of non-stop playing, he produces an unearthly improvisation, a 'music from another planet', which is lost to the world when he dies. He has also invented a simplified method of teaching children to play the violin, but can make nothing of it since no-one is interested, and so he leaves the way open for the later advent of Mr. Suzuki.

Mr. Burgess is fond of this sort of joke, and one must confess that there are some good ones here: *The Pianoplayers* is a funny book.

When her father dies, Ellen rapidly finds herself in a French convent, where she is taught the art of prostitution – yes, the art of prostitution, that's what I said. She becomes very successful, and in time sets up 'house', with herself as madame. Then she goes one better, and, with the help of a rich Singapore businessman, establishes a number of 'schools of love', where men will be taught to make love with the same skill and attention they would bring to pianoplaying.

Throughout, the lustre of her golden heart never dims. Now, in old age, she hires a wandering American, Rolf somebody, to tape her story and transcribe it to paper and thus we have *The Pianoplayers*.

It appears that Mr. Burgess set out to write a large, rowdy, rollicking book, a kind of latter-day Memoirs of a Lady of Pleasure, with a brief opening section set in his native Lancashire.

However, as we all know, the past is a strong force, and one suspects that, before he knew it, Mr. Burgess found himself revelling in memories of chip butties and HP sauce, seaside soubrettes, Woodbines, and, above all, those heart-breaking old tunes, with the titles of which he fills whole pages. And when the time comes to leave that world and follow Ellen on her adventures abroad interest seems to have wanted abruptly, so that the second half of the book seems perfunctory in the extreme.

Ellen's time as a prostitute, madame, and then love instructress, is skated over in the space of a few chapters, and suddenly we find ourselves in the midst of an entirely new yarn. This is the story of Robert, Ellen's son, who is also a pianoplayer, or, more properly, a pianist, as his grandfather Billy defined it.

Robert marries an Awful Girl, who brings her Awful Mother to live with them. They go on holiday to Europe in the Awful Mother's car, and in Italy the Awful Mother dies suddenly, and ... yes, you guessed it, it's the one about The Dead Mother-In-Law Strapped To The Roof Rack. And with this, admittedly funny, old chestnut, the book straggles to a close.

The reader's enjoyment of *The Pianoplayers* will depend entirely on what he or she expects from Mr. Burgess. Up to the time of, say, *ABBA ABBA*, his work was – with some large exceptions – firmly a part of the Joycean school, and as such it produced novels that were among the most interesting and exciting in the language. He had a gift, as did the master before him, of expressing a vast appetite for life in the strict forms of art.

His masterpiece of that period is surely *Napoleon Symphony*, a marvellously funny, moving novel composed around the model of the Eroica Symphony. Then came *Earthly Powers*, a stupendously bad, wonderfully entertaining saga which set its author firmly at the top of the best-seller lists.

The Pianoplayers is definitely a chip off that blockbuster. No doubt it will sell, and earn a great deal of pottage – which is nice, for who would begrudge Mr. Burgess his popular success at this stage of an impressive career? All the same, for this reader, at least, it is sad to see an artist of his skill and sensitivity allowing into print what is, by any standard of judgement, a botched book.

Notes

20   **A Liana / che conosce tutta la scala / cromatica dell' amore:** Italian, 'To Liana, who knows the entire chromatic scale of love'. Liliana Macellari Burgess (1929–2007) was Burgess's second wife, whom he married in 1968.

21   **Callian:** Burgess owned a house on 6 Rue des Muets, Callian, from around 1976. Callian is approximately 85 km west of Monaco, where the Burgesses had their main residence.

22   **Thus Spoke Zarathustra:** *Also sprach Zarathustra*, an orchestral tone poem written in 1896 by Richard Strauss, based on the philosophical novel by Friedrich Nietzsche.

22   **Sukiyaki Violin Method:** The Suzuki Violin Method was an approach to teaching the violin based on language acquisition techniques developed by Shinichi Suzuki (1898–1998). Sukiyaki is a Japanese hotpot-style dish.

23   **John le Carré:** (b. 1931), spy novelist. Burgess reviewed a number of Le Carré's novels, mainly unfavourably. Writing about *A Perfect Spy* for the *Observer* ('Defector as Hero', 16 March 1986) Burgess remarked that 'Mr le Carré's talents cry out to be employed in the creation of a real novel'.

24   **caporal:** a type of strong, dark tobacco.

25   **grenier:** French, 'loft'.

26   **It is his work, but the story is all mine. Meaning my father's story and mine:** In the 1982 manuscript draft of the novel these sentences read: 'The spelling and commas and so on are all his, but the story is all mine. Meaning me and

my father's story' (Anthony Burgess Papers at the Harry Ransom Center at the University of Texas at Austin, box 42, folder 5, p. 6).

28   **I was born while the First World War was hammering and clattering away with the loud pedal down:** The equivalent section in *Little Wilson and Big God* (1987) begins 'I was born when the war was at its grimmest' (p. 17) and the details of this part of *The Pianoplayers* closely match those given by Burgess in his autobiography. See Introduction, page 12.

29   **No. 81 Bagshot Street, Harpurhey:** Burgess was born at number 91 Carisbrook Street, Harpurhey, a district of north Manchester.

29   **Preston, Lancs:** city approximately 50 km north of Manchester. Like Billy Henshaw, Burgess's father was in the army when his wife and daughter died, but Burgess does not tell a story about him having a premonition of their deaths in his memoirs.

29   **Delauneys Road, Higher Crumpsall:** Delaunays Road. Compare *Little Wilson and Big God*: 'I came to full consciousness in a terraced house on Delauney's Road, Higher Crumpsall, in the care of my mother's sister' (p. 18). Higher Crumpsall is another district of north Manchester.

30   **Garveau of Paris, *Médaille d'Or* 1878:** Burgess kept a Gaveau piano that once belonged to the cabaret star Josephine Baker in his Monaco apartment. The first manuscript draft has the correct spelling but it is possible that this error was introduced deliberately for the second draft.

30   **Queen's Road, Miles Platting:** Queen's Road is a main thoroughfare in Miles Platting, another district of north Manchester.

30   **bob:** one shilling (twelve pence) in pre-decimal currency, also notated as 1/-.

30   **Golden Eagle, Lodge Street, Miles Platting:** Burgess lived in the Golden Eagle, a large and boisterous public house, of which his stepmother was the landlady between 1922 and 1924. He gives a detailed account of his life there and the

music that was played in the pub in *Little Wilson and Big God* (pp. 22–35).

32   **Rosie O'Brien**: Burgess's stepmother was Margaret Dwyer, also of Manchester Irish heritage.

32   **mardarse**: a pejorative for a sulky, spoilt person, from the Northern English dialect 'mardy', and 'arse'. See Jonathon Green, *Green's Dictionary of Slang* (Oxford: Chambers, 2010).

32   **Lincroft Street off Moss Lane East**: Burgess's father and step-mother ran an off-licence at 261 Moss Lane East, on the corner of Lincroft Street, close to their home at 21 Princess Road.

32   **Royal Cinema, run by Jakie Innerfield**: Jakie Innerfield was the proprietor of the Palace cinema in Manchester, and is presented by Burgess in *Little Wilson and Big God* as holding out stubbornly against the advent of talking pictures (p. 104).

32   *News of the World*: Sunday tabloid newspaper published between 1843 and 2011.

33   *The Singing Fool*: (1928), directed by Lloyd Bacon. A sing-ing waiter and composer (Al Jolson) loves two women (Betty Bronson, Josephine Dunn) and conquers Broadway. The final number as he holds his dying son is 'Sonny Boy'. Burgess gives a vivid account of his own experience of seeing this film in 1929 at the Claremont cinema in Manchester in *Little Wilson and Big God* (p. 103).

33   **Mendelssohn's Spring Song**: 'Frühlingslied' (1842–44), from *Lieder ohne Worte* (*Songs Without Words*) Book 5, Op. 62, No. 6, by Felix Mendelssohn.

34   **Poet and Peasant Overture**: the overture to the operetta *Dichter und Bauer* (1846) by Franz von Suppé.

34   **Rubinstein's Melody in F**: 'Melody in F', Op. 3 No. 1 by Anton Rubinstein.

34   **Paderooski**: Ignacy Paderewski (1860–1941), Polish pianist, composer and prime minister.

35   **Pretty Redwing**: 'Red Wing' (1907), a popular song with music by Kerry Mills and lyrics by Thurland Chattaway. It

was parodied during the First World War by British school-
children to amend the lyrics to mock Charlie Chaplin's
refusal to enlist.

35   **Charlie Chaplin**: Charlie Chaplin (1889–1977), comedian
and film actor. His stage career began in Manchester in 1899
with the troupe The Eight Lancashire Lads.

35   **Chester Conklin**: Chester Conklin (1886–1971), comedian and film actor. He and Chaplin starred in many films
together including *The Great Dictator* (1940).

35   **Bass's Pale Ale**: an English pale ale made in Burton-on-
Trent, Staffordshire, one of the bestselling beers of the
late nineteenth and early twentieth centuries. A particular
favourite of Burgess's father.

36   **a pair of wooden rickers**: rickers are simple percussion
instruments made from wood, bone or other hard material,
held between the fingers of one hand and brought together
to make a distinctive clicking sound. Here the effect seems to
be to mimic that of horses' hooves.

36   **Blue Danube waltz**: *An der schönen blauen Donau*, Op. 314
(1866) by Johann Strauss.

36   **There was this Mary Pickford film in which she sings
Home Sweet Home**: *Home, Sweet Home* (1914), directed
by D.W. Griffith. A silent film about the writing of the
song by John Howard Payne in 1822. Mary Pickford did not
appear in this film, which starred Dorothy Gish.

41   **Here Comes The Bride**: *Treulich geführt*, from the opera
Lohengrin (1850), by Richard Wagner.

41   **Get Out And Get Under**: 'He'd Have to Get Under – Get
Out and Get Under (to Fix Up His Automobile)' (1913), a
popular song with music by Maurice Abrahams and lyrics
by Grant Clarke and Edgar Leslie. It was a hit for Al Jolson
(1913) and Billy Murray (1914) and made fun of the trials of
car owners seeking to impress with their flashy but unrelia-
ble machines.

41   **The Roast Beef Of Old England**: a ballad by Henry Fielding,
part of *The Grub Street Opera* (1731) and traditionally sung

by theatre audiences before or after a performance of a new play.

41 **Wilson's the Tobacconist:** Joseph Wilson and Burgess's stepmother Maggie Dwyer ran 'Wilson's Tobacconists' at 47 Princess Road, Manchester. The family lived above the shop.

41 **Cigarette Girls' Chorus from the opera Carmen:** 'La cloche a sonné' from *Carmen* (1875) by Georges Bizet. Burgess's translation of *Carmen* was performed by the English National Opera in 1986 and was published by Hutchinson in the same year.

41 **Colonel Bogey:** 'Colonel Bogey March' (1914) by Kenneth J. Alford.

41 **Blaze Away:** 'Blaze Away March' (1901) by Abe Holzmann.

41 **God Bless The Prince Of Wales:** (1862) song with words by John Ceiriog Hughes and music by Henry Brinley Richards, written to mark the occasion of the marriage of the future King Edward VII of the United Kingdom to Alexandra of Denmark.

41 **Oh I Do Like To Be Beside The Seaside:** (1907) music hall song by John A. Glover-Kind about the pleasures of holidaying at English coastal resorts.

42 **Charlie Chase:** Charley Chase (1893–1940), comedian and film actor.

42 **Ain't She Sweet:** a 1927 song with music by Milton Ager and lyrics by Jack Yellen.

42 **Ben Hur:** *Ben-Hur: A Tale of the Christ* (1925), an epic silent film adaptation of the 1880 novel by Lew Wallace, directed by Fred Niblo.

42 **C A B B A G E F A C E:** Burgess claims in *Little Wilson and Big God* to have written and sold this song to 'a Manchester comedian' in 1937 (p. 163).

42 **Metro Polis:** *Metropolis* (1927), epic silent science fiction film directed by Fritz Lang that made a profound impression on Burgess when he saw it in Manchester. Later, Burgess accompanied a screening of the film at the University of Iowa in 1975, and selected it as one of his ten favourites for

a special season at the National Film Theatre in 1984. He writes in *You've Had Your Time* (1990) that 'My father had done this, twice nightly, thrice on Saturdays, but he had only the much edited reduction, which granted his hands a rest after ninety minutes. I played for nearly four hours' (p. 326).

48   **Lewis's**: part of a national chain of department stores, this was a large shop on Market Street, Manchester, open between 1877 and 2002.

49   **It's a long long lane / That has no turning**: lines from 'It's a Long Lane that Has No Turning' (1911) by Manuel Klein, popularised in the revue *Around the World* at the New York Hippodrome in 1912 and frequently revived.

49   **Boosey and Hawkes**: music publishers, formed in 1930 through the merger of the companies Boosey & Company and Hawkes & Son.

50   **ki-yike**: possibly leering suggestively. Compare *Enderby Outside* (1968): '[Easy Walker] stretched his left mouth-corner, as also the left tendon of his neck, and held the pose tremulously. This, Enderby seemed to remember, was known as the ki-yike' (p. 118).

50   **Skippers sardines**: a popular brand of tinned fish produced by Angus Watson & Co. in the 1920s.

51   **Lionel Monckton**: (1861–1924) popular writer and composer of Edwardian musical theatre.

51   **Ardwick Empire**: music hall in the Ardwick district of east Manchester.

52   **Vesta Tilley**: Matilda Powles (1864–1952), a music hall performer and one of the most famous male impersonators of the period.

52   **Guinness**: a brand of Irish stout. Nutritious but calorific.

53   **A negg and some nam and a nonion**: a song popularised by Ernie Mayne (1871–1937), music hall performer.

53   **Kruschens**: Kruschen salts, used as an aid to digestion.

53   **Charles Peace**: (1832–79), notorious burglar and murderer, hanged at Armley Prison in Leeds.

53   Fred Karno: Frederick Westcott (1866–1941), theatre impresario and music hall comedian. His company employed many
music hall stars at the beginning of their careers, including
Charlie Chaplin and Stan Laurel.

53   Casey's Court: the name of a sketch set in a courtroom produced by a group of performers working for Fred Karno.

53   Stan Laurel: (1890–1965), born Arthur Stanley Jefferson.
His early career in music hall, notably as Charlie Chaplin's
understudy, later developed into a successful film career
with Oliver Hardy.

54   Wild Woodbines: strong unfiltered cigarettes, sometimes
known as 'gaspers'.

55   King George V chocolates: a brand of chocolates sold
in half- and one-pound boxes and made by Cadbury
Bournville.

55   Trig: trigonemetry.

56   fags: cigarettes (British slang).

56   *The Light Of The World*: Compare *Little Wilson and Big
God*: 'We all, young as we were, recognised that sound
pushed back the art of film to the infantile. We missed the
old biblical epics *The Ten Commandments, Noah's Ark*
(Cecil B. De Mille [*sic*], like his master D.W. Griffith, knew
the appeal, before James Joyce, of a compound of myth and
contemporaneity)' (p. 105). *The Light Of The World* appears
to be an invention by Burgess.

56   Hymns Ancient and Modern: standard hymnal used in the
Church of England since 1861.

57   Housey Housey: bingo.

58   HMV portable: a brand of portable gramophone.

58   kalied: extremely drunk, likely to be from standard English
'alcohol'. Eric Partridge notes 'kali-water' for champagne
in the *Dictionary of Slang and Unconventional English*
(London: Routledge, 1969).

58   Adeste Fideles: 'O Come All Ye Faithful', in Latin.

59   In A Persian Market: piece of orchestral music from 1920
by Albert Ketèlbey (1875–1959). Ketèlbey's light classical

style was hugely successful in the 1910s and 1920s, and he wrote many pieces to accompany silent films.

61   **Faith Of Our Fathers**: an English Catholic hymn from 1849 sung to the traditional tune *Sawston*, with words by Frederick William Faber.

63   **stockingfeeter**: possibly a variant of 'stocking-foot(er)': military slang for a projectile approaching noiselessly (Partridge).

64   **Dr Crippen**: Hawley Harvey Crippen (1862–1910), homeopath and murderer. Hanged in Pentonville Prison, London, for the killing of his wife Cora, a music hall entertainer with the stage name 'Belle Elmore'.

64   **Smith, the Brides in the Bath murderer**: George Joseph Smith (1872–1915), bigamist and murderer. Smith drowned three of his wives in bathtubs in order to steal their money.

64   **Nearer My God To Thee**: One of the details of the 'Brides in the Bath' murder case was that Smith played this nineteenth-century hymn by Sarah Flower Adams on a harmonium while his victims drowned. The hymn is popularly believed to have been played by the band on the RMS *Titanic* as the liner sank in 1912. See Introduction and Appendix 1.

64   **shives**: slices, from 'shiv', a knife (Green).

64   **Heinz's 57 varieties**: a marketing slogan devised in 1896 by the Heinz company, bottlers and canners of beans, sauces and other products.

64   **jaxy**: arse (Green).

65   **Chorlton on Medlock**: an area of central Manchester, blighted in the early twentieth century by cotton mills and poor housing.

66   **the Maiden's Prayer**: *Modlitwa dziewicy* (1865), a sentimental piano piece by Tekla Bądarzewska-Baranowska.

66   **Bovril**: a brand of salty brown beef extract first sold in 1889, usually consumed as a hot drink or spread on bread.

66   **Barth and Parth and Clahss**: i.e. 'bath', 'path' and 'class' spoken with a long 'a', characteristic of British received

pronunciation and often taken to be a mark of privilege, especially in northern England.

67 **Cadbury's Milk Chocolate Fingers**: chocolate-covered biscuit confectionery made by the Cadbury company.

68 **Eyetie**: a pejorative for 'Italian' (Green).

69 **No. 88 Claremont Road**: Claremont Road leads from Princess Road (now Princess Parkway) in the Moss Side area of Manchester.

69 **2ZY**: the first local radio station in Manchester, which broadcast from a factory in the Trafford Park area from 1922.

69 **dandelion and burdock**: a soft drink made with extracts of these common English plants.

69 **Half a dollar**: slang for half a crown, which is to say two shillings and sixpence (thirty pence) in pre-decimal currency.

69 **the Age of Consent**: the legal age of consent to heterosexual activity has been sixteen years old in England since 1885.

70 **Mortal Sin**: a Roman Catholic category of sin that is particularly severe, having the characteristics of being a fault committed in full knowledge of the severity of the offence.

71 **a bit jiggered up**: exhausted, beaten (Green).

72 **Deansgate**: a major thoroughfare in central Manchester.

72 *The Jazz Singer* **with Al Jolson**. 1927 film directed by Alan Crosland. A major international success and the first feature-length film with synchronised dialogue. The account by Ellen here is accurate in that the film include less than two minutes of talking and the main audio is the musical numbers played from separate sound discs.

72 **Kol Nidrei**: Jewish traditional, sung at the beginning of the evening service at Yom Kippur (the Day of Atonement).

72 **I'd walk a million miles for one of your smiles my mammeeeeee**: 'My Mammy', popular song with music by Walter Donaldson and lyrics by Joe Young and Sam M. Lewis. A considerable success for Al Jolson, who performed it as part of the musical *Sinbad* in 1918, recorded it twice and performed it in three films: *The Jazz Singer* (1927), *The Singing Fool* (1928) and *Rose of Washington Square* (1939).

72   **Vitaphone**: an analogue system for presenting sound during films used by Warner Brothers between 1926 and 1931. Shellac sound discs would be played in tandem with the film reels by the projectionist.

73   *The Doctor's Secret*: 1929 film written and directed by William C. deMille and based on a play of the same title by J.M. Barrie.

73   *Weary River*: 1929 film directed by Frank Lloyd. A part-silent and part-talking hybrid.

73   *Broadway*: 1929 film directed by Pál Fejös. The first talking picture from Universal Studios with colour sequences. The actor Regis Toomey did not feature in this film but did appear in two others from that year, *Rich People* and *The Wheel of Life*.

73   *The Fox Movietone Follies of 1929*: a musical film with colour sequences released by Fox Film Corporation.

73   *Broadway Melody*: 1929 musical film with colour sequences and the first sound film to win an Academy Award for Best Picture.

73   *Innocents of Paris*: 1929 musical film directed by Richard Wallace and starring Maurice Chevalier, though not Claudette Colbert. Chevalier and Colbert appeared together in the 1930 film *The Big Pond*.

74   *The Secrets of the Soul*: *Geheimnisse einer Seele* (1926), a silent film directed by Georg Wilhelm Pabst. Burgess tells this story again in *Little Wilson and Big God* (p. 105).

74   **Snark**: informer (Green).

75   **french letters**: contraceptive sheaths, condoms (Green).

75   **HP Sauce ... Daddies and A1 and OK and Yorkshire Relish**: brands of brown sauce, a spicy and vinegary condiment.

76   **clemmed**: starving, wasting away from hunger (Green).

76   **alegar**: vinegar made from ale.

76   **marge**: margarine.

76   **grocer's peas**: dried peas, rehydrated and boiled to a pulp, usually known as 'mushy peas'.

76   **Eccles cakes**: a confectionery made from flaky pastry

and currants. Eccles is a town to the west of Greater Manchester.

76 **barmcake**: a large bread roll, baked on the floor of the oven. From 'barm', meaning yeast, and 'cake', meaning here a baked product (Partridge).

76 **Liptons or Seymour Meads**: brands of tea.

77 **Total Eclipse of the Sun**: On 29 June 1927 there was the first solar eclipse in England for 203 years. The event made a significant impression on Burgess, and as well as in *The Pianoplayers* he recalls it in *Little Wilson and Big God*, *The End of the World News* and the article 'Apocalypse and After' (reprinted as 'Endtime' in *Homage to Qwert Yuiop* (1986), pp. 12–16)

77 **Black Bottom**: dance craze in the US and UK during the 1920s, similar to the Charleston.

77 **Woolworth's**: chain of high street shops selling cheap household goods and sweets, trading between 1909 and 2009.

77 **a tanner**: a sixpence piece.

78 **He's Got 'Em On**: 'he's doing things in style'. Described in Eric Partridge's *Slang: Today and Yesterday* (London: Routledge, 1933) as 'ordinary Cockney' slang, i.e. non-rhyming. The song 'He's Got 'Em On' was written in 1891 by Fred Carlos.

79 **Yates's Wine Lodge**: pub chain founded in 1884 in the north-west of England.

79 **the Prom**: Blackpool Promenade, the main road along the seafront in the city.

79 **spotted dick**: suet pudding with dried fruit.

79 **Yorkshire pud**: batter pudding usually served with roast beef.

79 **When there's a snice smince pie**: 1914 comic song by Worton David and Burt Lee, and performed by Jay Laurier, music hall entertainer and film actor.

80 **Eiffel Tower Lemonade Crystals**: brand of concentrated lemonade crystals drunk when diluted with water, made by Foster Clark Ltd.

80   **Noah's Ark:** an immersive fun house experience based on the Biblical story, operational at Blackpool Pleasure Beach theme park between 1922 and 2008.

80   **Big Dipper:** wooden rollercoaster at Blackpool Pleasure Beach. The Big Dipper opened in 1923 and is still in use.

80   **Bradford and Chorley and Bury:** industrial towns in northern England.

80   **Wakes week:** originally religious festivals, wakes weeks became secular holidays in the north of England during the industrial revolution, when all factories and businesses from a particular town would close at once and the workers would decamp to the same resort.

80   **Southport:** fishing port and resort in north-west England.

83   **Marshall Aid:** The Marshall Plan was a US initiative to provide economic support to European countries after the Second World War.

85   **Monti's Czardas:** 1904 composition by Vittorio Monti (1868–1922), popular with so-called gypsy orchestras.

86   **Dancing On The Ceiling:** 1930 popular song composed by Richard Rodgers with lyrics by Lorenz Hart for the musical *Ever Green.*

86   **Dancing With Tears In My Eyes:** 1930 popular song by Joe Burke and Al Dubin.

86   **Dance Dance Dance Little Lady:** 'Dance, Little Lady', song by Noel Coward from the 1928 revue *This Year of Grace.*

87   **Up In The Garret Away From The Din:** 1929 song composed by Howard Fisher and with lyrics by Helen Taylor.

88   **Sparks:** 1927 march for xylophone and piano or orchestra by Kenneth J. Alford.

88   **On The Track:** 1934 march for xylophone and ensemble by Jack Simpson (1905–44)

89   **Hot Club de France:** the Quintette du Hot Club de France was an influential jazz group active between 1934 and 1948, founded by guitarist Django Rheinhardt (1910–1953) and violinist Stéphane Grappelli (1908–1997).

89   Pale Hands I Loved: 'Kashmiri Song' (1904) by Amy
          Woodforde-Finden (1860–1919). Popular drawing-room
          standard before the Second World War, and played
          during Christmas parties at the Golden Eagle in Miles
          Platting (*Little Wilson and Big God*, p. 27; also see note to
          p. 30).

91   Camp Coffee Essence: brand of coffee substitute.

92   printer's called Grigson's: Geoffrey Grigson (1905–85),
          poet, writer and critic, and Burgess's nemesis. Grigson
          reviewed Burgess's collection of literary journalism *Urgent
          Copy* unfavourably in 1968 and thereafter appeared as a vil-
          lain or an otherwise unattractive character in a number of his
          novels.

92   the Tower: Blackpool Tower (built 1891–94), a tour-
          ist attraction on Blackpool seafront inspired by the Eiffel
          Tower in Paris.

93   Lea and Perrin's: Lea & Perrins Worcestershire sauce, a
          condiment. Thinner and spicier than HP Sauce but equally
          brown.

94   Dempsey like the boxer: Jack Dempsey (1895–1983), world
          heavyweight champion between 1919 and 1926.

95   dago: a pejorative for 'Spanish' (Green)

98   kex: variant of 'kecks', from 'kicks', a dialect word for trou-
          sers (Green).

100   tubbing: washing (in a bath) (Green).

102   the opera Samson and Delilah: *Samson et Dalila* (1877),
          Op. 47, by Camille Saint-Saëns.

102   The Dying Swan: 'Le Cygne' from *Le Carnaval des ani-
          maux* (1886) by Camille Saint-Saëns ('Saint Sawn'), later so
          dubbed when choreographed by Fokine for Pavlova.

102   Barney's bull: Australian slang meaning extremely fatigued
          or physically distressed. Often added to the phrase 'bitched,
          buggered and bewildered' (Partridge).

104   a packet of Players: bestselling brand of filter cigarettes.

105   *The Well Of Loneliness*: 1928 novel by Radclyffe Hall
          (1880–1943) about lesbian relationships. Banned in the UK

after an obscenity trial on publication, the book eventually reappeared in 1949.

113   PT: 'pricktease', someone who appears to be offering unrestrained sexual favours but stops short of intercourse, leaving the male partner frustrated (Green).

113   the sculpture by Einstein called Genesis: a reference to the sculptor Jacob Epstein (1880–1959). Sculptures by Epstein including 'Genesis' and 'Adam', considered very controversial in the 1930s, were shown in Blackpool to enormous popular and critical acclaim by composer, music publisher and impresario Lawrence Wright. Wright also commissioned a companion piece 'Eve' and exhibited 'Jacob and the Angel' for two years from 1942. 'Genesis was gaped at with awe as indecent art. Indecency and vulgarity were all part of the Blackpool holiday' (Little Wilson and Big God, p. 129). The sculpture is now at the Whitworth Art Gallery, Manchester. See note to p. 131.

113   a clergyman who had been defrocked for dirty things and was trying to cash in on the scandal of the other one: a somewhat unlikely sideshow attraction. Harold Davidson (1875–1937), the Rector of Stiffkey, was an eccentric clergyman expelled from the Church of England in 1932 after a scandal related to his work rescuing young women from prostitution. Davidson resumed his career as an entertainer in Blackpool and exhibited himself in a barrel, ostensibly working on his legal case against the Church authorities, to be gawped at by holidaymakers. Ellen seems to be describing an attempt by another defrocked clergyman to cash in on this notoriety.

115   John Haig: a brand of Scotch whisky.

115   Salute Damoor: Salut d'Amour (1888) by Edward Elgar, a piece for violin and piano and one of the composer's most successful works.

116   soda fountain: small café-style concession selling soft drinks and ice-cream.

119   RCM: Royal College of Music, London.

119   **Tabs:** stage term for curtains.

120   **Pally Archie:** *Pagliacci* (1892), a popular opera by Ruggero Leoncavallo about the fatal jealousies among a troupe of travelling actors. 'Is not the actor a man with a heart like you' is a line from the Prologue.

122   **benza or bonza something:** the stimulant benzedrine.

125   **Craven A and Kensitas and Black Cat:** defunct brands of cigarettes.

125   **Swan Vestas:** a brand of matches.

126   **Avalon:** 1920 popular song and jazz standard by Al Jolson, Buddy DeSylva and Vincent Rose, and included in the musicals *Sinbad* and *Bombo*. Played at the Golden Eagle (see note to p. 30).

126   **Mountain Greenery:** 1926 song composed by Richard Rodgers, with lyrics by Lorenz Hart, for the musical *The Garrick Gaieties*.

126   **California Here I Come:** 1921 song for the musical *Bombo*, starring Al Jolson, written by Jolson, Buddy DeSylva and Joseph Meyer.

126   **Carolina In The Morning:** 1922 popular song with words by Gus Kahn and music by Walter Donaldson. Rerecorded many times including by Al Jolson in 1947.

126   **Happy Days and Lonely Nights:** 1928 song by written by Billy Rose and Fred Fisher, made popular by Ruth Etting.

126   **Beethoven's Mignonette in G:** *Minuet in G*, Op. 10, No. 2, by Beethoven.

126   **Paderooski's Mignonette:** *Minuet in G*, Op. 14, No. 1, by Paderewski.

126   **O Shinanacky Da He Play Guitar Outside De Bazaar Haha Haha:** traditional English song about Turkey. A hit in 1929 for Jack Hylton And His Orchestra, a leading popular and jazz ensemble active between 1923 and the Second World War.

126   **You Were Meant For Me:** 1929 song with by Nacio Herb Brown and Arthur Freed, featuring in the musical film *The Broadway Melody*.

126   **Sonny Boy**: closing number of the Al Jolson film *The Singing Fool* (1928).

126   **Für Elise**: Bagatelle No. 25 in A minor (1810) by Ludwig van Beethoven (1770–1827).

126   **Handel's Lager**: 'Handel's *Largo*', popular title for 'Ombra mai fu', the opening aria from the 1738 opera *Serse* by George Frideric Handel.

126   **In A Monastery Garden**: a 1915 piece of light classical music by Albert Ketèlbey. This was his first major success and sold over a million copies.

126   **The Sanctuary of the Heart**: music by Albert Ketèlbey, composed 1924.

126   **Handel's Water Music**: 1717, a collection of orchestral movements by Handel.

126   **Eine Kleine Something**: *Eine kleine Nachtmusik* (Serenade No. 13 for strings in G major, 1787): a chamber composition by Mozart.

126   **cavalry Rusticano**: *Cavalleria rusticana* (1890), a one-act opera by Pietro Mascagni. Often performed alongside *Pagliacci* (see note to p. 120) and here presented as part of a medley of well-known tunes from popular operas.

126   **Tan Houser**: *Tannhäuser* (1845), opera by Richard Wagner.

126   **Carnival of the Animals**: 1886 musical suite in fourteen movements by Saint-Saëns.

126   **Refuse in the Underground**: *Orpheus in the Underworld* (original French title: *Orphée aux enfers*), 1858 operetta by Jacques Offenbach (1818–90). The 'Infernal Galop' from the second act is better known as the music for the can-can.

126   **When It's Nighttime in Italy It's Wednesday Over Here**: 1923 song by James Kendis and Lew Brown. Burgess recalls in *Little Wilson and Big God* his stepsister Madge playing this at the Wilsons' house at 21 Princess Road, Manchester. 'One of the lines ran: "Oh, the onions in Sicily make people cry in California". So they ought to cry, the bewraying buggers' (p. 38).

126   **Rule Britannia Two Tanners Make A Bob**: variant of the

1740 British patriotic song by Thomas Arne, with obscene lyrics.

126   **the Marsellayse:** the *Marseillaise*, French national anthem.

126   **Over There Over There For The Yanks Are Coming:** 1917 patriotic song by George M. Cohan about the entry of America into the First World War.

126   **Keep The Home Fires Burning:** 1914 patriotic song by Ivor Novello and Lena Guilbert Ford.

126   **There's A Long Long Trail A-Winding:** 1914 song popular during the First World War written by Stoddard King and Alonzo Elliot.

126   **If You Were The Only Girl In The World:** 1916 song by Nat D. Ayer and Clifford Grey, written for the musical revue *The Bing Boys Are Here*. Now a standard and recorded many times. *The Bing Boys Are Here* was one of the most popular light entertainment shows in wartime London.

126   **Let The Great Big World Keep Turning:** 1916 song by Nat D. Ayer and Clifford Grey, written for the musical revue *The Bing Boys Are Here*.

126   **Yes We Have No Bananas:** 1922 novelty song by Frank Silver and Irving Cohen, which when recorded by Billy Jones became a number one hit in America for five weeks. Played at the Golden Eagle (see note to p. 30).

126   **I Lift Up My Finger And I Say Tweet Tweet Hush Hush Now Now Come Come:** novelty song recorded in 1929 by variety artist and radio entertainer Leslie Sarony, and Jack Hylton And His Orchestra.

126   **Never Be Cruel To A Vegitubel:** again recorded by Leslie Sarony and Jack Hylton And His Orchestra. Sarony made a 1928 short film which included him in character singing this song as a vegetable rights campaigner.

126   **Bye Bye Blackbird:** 1926 standard written by Ray Henderson and Mort Dixon. Recorded in 1929 by Jack Hylton And His Orchestra. Burgess recalls in *Little Wilson and Big God* that a record of this song was in the house at 21 Princess Road, Manchester (p. 38).

126   **Me And Jane In A Plane**: 1927 song written by Joseph George Gilbert. Recorded in 1927 by Jack Hylton And His Orchestra. Another record in the drawing-room at 21 Princess Road, and one for which Burgess writes out the lyrics in his autobiography. 'Why does one remember these vapidities so well?' (*Little Wilson and Big God*, p. 38).

126   **Poor Papa (He Ain't Got Nothing At All)**: 1926 song by Billy Rose and Harry Woods, a hit for Irving Aaronson and his Commanders.

126   **My Hero from the Chocolate Soldier**: a song from the 1908 operetta *The Chocolate Soldier* (*Der tapfere Soldat*) by Oscar Straus (1870–1954), based on George Bernard Shaw's 1894 play *Arms and the Man*.

126   **Show Boat**: Hugely popular and frequently revived 1927 musical by Jerome Kern and Oscar Hammerstein.

126   **Rose Marie I Love You**: song from the 1924 musical *Rose Marie* by Rudolf Friml, Herbert Stothart, Otto Harbach and Oscar Hammerstein. A film version appeared in 1928.

126   **Indian Love Call**: the biggest hit from the musical *Rose Marie*.

126   **The Man Who Broke The Bank At Monte Carlo**: music hall song from 1891, by Fred Gilbert (1850–1903). Popularised by the musical hall entertainer Charles Coborn (1852–1945) who claimed to have performed it more than a quarter of a million times and in fourteen languages.

126   **Daisy Daisy**: *Daisy Bell* (*Bicycle Built For Two*), composed by Harry Dacre in 1892.

126   **She Was A Sweet Little Dicky Bird**: music hall song from 1895 by T.W. Connor. The lyrics were often sung to the same tune as *Daisy Bell*, above.

126   **The Peer Gynt Suite**: popular classical music written in 1875 by Edvard Greig originally composed as incidental music to the play of the same name by Henrik Ibsen.

126   **Beethoven's Pathetic**: piano sonata No. 8 in C minor, Op. 13 (*Pathétique*) (1798) by Beethoven.

127   **Here's Another One Off To America**: 1904 song by Arthur
       Mills. Played at the Golden Eagle (see note to p. 30).
127   **Philadelphia In The Morning**: Irish traditional.
127   **Finnegan's Ball**: Irish traditional. A song played at the
       Golden Eagle (see note to p. 30).
127   **Phil The Fluter's Ball**: Irish traditional.
127   **After The Ball Is Over**: 1892 popular song by Charles Harris.
       The biggest-selling song in sheet music form in the history of
       Tin Pan Alley. The first verse and chorus appear in the musi-
       cal *Show Boat* to exemplify the musical style of the 1890s.
127   **Balls To Mr Bangelstein**: obscene song popular with
       rugby players and army soldiers with the tune of *Ach, Du
       Lieber, Augustin* (Viennese traditional). A version appears
       in Burgess's novel *Inside Mister Enderby* (1963) as 'Balls to
       Mister Enderby'.
127   **Over The Waves**: *Sobre las Olas* (1888), classic popular
       waltz by Juventino Rosas.
127   **Voices Of Spring**: *Frühlingsstimmen* (1882), waltz by
       Johann Strauss.
127   **Tales From The Vienna Woods** *Geschichten aus dem
       Wienerwald* (1868), waltz by Johann Strauss.
127   **The Skaters Waltz**: *Les Patineurs Valse* (1882) by Émile
       Waldteufel.
127   **They Call Me The Belle Of New York**: song from *The Belle
       of New York* (1897), a musical comedy by High Morton
       and Gustave Kerker. The first American musical to run for
       more than a year in the West End. A silent film version was
       released in 1919, directed by Julius Steger.
127   **Borodin's Polovsky Dances**: 'Polovtsian Dances' (first
       performed 1890) from the opera *Prince Igor* by Alexander
       Borodin.
127   **Lady Be Good**: song from the 1924 musical of the same
       name by George and Ira Gershwin.
127   **The Girl With The Flaxen Hair**: 'La fille aux cheveux de
       lin', the eighth in the first book of *Préludes* (1910) by Claude
       Debussy.

127   **Great Dirty Songs**: presumably a medley of these traditional tunes which are usually sung with obscene lyrics.

127   **Loch Lomond**: traditional Scottish.

127   **Ye Banks and Braes**: a version of *The Banks O'Doon* (1791) by Robert Burns. Burgess wrote a fugue for piano using the tune in 1981.

127   **Mother Macree**: traditional Irish.

127   **The Harp That Once**: *The Harp That Once Through Tara's Halls* by Thomas Moore (1779–1852). An Irish protest song.

127   **The Mountains of Mourne**: song by Percy French (1854–1920) to a traditional Irish folk tune.

127   **John Brown's Body**: traditional United States.

127   **Softly Awakes My Heart**: 'Mon cœur s'ouvre à ta voix', an aria from the Saint-Saëns opera *Samson et Dalila*.

127   **Wayward is Womankind**: a translation of 'La donna è mobile' from the 1851 opera *Rigoletto* by Giuseppe Verdi (1813–1901).

127   **The Bach Gounod Ave Maria**: a version of the Latin text *Ave Maria* by Charles Gounod (1818–1893), with a melody by him over the Prelude No. 1 in C major from Book I of J.S. Bach's *The Well-Tempered Clavier* (1722). Originally published in 1853 as *Méditation sur le Premier Prélude de Piano de J.S. Bach*.

127   **the other Ave Maria**: possibly *Ellens dritter Gesang* (1825) by Franz Schubert, one of his extremely popular settings from Walter Scott's poem *The Lady of the Lake* (1810).

127   **My Little Grey Home In The West**: sentimental 1911 song by Hermann Lohr (1876–1943).

127   **Smilin' Through**: 1919 ballad by Arthur A. Penn, the title music for a 1922 silent film of the same name, directed by Sidney Franklin.

127   **Somewhere In Sahara**: 'While The Sahara Sleeps', a 1927 song by Lawrence Wright composing as Horatio Nicholls. Burgess recalls this song and 'Shepherd Of The Hills' (below) in *Little Wilson and Big God*, p. 128.

127   **Shepherd Of The Hills I Hear You Calling**: 1927 song

by Horatio Nicholls and Edgar Leslie. Recorded by Jack
Hylton And His Orchestra in that year.

127 **Because You Come To Me With Naught Save Love:**
song by Guy d'Hardelot and Edward Teschemacher, first
published in 1902. Played at the Golden Eagle (see note to
p. 30).

127 **Pale Hands I Loved:** See note to p. 89.

127 **All Through The Night There's A Little Brown Bird
Singing:** 1922 ballad by Haydn Wood and Rodney Bennett.

127 **Little Brown Jug Don't I Love Thee:** 1869 drinking song
by Joseph Winner. Later popularised by Glen Miller And
His Orchestra during the Prohibition era.

127 **Beer Beer Glorious Beer:** 1895 drinking song by Steve
Leggett and Will J. Godwin.

127 **Dear Old Pals:** 1898 song by Will J. Godwin and Charlie
Chaplin.

127 **Come To Your Nabob On Next Patrick's Day Be Mrs
Mumbo Jumbo Jitterboo Jay O'Shea:** lines from 'I've Got
Rings On My Fingers', a 1909 popular song by Maurice
Scott.

127 **Just A Song At Twilight:** 'Love's Old Sweet Song' (1884),
parlour song and also a popular song at pub closing time by
James Lynam Molloy and G. Clifton Bingham. It was used
as the theme song for the film *The Sea Beast* (1926), an adaptation of *Moby-Dick* (1851) by Herman Melville directed
by John Barrymore. Molly Bloom sings this song in *Ulysses*
(1922) by James Joyce.

127 **The End Of A Perfect Day:** 'A Perfect Day' (1909) by
Carrie Jacobs-Bond. The most popular song of 1910 in the
US and UK.

127 **The Rosary:** 'A Soldier's Rosary' (1911), American popular
song by Joseph Burke and G.E. Dempsey.

127 **Slow Tune For Two Fingers:** likely to be an invention by
Burgess.

127 **Twinkle Twinkle Little Star:** English traditional nursery
rhyme.

127   **Alice Where Art Thou**: 1861 parlour song by Wellington Guernsey and Joseph Ascher.

127   **The Sunshine Of Your Smile**: 1913 song by Lilian Ray and Leonard Cooke.

127   **You Wore A Tulip**: 'When You Wore a Tulip and I Wore a Big Red Rose' (1914), song by Jack Mahoney and Percy Weinrich.

129   **Happy Days Are Here Again**: 1929 song by Milton Ager and Jack Yellen. Later used by Franklin D. Roosevelt as the campaign song for his 1932 US presidential campaign.

129   **The Sunny Side Of The Street**: 1930 song by Jimmy McHugh and Dorothy Fields. Now a jazz standard.

129   **first book of 48**: Book one of J.S. Bach's *The Well-Tempered Clavier* (1722).

129   **Another Little Drink Wouldn't Do Us Any Harm**: 1916 hit song by Clifford Grey.

129   **The Frothblower's Anthem**: 'The More We Are Together', drinking song to the tune of *Ach, Du Lieber, Augustin* (Viennese traditional). See note to p. 127.

129   **Daddy Wouldn't Buy Me A Bow Wow (Bow Wow)**: 1892 comic song by Joseph Tabrar about the disappointment of having a cat instead of a dog.

129   **A Bachelor Guy Am I**: 'A Bachelor Gay Am I' (1916) from the musical *The Maid of the Mountains* by Harold Fraser-Simson and Harry Graham. First performed at the Prince's Theatre on Oxford Road, Manchester, on 23 December 1916.

129   **Love Will Find A Way**: the hit song of *The Maid of the Mountains*. A soppy duet.

129   **Little Nelly Jelly**: 'Nellie Kelly, I Love You' from the old-fashioned but successful 1922 musical *Little Nelly Jelly* by George M. Cohan. Played at the Golden Eagle (see note to p. 30).

129   **I'm A Yankee Doodle Dandy**: US patriotic song from the Broadway musical *Little Johnny Jones* (1904) by George M. Cohan.

129   **Will Ye No' Come Back Again**: Scottish traditional tune with words by Lady Nairne (c. 1745) about the Jacobite uprising.

129   **Musetta's song from La Bohème**: 'Quando m'en vo', a soprano aria from the 1896 opera by Puccini.

130   **Ma He's Making Eyes At Me**: 1921 song by Sidney Clare and Con Conrad. Played at the Golden Eagle (see note to p. 30).

130   **Am I Blue**: 1929 song by Harry Akst and Grant Clarke, and featured in the film *On with the Show*, directed by Alan Crosland in the same year. The first film with sound and colour throughout.

130   **Body And Soul**: 1930 popular song by Edward Heyman, Robert Sour, Frank Eyton and Johnny Green. Now a jazz standard.

130   **big tune from Raspberry in Blue Jars**: likely to refer to the theme from *Rhapsody in Blue* (1924) by George Gershwin.

130   **The Stein Song**: also known as 'The Maine Stein Song', the anthem of the University of Maine. Written by Lincoln Colcord in 1902, it was popularised by Rudy Vallee in 1930 and became a number one hit in the US.

130   **The Birth Of The Blues**: 1926 popular song by by Ray Henderson, Buddy G. DeSylva and Lew Brown.

130   **Chloe**: song by Al Jolson and Buddy G. DeSylva, featuring in the musical *Sinbad* (1918).

130   **Wagner's The Master Singers**: *Die Meistersinger von Nürnberg* (1868) by Richard Wagner. This opera was selected by Burgess as one of his *Desert Island Discs* on BBC Radio 4 when he appeared on the programme on 28 November 1966.

130   **Tristan and Whatshername**: *Tristan und Isolde* (1865), opera by Richard Wagner.

130   **I Love Little Pussy Her Coat Is So Warm**: English nursery rhyme about being kind to a cat.

130   **In A Chinese Temple Garden**: 1923, piece of light classical music by Albert Ketèlbey.

130   **Pomp and Circumference March (the one with Land of**

Hope and Glory): March No. 1 in D (1901) of the *Pomp and Circumstance Marches* by Edward Elgar (1857–1934).

130   St Louis Blues: 1914 jazz standard by W.C. Handy.

130   Last Spring: *Våren* (1880), song by Edvard Greig.

130   I'll Sing You One Oh Green Grow the Rushes Oh What Is Your One Oh: English traditional.

131   Lawrence Wright latest hits by Horatio Nichols: Lawrence Wright (1888–1964) was a successful popular music composer and publisher, and wrote more than 600 songs under his own name and that of Horatio Nicholls. After running a music shop in London he moved to Blackpool in the early 1920s and became an impresario, promoting a show on the North Pier for 32 years.

131   The Rhine Gold: *Das Rheingold* (1869), opera by Richard Wagner.

131   The Twilight of the Gods: *Götterdämmerung* (1876), opera by Richard Wagner.

132   The Desert Song: 1926 light opera by Sigmund Romberg and Oscar Hammerstein.

132   The Student Prince: 1924 light opera by Sigmund Romberg and Dorothy Donnelly.

132   How Beautiful They Are The Lordly Ones: the hit song of the music drama *The Immortal Hour* (1914) by Rutland Boughton.

132   There Are Fairies At The Bottom Of Our Garden: 1917 musical setting of the children's poem by Rose Fyleman composed by Liza Lehmann.

133   I Love The Moon: 1912 song by Paul Rubens.

133   the Strippers' Anthem (Hair on the G String): arrangement by August Wilhelmj for the lowest string of the violin of the second movement in Johann Sebastian Bach's Orchestral Suite No. 3 in D major.

133   The Golliwog's Cakewalk: the sixth piece in the *Children's Corner* suite (1908) for solo piano by Claude Debussy.

133   Darktown Strutter's Ball: 1917 popular song by Shelton Brooks. Now a jazz standard.

133 **Demande et Réponse:** the second part of the *Petit Suite de Concert* (1911) by Samuel Coleridge-Taylor.

133 **Tosti's Goodbye:** 1881 song by Paulo Tosti and George J. Whyte-Melville.

133 **Swan Lake:** 1876, one of the most popular ballets, composed by Pyotr Tchaikovsky.

133 **Coppelia Ballet:** *Coppélia* (1870), comic ballet composed by Léo Delibes.

133 **Call Call Vienna Mine:** 'Vienna, City of My Dreams' (*Wien, du Stadt meiner Träume*, 1914), song composed by Rudolf Sieczyński.

133 **Down In The Forest Something Stirred:** 1915 song by Landon Ronald.

133 **Where The Bee Sucks There Suck I:** a setting of 'Ariel's Song' from *The Tempest* by William Shakespeare.

133 **The Death Of Nelson:** patriotic song by tenor and composer John Braham, from the opera *The Americans* (1911).

133 **Asleep In The Deep:** 1897 song by Arthur J. Lamb and Henry W. Petrie.

133 **Hush Hush Who The Hell Cares Christopher Robin Has Fallen Downstairs:** parody of 'Vespers' (1924) by A.A. Milne and in a setting by Harold Fraser-Simon. The original is extremely saccharine and infantile.

133 **Three Green Bonnets:** 1901 song by A.L. Harris and Guy d'Hardelot.

133 **The Intermezzo to Guy Domville:** an invention by Burgess, presumably music to be played during the interval to *Guy Domville* (1895), the last and worst play by Henry James.

133 **Mighty Lak A Rose:** 1901 popular song by Frank Lebby Stanton and Ethelbert Nevin.

133 **Loola Loola Loola Loola Byebye:** 'My Curly-Headed Baby', a traditional lullaby from the American South.

133 **Mr Flanagan and Mr Sheen:** 'Mister Gallagher and Mister Shean' (1922), vaudeville song popularised by the double-act of the same name from *The Ziegfeld Follies* from that year.

133   **Give My Regards to Broadway:** song from the Broadway musical *Little Johnny Jones* (1904) by George M. Cohan.

133   **Moonlight Sonata:** piano sonata No. 14 in C sharp minor (1801) by Beethoven.

133   **Purcell's Trumpet Voluntary:** possibly *The Prince of Denmark's March*, a popular piece of wedding music thought to have been composed by Henry Purcell but now known to be the work of Jeremiah Clarke in c. 1700.

133   **Fairest Isle All Isles Excelling:** an aria from the opera *King Arthur* (1691) by John Dryden and Henry Purcell.

133   **When I Am Laid In Earth:** Dido's final aria from the opera *Dido and Aeneas* (1688) by Nahum Tate and Henry Purcell.

133   **the Ode to Joy of Beethoven:** the tune from part of the final movement of Beethoven's Symphony No. 9 in D minor (1824).

133   **Chopin's Waltzes:** solo piano pieces written between 1831 and 1847 by Frederic Chopin. The waltz in D flat major is also known as the Minute Waltz or the *Valse du petit chien*, the *Little Dog Waltz*.

133   **Lager from the New World:** 'Largo', the second movement of Symphony No. 9 in E minor, 'From the New World' (1893), by Antonin Dvorak.

133   **Felix Kept On Walking:** 1919 song by Hubert W. David and Ed E. Bryant, issued in conjunction with the popular 'Felix the Cat' cartoons that appeared in silent cinemas during the period.

133   **Horsey Cock Your Tail Up:** 'Horsey! Keep Your Tail Up (Keep the Sun out of My Eyes)', 1923 children's song by Walter Hirsch and Bert Kaplan.

133   **Valencia Land Of Orange Groves And Sweet Content I Saw You From Afar:** 'Valencia', 1926 Spanish song by Jose Padilla with English lyrics by Eric Valentine.

133   **The Red Flag:** 1889 socialist song by Jim Connell and Ernst Anschütz. Traditionally sung at the end of Labour Party conferences.

134   **Jambes:** French, 'legs'.

135   **the Poem of Ecstasy by Scriabin:** *Le Poème de l'extase* (1908), orchestral work by Alexander Scriabin.

135   **an Opera made up as it goes along:** What follows is a description of a version of Burgess's unpublished and unproduced opera 'Trotsky's In New York!', completed in 1979. See Introduction, p. 7.

140   **You was meant for me:** lyrics from 'You Were Meant for Me', a song by Nacio Herb Brown and Arthur Freed from the musical *Broadway Melody* (1929).

142   **Jeremiah Feldfloh:** This dubious character may owe something to the reputation of Albert Feldman, music publisher and owner of Feldman's Arcade on Blackpool Promenade. Feldman's Arcade was a live music venue during the 1920s, with many stages and rooms where performers would present the new songs of the day to the public who were then encouraged to purchase the sheet music. Feldman's shrewd business sense and aggressive marketing techniques made him hugely successful. His great rival was Lawrence Wright, whose twenty song booths along the Promenade and on the pier competed with Feldman for the custom of holidaymakers. The Cyril Critchlow Collection at the Local and Family History Centre, Blackpool Central Library, contains a wealth of material about the entertainers of Blackpool during this period.

143   **Midland:** The Midland Hotel opened in 1903 and was the grandest hotel in Manchester for many years. In 1993 Burgess wrote 'it is still worth travelling to Manchester merely to eat of the roasts of the buffet in the Midland' ('Manchester As Was', reprinted in *One Man's Chorus*, ed. by Ben Forkner (New York: Carroll and Graf, 1998), p. 91).

144   **real brass monkey weather:** extremely cold, as in 'enough to freeze the balls off a brass monkey' (Green).

145   **the Mannequin Piss:** the 'Manneken Pis', a small bronze statue of a boy urinating into the basin of a fountain and symbol of the great city of Brussels.

148   Je suis tout à fait ravie monsieur de faire votre connai-
       sance: French, 'I am delighted to meet you, sir'.

148   vous pourrez faire ce que vous désirez cher monsieur ce
       m'est tout à fait égal: French, 'you must do whatever you
       please my dear sir, it's all the same to me.'

149   Je vous remercie Madame de votre gentillesse. Je suis sûre
       que je serai heureuse chez Madame Recamier: French, 'I
       am grateful for your kindness, ma'am. I am sure that I will
       be happy with Madame Recamier.'

149   Bien, ma petite. Alors, après demain: French, 'Very well,
       my child. So, until the day after tomorrow.'

150   Malmaison, which is where the house of Josephine was:
       Château de Malmaison, a large estate to the west of Paris.
       Joséphine de Beauharnais, Napoleon's wife, created one of
       the grandest gardens in Europe there.

150   fais moi le pompier ma petite: French, 'put out the fire for
       me, little one.'

150   the foul Boche, il faut en finir: 'Boche' is a derogatory term
       for Germans, specifically German soldiers. French, 'they
       must be finished off'.

151   Chamberlain, or J'aime Berlin: Neville Chamberlain (1869–
       1940), British prime minister 1937–1940 and best known for
       a policy of appeasement towards Adolf Hitler's Germany,
       and particularly for the Munich Agreement of 1938, which
       conceded the Sudetenland to Germany in return for a prom-
       ise from Hitler not to invade Poland.

151   Chiswick: a town in west London. Burgess lived at 24 Glebe
       Street, Chiswick, between 1963 and 1968.

151   the Doves on the river: The Dove, a late eighteenth-century
       public house situated on the bank of the river Thames in
       Hammersmith in west London.

151   a bit of a blow on Chiswick Mall: getting some fresh air on
       Chiswick Mall, a riverside path and gardens near Chiswick.

151   Albert Ross ... like the bird in Coleman's or Selfridge's
       poem: the albatross in Samuel Taylor Coleridge's poem The
       Rime of the Ancient Mariner (1798).

151   **Round The Worlds to Yank clients:** 'Around the world' is a service offered in a brothel in the novel *From Here to Eternity* (1951) by James Jones, which deals with the misadventures of American soldiers posted to Hawaii in 1941. Burgess compares this novel unfavourably to *The Caine Mutiny* (1951) by Hermann Wouk in his survey *99 Novels* (London: Allison & Busby, 1984).

151   **King Bomba in Soho:** an Italian delicatessen.

152   **Caxton Hall:** building used as a register office in Westminster until 1979, popular with celebrities.

152   **London Clinic:** an exclusive private hospital on Harley Street, central London.

152   **Horsham:** a market town in Sussex, south of London.

152   **Free French:** the forces under Charles de Gaulle during the occupation of France during the Second World War.

152   **Vous avez absolument raison, mon capitaine, vous avez les droits du mari:** French, 'You are perfectly justified, Captain, you have conjugal rights.'

154   **Sir Stafford Cripps:** Labour politician, Chancellor of the Exchequer 1947–50. His austere policies kept rationing in place to control consumption while Britain rebuilt its economy following the war.

154   **I Scream You Scream We All Scream For Ice Cream:** 1927 novelty song and later jazz standard, by Howard Johnson, Billy Moll and Robert King.

154   **Pink Elephants On Parade:** song from the cartoon *Dumbo* (1941), by Oliver Wallace and Ned Washington.

154   **Begin The Beguine:** 1935 popular song by Cole Porter.

154   **That Old Black Magic Has Me In Its Spell:** 1942 song by Harold Arlen and Johnny Mercer, popularised by Glen Miller And His Orchestra.

154   **The Scar On Your Nose:** this and the other songs in the list are inventions, as Ellen indicates.

155   **Mauser:** a German gun manufacturer. Among other weapons Mauser produced a range of small pistols.

155   **Les Halles:** the central market area in Paris.

157   *hôtel de passe*: French, 'short-stay hotel'.

157   **American organ**: a harmonium. See 'An American Organ' (Appendix 1) and Introduction, p. 6).

158   **P'tites Sœurs des Cœurs**: 'Petites Soeurs des Sacrés Coeurs', a Catholic religious order.

158   **Tout se passe le mieux du monde mais au moment stratégique, dans l'impossibilité de dominer son émotion, notre abbé s'écrie: Ah! ma fille! Le bon Dieu est avec nous! Bon d'accord, rétorque la môme, mais dans ce cas, c'est tarif double!**: French, 'Everything was going extremely well but at the critical moment, finding it impossible to contain himself, our priest cried out: Oh! My child! The good Lord is with us! Well that's just fine, she retorted, 'but in that case the price is doubled!'

158   **sireh**: betel leaf, a mild stimulant.

158   **Belles du Jour**: a pun on 'belle de nuit', a lady of the night or prostitute; the phrase was popularised by Luis Buñuel's 1967 film *Belle du jour* starring Catherine Deneueve, based on the 1928 novel of the same name by Joseph Kessel.

158   **Eton or Harrow College**: expensive English independent schools.

158   **Straits dollar**: the currency used in Malaya, Brunei and other British territories in south-east Asia between 1898 and 1939.

158   **Johore over the border**: Johore, a state of Malaya adjacent to Singapore.

158   **Topeka**: city in the state of Kansas.

158   **UCLA**: University of California at Los Angeles.

159   **Rotary**: an international networking club for businesspeople.

159   *Hsieh hsieh*: Chinese, thank you.

159   **flower lei**: Hawaiian garland.

159   **camphorwood chest**: Burgess owned a camphorwood chest himself, which appears in a similar context in his novel *One Hand Clapping* (1960), p. 203.

159   **Shantung silk**: very fine silk from the Chinese province, often used in bridal gowns.

160   hard boiled hundred year old eggs: eggs preserved in ash, a traditional Chinese dish.

160   the strong men of one of the musical Gong Societies: experts in the martial arts practice gongfu, or kung fu.

161   Oscar Peterson: (1925–2007), jazz pianist and composer.

161   Lord Soper: Donald Soper, Baron Soper (1903–98), prominent Methodist minister known for radical pacifist and socialist views.

161   the Archbishop of Birmingham, who I'd met once as a kid in Manchester in his mother and father's greengrocer's shop: George Dwyer (1908–87), Catholic archbishop of Birmingham between 1965 and 1981. Dwyer's father was a wholesale potato and egg merchant in Manchester. Burgess's stepmother was Margaret Dwyer, George Dwyer's cousin. Burgess's relationship with George Dwyer is described in Andrew Biswell, *The Real Life of Anthony Burgess* (London: Picador, 2005), pp. 276–7.

162   the Dorchester which was not run by the Arabs in those days: luxury hotel in Park Lane, London, which opened in 1931. The Dorchester was purchased by the Sultan of Brunei in 1985.

162   Tonight and Every Night: *Tonight* was a BBC current affairs and culture magazine programme presented by Cliff Michelmore which was broadcast live on weekday evenings between 1957 and 1965. Burgess's first television appearance was on the show in 1962, when a dramatised extract from *A Clockwork Orange* was broadcast. *Tonight and Every Night* was a 1945 musical film about a romance during the Blitz directed by Victor Saville and starring Rita Hayworth.

165   Salopian Tubes: i.e. fallopian tubes. 'Salopian' means of or from Shrewsbury, a market town in Shropshire, England.

165   Bugatti: French marque of high-powered cars, flourishing between 1909 and 1947.

165   Haywards Heath: a town in west Sussex, south of London.

166   Bognor Regis: seaside resort town in west Sussex.

167   **pppp**: pianississississimo, a musical direction meaning very quiet.

168   **Emergency Ward Ten**: *Emergency Ward 10*, a hospital-based British soap opera and one of the first of its kind to be broadcast, screening between 1957 and 1967. Burgess saw a fondness for the programme as a marker of a lack of an inner life, gloomily referring to his first wife Lynne watching it while he wrote novels in *You've Had Your Time* (p. 37) and the idle inhabitants of Bradcaster watch it in *One Hand Clapping* (p. 39).

168   **Fiat**: mass-market Italian marque.

169   **bird's eye maple**: maple that has grown with the branches failing to form properly, giving an unusual pattern on the wood. Sometimes used to give visual interest in piano manufacture.

170   **Clacton**: Clacton-on-Sea, a resort on the Essex Sunshine Coast east of London.

170   **Hastings St Leonards**: a resort on the east Sussex coast, slightly further from London than Clacton-on-Sea.

172   **Gesualdo**: Carlo Gesualdo (1566–1613), Italian aristocrat, technically innovative composer and musician, and brutal murderer of his wife Donna Maria and her lover Fabrizio Carafa.

172   **Dover**: coastal town in Kent, the most convenient ferry port from London.

173   **Nice**: port on the south coast of France.

173   **Ventimiglia**: coastal town in north-western Italy, close to the border with France.

173   **Albenga**: coastal town in north-western Italy, slightly further on than Ventimiglia.

175   **Fermata**: musical symbol requiring that a note or rest be held or paused longer than the notation would ordinarily demand.

176   **Vieni qua Bruno**: Italian, 'come here, Bruno'.

178   *zuppa di verdura*: Italian, 'vegetable soup'.

178   *spaghetti alla vongole*: Italian, 'spaghetti with clams'.

180   **AGIP:** Azienda Generale Italiana Petroli, General Italian Oil Company. Their garages were ubiquitous throughout Italy.

183   **sweating cobs:** 'Cob' means a rounded lump; the reference here is to large globules of perspiration (Green).

184   **Lucretia Borgia:** Lucrezia Borgia (1480–1519), villainous daughter of Pope Alexander VI rumoured to have poisoned various rivals for her own gain.

185   **There is a lot of kidnapping in Italy:** Burgess claims in *You've Had Your Time* that a 'retired mafioso' came to warn him in 1975 that his son Andrea was 'on the kidnap list [...] It was to be a group whose location and membership he knew but would not divulge; he could vouch for both its greed and efficiency. We had better get out of Bracciano. We were, I said leaving anyway' (p. 321).

185   **film called Casanova by Fellini or Fellazione:** *Il Casanova di Federico Fellini* (1973), a fictional telling of the story of the famous libertine.

185   **Questura:** police headquarters.

186   **Mulberry Street in New York:** a street running through the Little Italy area of New York City.

187   **There's some corner of a foreign field / That is for ever Mrs Aldridge:** parody of the poem 'The Soldier' by Rupert Brooke (1887–1915).

189   **Sèvres:** high-quality manufacturer of porcelain from France.

189   **complete Constable tea set:** a range of china crockery with designs by John Constable (1776–1837) made by Broadhurst from 1976 to mark the bicentenary of the painter.

190   **Wedding March from Low and Grin:** i.e. *Treulich geführt* from the 1850 opera *Lohengrin* by Richard Wagner.

192   **Richard Rodney Bennett:** (1936–2012), pianist and composer of film, television and concert music.

193–4 **Fingers Off:** this piece is composed by Burgess, and a sketch of the score and an account of its composition is given in *This Man and Music* (1982): 'In 1947 I wrote violin exercises, with piano accompaniment, designed to make melodic sense of open-string playing [...] I called the compilation *The*

Young Fiddler's Tunebook and sent it to Messrs Curwen, the music publishers. They liked the idea, they said, but they could not as yet hold out hope of publication because of the post-war paper shortage. It didn't matter. The young fiddler I had written for was my long-dead self' (p. 15).